WELCOME TO
HOMETOWN REUNION

Twelve unique stories set in Tyler.

Where you can find romance and adventure, bachelors and babies, feuding families, a case of mistaken identity, and a mum on the run!

Join us in America's favourite town and experience the love and the laughter, the trials and the triumphs of those who call it home.

*First published in Great Britain 2000
by Harlequin Mills & Boon Limited,
Eton House, 18-24 Paradise Road,
Richmond, Surrey TW9 1SR*

HERO IN DISGUISE © Harlequin Books S.A. 1996

Vicki Lewis Thompson is acknowledged as the author of this work.

ISBN 0 373 82552 8

110-0700

*Printed and bound in Spain
by Litografia Rosés S.A., Barcelona*

VICKI LEWIS THOMPSON

Hero in Disguise

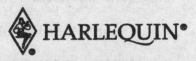

HARLEQUIN®

TORONTO • NEW YORK • LONDON
AMSTERDAM • PARIS • SYDNEY • HAMBURG
STOCKHOLM • ATHENS • TOKYO • MILAN • MADRID
PRAGUE • WARSAW • BUDAPEST • AUCKLAND

WELCOME TO A
HOMETOWN REUNION

**Twelve books set in Tyler.
Twelve unique stories.**

Vicki Lewis Thompson lives in Arizona, USA, with her husband and a cat called Moppet. Vicki, a former journalist and English teacher, spent childhood holidays with her grandparents in a small town that she remembers being very much like Tyler. Keep an eye out for Vicki's latest Sensual Romance™, *Operation Gigolo*, available in September 2000.

For Audrey Sharpe and Laura Chesler, two friends who understand the true meaning of the word. And for a very special performer with the Cirque du Soleil troupe. Remember, Audrey and Laura?

CHAPTER ONE

"SHEILA." Abby Triblett grabbed Sheila's arm. "Look!"

Sheila Lawson glanced up from the Timberlake Lodge registration desk, where she'd been helping Abby untangle a booking error.

"The guy heading for the bar," Abby said in the same urgent undertone.

Sheila looked toward the bar entrance and caught her breath. A dark-haired hunk in tight buckskin breeches and a formfitting buckskin shirt strode into the dim interior, his moccasined feet making no sound on the polished wood floor. "Be still, my heart," Sheila whispered.

"Who do you suppose he is?"

Sheila edged down the length of the registration desk and leaned over the far end to track the man's progress into the bar. "One of the reenactors from the encampment, I guess," she said in a low voice.

"You didn't say any of those history nuts would look like *that*."

"The one who made all the arrangements didn't look *anything* like that." Sheila grinned at Abby. "Ready to make a foray down to their encampment by the lake?"

"First let's find out if he's the exception or the rule."

"How do you propose to do that?" Sheila watched him skirt the tables and saunter over to the bar. He propped one foot on the brass railing running in front of it as he gave his order to the bartender, then shifted his weight, stretching the buckskin tight across his backside.

"One of us will engage him in conversation." Abby nudged Sheila with her hip. "Don't hog the view." As she craned her neck for a better look, she sighed. "He has nicer buns than Joe Montana."

Sheila agreed. She also took note of wavy hair a little too long to be fashionable but just right for a woman to comb her fingers through. "He could have an ugly face."

"God wouldn't do that to me."

Sheila poked Abby with her elbow. "You realize this conversation is sexist and superficial."

"I won't tell anybody about it if you won't. Check out those shoulders! Now there's a man who could carry me up the staircase."

Sheila fantasized about his strong arms sweeping her into an embrace and felt goose bumps prickle her arms. "He's probably married."

"Then why isn't his wife in there having a drink with him?"

"Good point."

"I'll bet he's single. Sheila, we have to think up a reason for one of us to go in there and talk to him."

"That's easy." A thrill of anticipation shot through her. "We'll ask about his costume. Trust me, history buffs love explaining things like the origin of fringe."

"I'd like him to explain how he makes that fringe ripple. Yum. I love fringe."

Sheila laughed. "I never would have guessed. How many times did you see *Last of the Mohicans?*"

"Eleven, but who's counting? Okay, we have our topic of conversation. How do we decide which one of us goes?" Abby glanced at Sheila. "You're my boss, so I guess you could pull rank."

"Not a chance."

"Then let's flip for it."

"I have a penny." Sheila reached in her skirt pocket for

the one she'd found, heads up, in the lodge parking lot on the way to work that morning. "Call it." She flipped the coin in the air.

"Heads."

Sheila slapped the coin onto the back of her wrist and lifted her hand. Tails.

"Damn," Abby murmured. "Two out of three?"

"Nope." Sheila slipped the penny back in the pocket of her wool skirt and pushed open the swinging door that separated the registration counter from the lobby. "He's mine."

"Maybe it'll turn out that he likes brunettes better than blondes," Abby said hopefully.

Sheila evaluated the physique of the man leaning against the bar. She turned back to Abby. "Some things are worth dyeing for," she said with a wink.

"Very punny. Look, if you strike out, I think I deserve a turn at bat."

"Abby, my dear, I plan to clean the bases." Sheila turned and started for the bar, feeling much less confident than she'd sounded with Abby. But darn it, she hadn't had a date since she'd moved back to Tyler six months ago and it would be very nice to catch a movie or share a meal with someone of the opposite sex. Especially someone as gorgeous as the man leaning against Timberlake's polished mahogany bar.

The only reenactor she'd met, Charles Ridenour from Milwaukee, had told her that the group drew members from all over Wisconsin, so this cutie-pie could be from anywhere in the state. Sheila hoped he didn't live too far away from Tyler.

At four in the afternoon the bar wasn't busy. Aside from the buckskin wonder, only one couple occupied a far corner table. In fact, the lodge itself was low on bookings this weekend, probably due to March's unpredictable weather,

Sheila had concluded. The reenactment group hadn't wanted any rooms, so she'd worked out a rate for camping on the grounds. The *Tyler Citizen* had run a story about the mock battles to be staged on Saturday and Sunday afternoons, and spectators should fill the Timberlake dining room on both days, at least. Too bad the newspaper story hadn't included a picture of the man in buckskins, she thought. Female attendance would have tripled.

As she entered the bar, she framed her first question. *I couldn't help noticing your costume.* Now there was an understatement. *Who do you represent?* Or was it *whom?* Oh, well. If he cared that much about grammar, she wasn't interested, anyway. She reached up to tap him on the shoulder just as he put down his empty glass and turned, nearly colliding with her. She gasped. "Mr. *Wagner?*"

Startled, he stepped back. "Why, it's Sheila. Sheila Lawson. Sixth-period government."

"Class of eighty-three," Sheila said automatically as she stared in dismay at her high-school history teacher. Her married high-school history teacher. She knew the blush was coming and could think of no way to hide it. She'd been admiring Mr. Wagner's buns. Abby would split a gut. "I—I didn't recognize you from the back." She closed her eyes in mortification. "I mean…the buckskin makes you look different. I never dreamed you were…Mr. Wagner."

His eyes twinkled. She'd never realized they were such a captivating shade of green. "I'll admit the costume's a little tight," he said. "The guy who played Chief Black Hawk before me was smaller, but he insisted I had to wear this. Hand-beaded buckskin isn't that easy to come by."

"Chief Black Hawk?" She registered the scent of his aftershave, a woodsy fragrance she remembered from the hours she'd spent in his classroom.

"Come on, Sheila." He smiled, and she remembered the smile, too. It had always made her feel wonderful. "Don't tell me I wasted my time on that statehood unit. Surely you know who Black Hawk was."

Suddenly she was seventeen again, sitting in the front seat, third row, and she hadn't done her homework. She struggled to think of something, anything about Black Hawk. "He was good-looking," she blurted.

He rolled his eyes.

"Okay. Okay, now I remember. He couldn't get the other tribes to help win back their land, so he and his braves had to fight alone. I think you compared his idealism to Don Quixote's."

"So you *were* paying attention."

Sometimes, she thought. And sometimes she'd day-dreamed in a vague, seventeen-year-old fashion about what it would be like to be married to him, although she'd never admitted that to anyone for fear of ridicule. All his students had known he was practically engaged to a woman who taught over in Sugar Creek.

"You were a good teacher," she said. "It's just that I haven't thought about history in years." Or that other business, the matter she'd pushed to the back of her mind. The last time she'd had a conversation with this man, she had admitted to plagiarizing a friend's essay. To hope he'd forgotten would be stupid. He was a history teacher and re-calling the past was his specialty.

"You probably don't have much reason to think about Black Hawk these days," he said. "I'm sure you have a very successful career by now, and I doubt it has anything to do with Wisconsin history."

She was surprised he'd assume she was successful, con-sidering what his opinion of her must have been thirteen years ago. "Actually, I'm the manager here at Timber-lake."

"Really? That's great." He glanced up at the beamed

ceilings. "I'm glad Judson Ingalls's granddaughter talked him out of tearing the place down."

"Liza's very protective of Timberlake. In fact she got me the job as concierge here five years ago."

"That's right. You and Liza were in the same class." He leaned a hip against the bar. "So you've been working here five years?"

"No, Mr. Wocheck sent me to intern with one of the Addison chain's Chicago hotels. Six months ago I transferred back here."

"You know, when Wocheck bought this for the Addison Corporation, I figured the special character of the lodge would disappear, but it hasn't."

"I think Liza had a lot to do with that."

"Probably." He smiled. "I remember she always had a tendency to get her way. I saw her the other day in the library with her daughter. I never thought Liza Baron would settle down, but here she is, a happily married lady with a four-year-old." His glance flicked down briefly to her left hand. "How about you?"

She held up her ringless hand. "No husband and no kids."

He nodded, as if in approval. "There's no rush. I'm just glad you didn't end up with Dennis Hopkins."

So was she, but she was amazed that Mr. Wagner remembered who her steady had been back in high school. "He had a convertible, and he was a jock," she said with a dismissive shrug. "Those things impress you when you're young."

He chuckled. "And now you're an old lady? What does that make me?"

She glanced at him. She'd never really thought too much about his age. He'd been her teacher, so he'd been older, wiser, superior to her in every way. Yet if she set that aside and looked at him simply as a man, he didn't seem any older than other men she'd dated. His hair was dark and full, with no traces of gray, his skin supple, and his body…well, she'd already evaluated his body, and she'd be wise not to think of that now at the risk of blushing all over again. But she was curious about his age, now that he'd brought it up.

"I'm thirty-five," he said, as if reading her mind.

She made a quick calculation. "You were only twenty-two when I was a senior?"

"Barely twenty-three. Fresh out of college and so green I was sure all of you would see right through me."

"No way! We thought you knew everything."

He laughed.

"No, really. I don't think anybody ever stumped you with a question."

"I prepared for those classes like you wouldn't believe."

She was intrigued with the idea that he hadn't been as confident as he'd seemed. "Just about everyone admired you, especially the kids in the scuba club. That was when the first Indiana Jones movie had come out, and we pictured you going all over the world looking for treasure like he did, only underwater instead of on land."

His smile faded, and a haunted look came into his eyes. "I was no Indiana Jones."

Just like that, the cheerful atmosphere had evaporated, and she had no idea why. Uncomfortable with the tense silence, she searched for something more to say. "Do you still sponsor the club?"

"No."

It was obviously a sore subject, but she didn't know him well enough to ask any more questions. "That's too bad," she said lamely. The conversation seemed to have hit a snag, and Sheila decided the safest plan was to extricate herself and go back to work. "Well, it was great seeing you again, Mr. Wagner." She held out her hand. "Have fun with the encampment."

He seemed to pull himself back from the dark place to which he'd retreated. His smile looked a little forced, but his eyes focused on her with a new intensity as he took her hand. "First of all, I'd count it a big favor if you'd call me Douglas instead of Mr. Wagner. When a thirty-year-old woman calls me Mr. Wagner, I feel about a hundred and two."

The request tantalized her with renewed awareness of him as a man, not an icon, and the firm pressure of his hand closing over hers set off a little explosion of unexpected pleasure. "All right." She looked into his eyes and tried out his name. "Douglas." Immediately she felt an erosion of formality, an expansion of possibilities.

"Second of all, can you get away from your job anytime tomorrow and visit the encampment? I think you'd be interested."

It was an invitation that could be interpreted many different ways. Perhaps it was an empty courtesy, although the warmth in his eyes belied that assumption. Or maybe he was only behaving like a teacher who jumped at every chance to instruct an available student. Or he might be asking her as a man would ask a woman to spend time with him. The last possibility had her heart beating faster. Then she remembered his wife. A year after Sheila graduated he'd married the teacher from Sugar Creek.

She pulled her hand from his and pasted on a smile. "I can sure try, Mr. W—Douglas."

"Good. I'll look for you. I'd better get back, and I'm sure you have work to do. See you tomorrow."

He left before she could throw out some statement about not being positive she could make it. She was pretty certain that he expected her, but she didn't want to go. There was no point in kidding herself; she was still attracted to him.

In high school she'd thought of it as a hopeless crush, considering that he was a teacher and had a girlfriend. Thirteen years later it was still a hopeless crush, unless Douglas was the kind of man who didn't let marriage stop him from engaging in flirtations or even full-blown love affairs. She didn't want to discover that about somebody she'd always admired.

With a sigh she returned to the registration desk.

Abby was busy with a couple who needed directions to Gates Department Store on the square in downtown Tyler. Abby obviously hadn't recognized Douglas Wagner as he walked out, either. When she'd supplied the couple with a map and sent them on their way, she turned expectantly toward Sheila. "Well? Got a date with that handsome devil?"

"You mean that handsome devil who's taught government at Tyler High for thirteen years?"

"Get out of here! That wasn't Mr. Wagner!"

"I'm afraid it was."

"I don't believe it," Abby sputtered. "It's not possible. Not with a behind like that." She clapped a hand over her mouth in horror and glanced around, as if worried that someone might have overheard her. "You're not kidding me, are you? It really was him?"

"Yes, it most certainly was. You were drooling over your high-school history teacher."

"How embarrassing! I'll bet you just about died. Did he recognize you right away?"

"Right away." Sheila hadn't thought much about it at the time, but it was remarkable, considering he'd had hundreds of students over the years.

"Well, your hair's the same color, and you still look a lot like you did back then. I'll bet he wouldn't remember me, though."

Sheila thought of Abby in high school, a chubby girl

with dyed blond hair and a fondness for old Army jackets and ripped jeans. Sheila had been a model student, so Abby's grungy style and rebellious attitude had kept Sheila from pursuing a close friendship. Now brunette, slim and tastefully dressed, Abby didn't look anything like her high-school self and had mellowed considerably. She'd become Sheila's frequent companion for movies and shopping expeditions. "Even I didn't recognize you when I walked in here the first day on the job," Sheila admitted.

The switchboard buzzed, and Abby picked up a headset and transferred the call while Sheila checked the computer to see how reservations were going for the month. She had a hard time concentrating on the screen. She kept seeing the change in those brilliant green eyes when she'd mentioned the scuba-diving club.

Abby finished with the phone call and came to stand beside her. "So our hunk of burning love turns out to be Mr. Wagner. Not that Mr. Wagner isn't kind of cute. Lots of us had crushes on him, remember?"

Sheila pushed a button and scrolled through the next few days of reservations. "Weren't you the one who baked him cookies every week?"

"Yeah, and it didn't help my grade one bit, either. It's a sorry situation when a teacher can't be bribed with chocolate chip cookies."

"Did you know he's only five years older than we are?"

"What, you asked him his age?"

Sheila focused her attention on the computer screen. "No, he volunteered it."

"That seems like a strange thing to do."

Perhaps it was, Sheila thought, growing more uncomfortable with the situation. She sincerely hoped Mr. Wagner hadn't been flirting with her.

"Exactly what did you two talk about?" Abby persisted.

"Chief Black Hawk, and the fact that I dated Dennis

Hopkins in high school. And then I asked him if he was still sponsoring the scuba club. That's when he sort of spaced out on me.''

Abby slapped her forehead and groaned. ''You brought up the scuba club?''

Sheila turned from the screen, puzzled by Abby's stricken expression. ''What was wrong with that?''

''You don't remember?''

''No.''

''His wife died in a scuba accident four years ago.''

Sheila caught her breath as relief that he wasn't a sleaze-ball was followed swiftly by regret for her insensitive comments. ''Oh, God. No wonder he looked like that while I prattled on about his Indiana Jones image, roaming the seas looking for treasure. How awful. How perfectly awful.''

''I guess you were working in Chicago then, but I'm surprised somebody didn't tell you in a letter or on one of your visits home.''

''I wish somebody had! It would have saved me from making a fool of myself and causing him to get upset. Damn. Now I suppose I should go tomorrow, just so I can apologize, although I'm not looking forward to it, under the circumstances.''

''Go?'' Abby cocked her head. ''You're going somewhere with him?''

''He threw out the suggestion that I might be interested in visiting the encampment tomorrow. It's no big deal.''

''Was this before or after you put your foot in your mouth?''

''After.''

Abby leaned on the desk and propped her chin in her hand as she studied Sheila.

''Why are you looking at me like that?''

''I'm thinking about the fact that he told you his age, remembered you right away and asked you down to the encampment. Add that to the information that he's a widower, and what do you get?''

Secretly Sheila had been thinking the same thing, but Abby's obvious insinuation brought heat to her cheeks and a curl of tension to her stomach. ''For goodness' sake! He's Mr. Wagner, our old history teacher!''

''Not so old, apparently. And judging from the way he filled out that buckskin, he's holding up well for his age.''

''Abby, it feels so *strange* to think of him like that. I can't imagine actually going out with him, can you?''

''Going out with our history teacher, Mr. Wagner? No. Having a wild fling with that beautiful man in buckskin? Definitely. I just have to make some mental adjustments to superimpose one image over the other. I'm off duty in the morning, and I'll bet the lodge could survive without you for an hour or so. Why don't we go down to the encampment together?''

Sheila's heart thumped erratically. ''I don't know about this, Abby.''

''I do. You may have reservations about taking up with a former teacher, but I don't. He invited you, so I'll just tag along and check him out. Sounds like he might be getting lonely.''

As much as Sheila resisted the idea of Douglas Wagner as a potential date for herself, she wasn't quite ready to turn him over to Abby, either. ''Don't forget I won the toss.''

''Oh, ho! You're not as reluctant as you pretend!''

A vision of Douglas's green eyes and broad shoulders vied against an older picture of an unapproachable role model. ''I don't know what I am, except very confused.''

''Look, it's simple. We'll meet in the parking lot at nine in the morning and walk down to the encampment together.

I think we'll know very shortly if he's interested in either one of us.'' Abby grinned. ''And may the best woman win.''

CHAPTER TWO

DOUGLAS'S FOOTSTEPS crunched across the frozen grass and his breath fogged the air as he neared the encampment. At his approach, a white-tailed deer that had been foraging in the meadow bounded away into the protective covering of the trees. Cold crept through the laces fastening Douglas's shirt, and he looked forward to the warmth of a buffalo robe around his shoulders and the heat of a fire.

The scent of wood smoke and the aroma of cooked food drifted toward him. Beside the frozen lake, eight dome-shaped wigwams housed the Native American side of the conflict, ten Army tents the men portraying frontier soldiers. Historically, wives wouldn't have accompanied their husbands on an Indian campaign, so the women reenactors played camp followers, the frontier version of prostitutes.

Valerie Positano had no husband, however, and she seemed to be taking the camp-follower role seriously when it came to Douglas. He'd retreated to the lodge for a drink in order to escape her. As he walked toward his wigwam he glanced around warily, but didn't see her lurking anywhere nearby. He did, however, see his old college buddy, Charlie, dressed in a navy blue wool Army jacket and white breeches, coming out of the woods with an armload of firewood. And Charlie had much to answer for.

Douglas walked over to meet him. "What did you tell that woman about me, Charlie?"

Charlie tried to look innocent behind his bushy red beard. "You mean Valerie?"

"You know damn well who I mean. When I agreed to spend this weekend as a reenactor, I didn't think you had ulterior motives."

"I didn't. Swear to God. Bringing Valerie along was Cathy's idea, not mine."

"Oh, sure. Blame Cathy."

Charlie had the grace to look uncomfortable. "Okay. When Cathy pointed out that you aren't seeing anybody, I sort of agreed it would be good for you to meet some single women. Tyler's a small town, and if you'll pardon my saying so, teachers have a boring image to uphold."

"Is that so?"

"Face it, Douglas. With your job, you have to come across as sexless, especially in this day and age of lawsuits. Cathy thought this weekend would give you a chance to loosen up."

"I see."

Charlie shifted the wood in his arms. "You have to admit you don't have much of a social life down here. If you'd take a teaching job in Milwaukee, we could introduce you to lots of—"

"Hey, I like Tyler, and I don't feel desperate about beefing up my social life. Tell Cathy to stop worrying about me."

"It's not just Cathy," Charlie admitted. "I'm worried, too. Look, we've been friends for a long time—you, me, Cathy…and Joanne, God rest her soul. I miss her, too, and so does Cathy. But life goes on. I may complain about the twins, but I wouldn't give up those little girls for the world." He grinned. "Although I'm willing to forgo their presence for a weekend alone with Cathy."

Douglas fought a pang of envy. Charlie and Cathy had the kind of lusty, loving relationship he'd always wanted and never really had, not even with Joanne. And he was glad for his friends' happiness. But sometimes, when he happened to catch Charlie giving Cathy an affectionate pinch on the behind, or he heard her whisper something suggestive in Charlie's ear, Douglas felt very deprived, indeed.

"Anyway, to put it bluntly," Charlie continued, "if you still want to have kids…"

Douglas sighed. Charlie was the only person in the world he would suffer through this conversation with, and he still wasn't crazy about doing it. "Of course I want to have kids. But I refuse to grab the first fertile woman I can find and start breeding. I have these quaint ideas about love and shared values."

"I take it Valerie's not your type."

"Do *you* think she is?"

"No." Shorter by five inches, Charlie glanced up at Douglas. "But you have to start somewhere."

"I don't plan to start with Valerie. I've tried to be polite because she's Cathy's cousin, but the woman is unbearably persistent."

Charlie grinned. "From the comments I've heard from some of the women, it's mostly your fault. Even Cathy's noticed how studly you look in that buckskin. You've been compared favorably with Daniel Day-Lewis."

"Wonderful. Just wonderful."

"Hey, don't knock it. Valerie may not be right for you, but we'll draw a crowd of spectators in the next two days. Maybe someone more compatible will show up. Women usually love watching the hatchet-throwing contest. You're still competing in that event, right?"

"Yeah. I was planning to get in some practice tomorrow morning." Douglas flexed his shoulders. "Now that I realize how tight this thing is, I'm afraid I'll split the shirt with the first throw."

Charlie waggled his eyebrows. "Then undo the laces. You'll have women falling at your feet."

Douglas braced his hands on his hips and studied his friend, who was beginning to get on his nerves with this constant theme of finding him a woman. "If I didn't know better, I'd think this whole weekend was some elaborate plot you and Cathy cooked up just so I could get lucky."

"I wouldn't say that, but if opportunity knocks, don't slam the tent flap on her, my friend. See you around the fire circle tonight." Charlie started toward the large bonfire already blazing in the middle of the clearing.

"Unless Cathy says something to Valerie, I'm making myself scarce for the next few hours."

Charlie paused and glanced back at him. "That bad, huh?"

"From the signals she was giving off, I'm afraid if I'm even remotely friendly she'll appear unannounced in my tent tonight. If she does, I'm sending her back out, which would embarrass us both."

"Valerie doesn't usually come on so strong. I'll bet it's the widower thing. Women are sure you need tending to, if you know what I mean."

Douglas sighed. "Maybe Cathy can convince her otherwise."

"I'll see what I can do."

"Thanks."

"But keep your powder dry, buddy. You never know who else might turn up in the next couple of days."

Douglas groaned and headed for his wigwam to get his cooking utensils for dinner. Charlie and Cathy were both good friends, but he'd have to convince them to stay out of the matchmaking business. When it came to that area of his life, he wanted to make his own choices.

Which might explain why his thoughts kept turning to Sheila Lawson. Her intelligent hazel eyes and shiny blond hair were just as he'd remembered them from when she'd sat in his class years ago. But her bearing was more confident now and her voice well modulated instead of breathy and filled with giggles. Of course he'd been pleased to see her. Anytime an ex-student showed up who seemed to be doing well, he was gratified.

Was that why you asked her to visit the encampment in the morning? questioned an inner voice.

Sure it was, he told himself. He'd always liked Sheila Lawson—as a student, of course.

He ducked under his tent flap and rummaged through his knapsack for a cast-iron skillet and a wooden spatula. To be honest, he'd been somewhat attracted to Sheila once. That could happen when a teacher was almost as young as his students. He might have fantasized about her a little. No harm in that.

He paused and muttered a soft oath. Whom was he kidding? He'd been so worried about his attraction to Sheila that he'd all but abandoned his responsibilities as her teacher. He had thrust that guilty knowledge away thirteen years ago, but the sight of her today had brought back the whole nasty episode.

Maybe he'd invited her to the encampment because he wanted to assure himself that she hadn't been handicapped by his negligence. Or maybe he hoped that he'd finally be able to explain and ask her forgiveness. Or maybe it had nothing to do with assuaging his guilt. Because when he'd seen her looking up at him with that special light in her eyes that he remembered all too well, he'd realized that his fantasies about Sheila Lawson had never really disappeared.

SHEILA MADE SURE everyone on the evening staff had reported for work before she left the lodge at six that evening. Then she walked out on the darkened veranda, where a newly risen moon glinted off the frozen lake. Snowmobiles and four-wheel-drive vehicles had swirled patterns in the patchy snow until it looked like the top of a vanilla frosted cake.

To her left near the edge of the lake the reenactment camp was clustered. Inside the circle created by wigwams and Army-style tents burned a large bonfire. Smaller fires in the wigwams made the dome-shaped structures glow like lamp shades in the deepening twilight. An elongated shadow caressed one of the wigwam walls, and Sheila wondered if it was Mr. Wagner. Douglas. She wondered if Abby had guessed right, that he was interested in a relationship beyond that of student and teacher. A tightening coil of anticipation made her shiver and button her wool coat.

After watching the flickering shadow for a moment, she glanced to her right, far out across the lake. Sure enough, a square of light shone from the window of a dilapidated fishing shanty, indicating her father was still there. She could just make out the shape of his snowmobile parked beside it. About fifty yards beyond sat Gus Lemke's shack, with a twin square of light reflected on the ice. Every ice fisherman on the lake had called it quits for the season except Gus Lemke and Emil Lawson. Locked in a sixty-year rivalry, they were determined to use the lake's non-regulated status to catch Jumbo. On most other Wisconsin lakes, the huge walleye would have been out of season after March 1.

Next week both men would be forced by Wisconsin fishing regulations to remove the wooden shanties and replace them with portable canvas ones that could be dismantled each evening. Sheila was campaigning for Emil and Gus to end the season and not bother with the portable shelters, but she didn't hold out much hope that either man would listen to her. The annual fishing contest had sapped their good sense. Sheila fingered the whistle in her pocket as she started toward the lake on a path crusty with dead, half-frozen clumps of grass.

As she walked, she glanced toward Timberlake Lodge's old boathouse on the north side of the lake. Liza and Cliff Forrester had converted the upper level into an apartment, and lights shone from the windows as dusk settled in. The boathouse had served the couple and their daughter well for the past few years, but Liza had mentioned to Sheila that they wanted to relocate and build a log house. Sheila was glad they hadn't moved yet. Living in the boathouse, they might hear a cry for help if Gus's or Emil's luck ran out. The risk of thin ice would be dangerous for younger men, let alone two guys past seventy.

Standing on the shore of the frozen lake, Sheila tried to gauge its safety. The weather had stayed unseasonably cold and the lake looked solid, but Sheila didn't trust it. She wished her father would give up and let Gus win this season's contest, but her arguments seemed to make no dent in his resolve. She put the whistle to her lips and blew.

Within thirty seconds her father appeared at the door of his shack, as did Gus. Their casual behavior indicated neither of them had come up with any prizewinners that day. They turned off their Coleman lanterns, climbed on their respective snowmobiles and traced a zigzag path over to Sheila. Emil reached the edge of the lake first, by a nose.

"Gotcha!" he called to Gus as he stopped next to Sheila and pushed his goggles up over his stocking cap. "Gus and me lost track of the time, as usual," he said.

"But you know it's late when you have to use the lanterns to see."

A grin flitted across his weathered face, revealing the missing front tooth in his set of dentures. "To tell the truth, Sheilie, when you're working at the lodge, we kind of wait for your whistle."

"As I suspected." She surveyed the two men. *Thank*

God for Gus, she thought. Without him her father would really be alone. "What if I forgot to blow the whistle some evening? Would you two fish until midnight?"

"Could be," Gus said cheerfully, his round face pink from the cold air and the six-pack he and Emil split every afternoon.

"I take it nobody's bringing fish home tonight."

"There's enough fish in our freezer to last a year," her father said.

"Same here." Gus wrapped his muffler tighter around his neck. "Faye would kill me if I brought fish home. I'm just waiting for Jumbo."

"You'll freeze your butinski waiting, too," Emil said. "That fish is mine."

"Ha!" Gus revved his snowmobile engine and started away from the lake. "The day you catch Jumbo is the day I streak nekked through town!" he called over his shoulder.

"Then you'd better practice running nekked, Gus-Gus!" Emil shouted back. Then he turned back to Sheila and winked. "Don't that paint a picture? Gus-Gus streaking past Worthington House one fine spring day with the Quilting Circle in session on the front porch?"

Sheila laughed as she watched the bobbing headlight that indicated Gus's progress along the trail leading through the woods to the Lemke farm. At age four she'd nicknamed him Gus-Gus, after one of the mice in Walt Disney's *Cinderella,* and the nickname had stuck. "That would be a sight, Pa."

Emil smiled and replaced his goggles. "Hop on. I'll give you a ride to the parking lot."

"I don't know if you should. The snow's getting patchy between here and there."

"You are the biggest worrier in the world. Here. Hold my fishing pole."

Sheila considered it her job to worry about him, now that

her mother was gone. It was the reason she'd moved back to Tyler, although she would never admit that to him. He thought she'd become homesick for small-town life after several years in Chicago.

Clutching the precious pole, one that Emil's father had given him, Sheila hitched up her skirt and climbed onto the snowmobile. She wrapped an arm around her dad, which wasn't hard to do. Emil Lawson always said he had to stand twice in the same place to cast a shadow. His wool coat smelled of Borkum Riff and fish, a combination Sheila would always associate with him.

"Gus is scared," Emil said. "He knows I'm gonna catch that big walleye. I've seen that fish cruisin' past the hole twice now."

"I hope you catch him soon, Pa. This weather can't hold much longer."

"Tomorrow. I'll catch him tomorrow. Wait and see. This is my year. And I'm going to order that winter special Marge has at the diner, with meat loaf, mashed potatoes and gravy, that fancy Jell-O thing and a huge piece of pie for dessert. Ha! And Gus-Gus will have to pay for it. Then he'll have to drive past my house every day and see the flag flying from *my* porch, just like I've had to put up with him having it all this time. Boy, that'll be sweet."

Sheila treasured the spirit her father showed when he was embroiled in this contest with Gus. Here on the lake he was the father she remembered, but when he got back home, she knew from experience he would deflate like a pricked balloon. She'd wondered if they should sell the farm with all its poignant memories, but that might be worse, especially because Gus Lemke would no longer be a neighbor if she and her father moved into town.

At least living next to Gus, Emil had focused on winning back the fishing flag, a tattered and faded piece of blue-and-gold canvas that had been in contention for as long as

Sheila could remember. Aside from winning that darned
flag and the celebration meal at Marge's Diner, Emil didn't
seem to have much to live for anymore. He even refused
to get his dentures fixed, claiming that he wouldn't need
them that much longer. Friends had told Sheila that the first
year after a spouse died was critical, so she was watching
her father carefully. She was counting on Gus having more
sense than Emil, and calling an end to the contest before
the ice gave way beneath them.

ALTHOUGH MARCH 20 was more than two weeks away,
spring seemed to arrive the following morning. But as
Sheila drove under sunny skies to Timberlake Lodge, the
radio weather report predicted snow by afternoon.

"No way," Sheila said, glancing out through the car
windshield at the cloudless sky. A crocus had poked up in
the front yard that morning, a royal purple daub against a
patch of dingy snow. Winter was over and this had to be
the last day her father and Gus spent ice fishing. She would
put her foot down tonight.

As she pulled into the lodge parking lot she was glad to
see Abby's old van already there. Dressed in jeans and a
sweater, Abby leaned against the fender. The prospect of
being with Douglas again had interrupted Sheila's night
with a series of X-rated dreams that woke her several times
with their potency. When she dragged herself out of bed in
the morning she'd decided she didn't need the extra stress
of a man in her life right now, especially with all the complicated baggage of their past history together. If Douglas
showed interest in Abby, so much the better. Yesterday's
commotion surrounding Douglas Wagner in buckskins had
temporarily distracted Sheila from her goal—to make sure
her father survived the first year without his wife.

She'd dressed for work in a forest-green jersey with a
slim skirt and long sleeves. The sun beamed down with

such warmth that she left her coat unbuttoned as she walked over to Abby's van.

"From your expression, anyone would think you were heading for a hanging in the public square," Abby said. "This is supposed to be in the spirit of fun, remember?"

"I fold," Sheila said, shoving her hands into her coat pockets. "If you want Douglas Wagner, he's all yours."

Abby pushed away from the fender. "Don't you dare tell me you're not even going down there. I'm brave, but not that brave."

"I'll walk down with you. Somebody has to introduce you, after all, and I said I'd be there. But I don't expect to stay long."

Abby shook her head. "This business of him being a teacher really has you going, doesn't it?"

"I guess it does. Come on. Let's get it over with." As Sheila started across the parking lot, a thin film of ice covering the asphalt crackled under her boots. Squinting, she realized she'd left her sunglasses in the car, but she didn't want to go back for them.

Abby hurried to catch up. "Did something happen in high school I don't know about?"

"Well, he thought I copied Beverly Sadler's citizenship essay for the college scholarship contest, if you call that something."

"Uh-oh. Did you?"

"Not exactly." Sheila noted that the path would soon turn to mud if the sun kept shining like this. Maybe she should have cinders spread. "It was a complicated situation and I just let him think what he wanted to."

"Beverly got that scholarship, didn't she?"

"Yes." Sheila had known it was her friend's only chance to go to college after Beverly's alcoholic father had squandered all her tuition money on booze. But Sheila hadn't realized her own father's dairy business was in trouble and there would be no money for her college education, either.

"I'll bet Mr. Wagner's forgotten all about that essay contest," Abby said. "So if that's what's tied you up in knots, I'd advise you to put it out of your mind."

Easier said than done, Sheila thought, for someone who prized honesty as much as she did. "I guess you're right." She took a deep breath and let it out. "The other problem is that I should tell him I'm sorry about his wife, but you know what? I can't remember much about her, not her name or even what she looked like."

"They weren't married yet when we were seniors, and I don't think he brought her to any school functions, so you'd have no reason to remember."

"I guess." The scents of bacon and coffee mingled with the aroma of burning cedar wafting up from the encampment. Sheila had been too nervous to eat breakfast, but now the food smelled really good.

"It was a bummer that he lived in Sugar Creek back then. We could never harass him. It was too far to go, so we couldn't TP his house, or put a stink bomb in his mailbox, or anything. Not that *you* ever did those things."

Sheila laughed. "With your new image I keep forgetting what a little troublemaker you were, Abby."

"Yeah. If anybody has a bad rep with this guy, it's me. I came close to flunking his class, despite the cookie bribes. He was so untouchable we used to call him Eliot Ness."

"That's exactly the point." Sheila watched as a regiment of soldiers in blue coats and white breeches marched into a clearing to the left of the camp and began to drill. "Of all my teachers, he was the one I admired the most. I can't throw a switch in my brain and start thinking of him as a date. It's too big a leap." Yet in her dreams the night before Douglas had been much more than a date. The memory made her flush with embarrassment.

"Okay," Abby said. "You've convinced me that you're too hung up on your past relationship with him for your hormones to function properly. Let's go find this paragon and I'll take a shot at him. I'm guessing he might be over there." Abby pointed to a group down by the lake. "That's the bunch wearing beads and feathers."

Sheila had figured out the same thing after visually searching the area without finding a tall, dark-haired man in fringed buckskin. As she and Abby drew closer, she heard the solid thunk of metal biting into wood, and a cheer went up from the group.

"What's happening?" Sheila asked a woman wearing a beaded dress.

"Some of the men are practicing the hatchet throw for the contest this afternoon," she said, moving aside. "If you squeeze right through here you can see."

Sheila stepped around the woman and her breath caught in her throat.

Poised not five yards away stood a magnificent Indian brave, his face in profile, two feathers woven through his jet-black hair. The noble sweep of his brow and the flare of his nostrils made her heart stumble. Then she noticed that the laces down the front of his buckskin shirt were undone, revealing a mat of black chest hair. She swallowed.

Gazing straight ahead, he flexed his powerful shoulders. She'd seen the play of those muscles in her dream, had run her hands over them in wonder. A flash of elemental desire took her by surprise, leaving her trembling in its wake. Bewildered by raw emotions she'd never acknowledged in herself, she put a hand over her racing heart and prayed that no one would notice her response. Yesterday's ogling with Abby had been nothing more than a silly game, but this... She had no experience of such a primitive reaction to a man.

He leaned down and pulled out a hatchet embedded in a

tree stump in front of him. As he grasped the implement, Sheila stared at his hand as if she'd never seen it before. And indeed she hadn't seen it like this—through a filter of lust that made her clench her jaw to keep from whimpering. She mentally traced the faint blue veins on the back of his hand and stroked the length of his tapered fingers. She craved the touch of those fingers, feeling as if her skin would wither without it.

Taking a deep breath, he reared back to throw, and Sheila's mouth went dry at the coiled strength in his lithe body. His breath came out in a rush as he hurled the hatchet toward a target pinned to a dead tree about thirty yards away. The hatchet wheeled end over end and landed with a heavy thud, penetrating deep to shred the target's center. Sheila felt as if something deep within her had been struck, as well.

"Way to go, Black Hawk!" someone next to Sheila called out. "Best throw of the morning!"

He turned toward the speaker, a grin of triumph on his face, and looked directly into Sheila's eyes. She had no time to mask her passion with a more civilized expression. The moment stretched between them as the shock of recognition gave way to an answering flame licking from the depths of his eyes. Warmth surged through her. Propriety told her to look away, but desire fed on his heated gaze, and desire was in command.

He started toward her.

CHAPTER THREE

"YOU CAME," Douglas said, gazing down at Sheila.

"Hell of a throw, Douglas!" said the man standing next to her as he clapped Douglas on the shoulder, jostling Sheila in the process.

"Thanks, John." Douglas's attention flicked to the man briefly before returning to Sheila.

Shaken out of her daze, she scrambled for composure. She'd had a plan, but couldn't remember it. Abby. She'd planned to introduce him to Abby and retire from the field. "I brought along a friend," she said. Her breath hitched as if she'd been running. She turned to discover Abby watching her with a knowing smile on her face. "Do you remember Abby Triblett from my graduating class?"

He shot a puzzled look in Abby's direction. "Yes, but—"

Abby stuck out her hand. "Picture me with blond hair and an extra thirty pounds, and you might see the resemblance, Mr. Wagner."

Douglas studied her as he shook her hand. "It's good to see you again, Abby. I confess I wouldn't have recognized you."

"That makes us even. I didn't recognize you when you walked into the lodge yesterday afternoon, either."

"Now I remember where I've seen you recently. You were behind the registration desk when I left."

"That was me." Abby gave him a broad smile. "And in that buckskin, with your hair longer, I would never have guessed you were my history teacher. You look a lot like an Indian, except for those green eyes.''

Sheila found herself resenting Abby's glib interchange with Douglas, but was too caught up in her churning emotions to think of anything clever to say herself.

''There is some Sauk blood in my family tree,'' Douglas said. ''But in order to be completely authentic, I should have shaved my head and my chest.'' His glance was teasing. ''That's what Black Hawk really looked like.''

Abby combed her hair back from her forehead with her fingers. Sheila had never thought of it as a provocative gesture, until now. And Abby's gaze as she looked up at Douglas was filled with invitation. ''You're probably one of those men who'd look good shaved.''

''He wore earrings, too.''

''So did pirates,'' Abby said. ''Earrings can be very sexy on a man.''

''Call me traditional, but I prefer seeing them on women.'' Douglas seemed oblivious to Abby's flirtation as he abruptly turned his attention to Sheila. ''Ready for a tour of the encampment?''

She found her voice. ''Sure.''

''I have to put the hatchet away, and then I'll show you and Abby around. Be right back.'' He headed off toward the dead tree where he'd recently embedded the hatchet blade.

When he was out of earshot, Abby leaned close to Sheila. ''I'm outta here. Give my regrets to our good-looking tour guide.''

Sheila gave her a startled glance. ''You're leaving? Why?''

''I gave it the old college try, but as the song goes, he only has eyes for you.'' Abby's smile was gentle. ''I'd just be spoiling the party.''

Panic-stricken at the thought of interacting with Douglas

by herself, Sheila grabbed Abby's arm as her friend turned to leave. "That's silly. Stay and see the encampment with me."

Abby shook her head. "I'm no more interested in history than I was in high school. I'd be bored silly. I came this morning on the off chance that our man in buckskin wasn't specifically interested in you. It's pretty obvious that he is, so I'm heading home. I have a stack of laundry a mile high, anyway." She gave Sheila a nudge. "Now go and have fun."

"Abby…" But it was no use. With a cocky salute, Abby headed back up the hill toward the parking lot.

Sheila turned. There was an air of inevitability in the way Douglas came toward her, the fringe of his shirt undulating in the breeze. He clasped the hatchet loosely by its head and absently tapped the handle against his thigh as he walked. To Sheila's heightened awareness, every gesture seemed filled with sensuality. He paused as a bearded man in a soldier's uniform put a hand on his arm and said something that made Douglas laugh and shake his head. The cadence of his laughter tantalized Sheila with the power of a caress.

Then the man turned toward Sheila and waved, and she recognized Charles Ridenour. As she waved back, she remembered Charles had mentioned having an old college buddy in Tyler. Apparently that was Douglas.

After one last comment to Charles, Douglas started toward Sheila. "Where's Abby?" he asked as he approached.

"She…just realized how late it was getting. She has a lot to do today."

Douglas grinned. "If I remember Abby, she just smelled a history lecture coming and decided to beat it."

"Oh, I'm sure she didn't—"

"It's okay. You don't have to spare my feelings. Besides, you were never any good at stretching the truth."

She looked into eyes warm with compassion and humor. She wondered if he could possibly be thinking of that afternoon so long ago when she and Beverly had sat with him in an empty classroom and discussed their very similar essays. She wasn't prepared to bring up the subject.

"You don't have to tour the encampment, either, if it will bore you," he said.

"It wouldn't."

"Good. I didn't think so." He lifted the hatchet dangling from his hand. "I have to put this away, so we might as well begin with the wigwams. Mine's down at the far end of camp."

Sheila fell into step beside him as he walked toward the semicircle of wigwams. With Abby gone, she was the only one around in modern dress, and she felt like a time traveler propelled backward 150 years. The crunch of her boots against the ground sounded harsh compared with the sibilant whisper of Douglas's moccasins. She could easily understand the appeal of experiencing this way of life for short periods of time. "Have you been part of this reenactment group for long?" she asked.

"This is my first weekend." Douglas called a greeting to a couple sitting on tree stumps drinking coffee in front of their wigwam. "My friend Charlie's been bugging me for years to get into it. Last summer he got me hooked on the hatchet-throwing competition, and when the encampment turned out to be in Tyler this time, I could hardly refuse to come. I think Charlie planned it that way."

"So maybe it was you and not my great ad campaign that brought the reenactors here."

"Oh, no. It was definitely your ad. Charlie mentioned how innovative the lodge's manager was. I just didn't realize until yesterday he was talking about you. It was a nice surprise."

The casual compliment warmed her. "And what do you think of the encampment so far?" she asked.

"Charlie was right. It's a natural for a history teacher. One night spent in a wigwam is worth a hundred filmstrips on the life of Native Americans."

"Isn't it cold at night?"

He glanced at her with a spark of awareness in his eyes, and she realized it was a rather intimate question. For all she knew he shared the wigwam with a woman who helped keep him warm. "No, it's not cold," he said. "There's ventilation through the roof, so I keep a fire going all night, and I have a buffalo robe bedroll that's probably a lot like the Indians used. I figure if they could make it through an entire Wisconsin winter, I can manage a couple of nights in March."

Sheila realized this topic contained too many potent images of Douglas stretched out on a buffalo robe dressed in nothing but a loincloth. She gestured toward the row of wigwams. "Did you help put these up?"

"You bet I did, which gave me even more respect for the process. It was a lot of hard work, and we didn't have to cut and bend trees for the frame, or tan the hides to cover them. The group has collected its supplies over the years, and some generous soul donates an old barn to store everything in." He paused outside the last wigwam and pulled back the flap over the door. "Want to see what it looks like inside?"

To refuse seemed cowardly. "Sure."

"Just slip your boots off as you step in. Hard soles are rough on the fur mats, and they don't belong to me."

As she balanced on one foot to take off her boot he steadied her with a hand at her elbow, and his firm touch destroyed what little composure she'd scraped together. She hurried through the process of removing her boots and ducked under the flap he held open. Immediately her stock-

ing feet sank into plush fur, bringing a sigh of pleasure to
her lips.

Douglas followed her in and allowed the flap to close
behind him. Suddenly the domed enclosure seemed too
small and private to share with this problematic man, but
she didn't know what to do about it. She couldn't put more
distance between them; only the area where they stood,
near the charred fire circle, was high enough to keep from
stooping.

She decided to concentrate on her surroundings and
block out the knowledge that she was alone with Douglas
Wagner for the first time in her life. Of course the area
outside the wigwam swarmed with people, and anything
she and Douglas said to each other could be heard, but it
was the unspoken messages he sent with the merest glance
that made her heart pound.

As he pulled a leather cover over the hatchet blade, she
surveyed the wigwam's interior. It was mostly bed. The
buffalo robes, rumpled and inviting, took up nearly half the
floor. Sun shining through the hides covering the frame-
work bathed everything in soft golden light, and the air was
warm and still sweet with wood smoke, although the fire
was out. Sheila had never encountered a setting this erotic
in all her thirty years.

"If this were set up exactly as the Sauk would do it,
there would be slatted benches along the wall, but the reenactors haven't gotten around to building them, so those of
us who are supposed to be Native Americans sleep on the
ground." Douglas crouched next to the fire, picked up a
stick and stirred the cold ashes, almost as if he needed
something to do with his hands.

Sheila watched the movement of his broad shoulders under the buckskin and moistened her dry lips. She wondered
if he had any idea how seductive he looked in that outfit.

"The fire gets oxygen from that little ditch that runs from

the edge of the fire circle out to the edge of the wigwam."
He pointed with the stick to a small trench dug into the dirt
floor. "Smoke goes up through the roof. I made sure the
fire was out before I left this morning, but at night it gives
off a lot of heat." He stood, tossed the stick aside and
brushed off his hands. "Listen to me lecturing. No wonder
Abby took off."

"It's very…interesting," she said around the dryness in
her throat.

"It's basic," he said. "There's a certain appeal in the
simplicity of the Native American lifestyle."

No kidding, she thought. This man in this setting
plumbed a bedrock of instinctual desire she'd never tapped
before. To keep from flinging herself into his arms and
dragging him down to the buffalo robes, she looked away
from those beguiling green eyes. "I can see why you'd be
intrigued."

Apparently he misinterpreted her lack of eye contact. "I
am intrigued, but you're probably getting bored. We can
go."

Bored? She found the courage to meet his gaze. "You
aren't boring me."

He rested his hands on his hips. "That's a small miracle.
Put me in front of a classroom full of teenagers and I can
talk for hours." He smiled sheepishly. "As I'm sure you
remember. But I'm out of practice for what to say when
I'm alone with a beautiful woman."

His admission of vulnerability, considering how imposing he looked standing before her, was stunning. The balance between them shifted a fraction. "I never would have
guessed Mr. Wagner would be at a loss for words," she
teased gently.

"Mr. Wagner isn't. Douglas is."

Her heart swelled in wonder as she watched the barriers
between them begin to crumble. Perhaps it wasn't an im-

possible situation, after all. She followed her instincts. "And how about Black Hawk? How would he react?"

He seemed taken aback. Then his eyes slowly filled with a roguish light. "To a beautiful white captive, a young woman with yellow hair?" His gaze darkened. "I don't think you're ready for that." He took a step closer, and for one heart-stopping moment she thought he might kiss her. "I promised you a tour," he said, moving past her and opening the tent flap. "If we don't get out of here, you won't get one."

FOR THE NEXT half hour, as Sheila walked with Douglas through the encampment, she mulled over the encounter in the wigwam. She was sure he'd been fighting the urge to take her in his arms when he'd abruptly ushered her out. The prospect made her feel as if she carried a glowing ember deep within her, one that needed a mere feather touch to cause it to burst into flame. But the encampment filled with more residents of Tyler, including several of Douglas's students, and that feather touch never came.

At last Sheila consulted her watch and announced that she'd better get back to the lodge and begin her workday. Kathleen Kelsey, Edward Wocheck's executive assistant, had scheduled a meeting at eleven for an update on Sheila's plan to bring publicity-generating conventions to the lodge.

"Charlie said there would be a brunch there tomorrow for the reenactors," Douglas said, gazing down at her. "Are you organizing that?"

"Yes."

"Then I should see you tomorrow up at the lodge."

"I expect you will." She paused, hoping he might mention something more immediate. She finished work at six and had the evening free. "Thank you for the tour."

"My pleasure."

In the unfilled silence between them she realized he

wasn't going to invite her to the encampment for the evening. He'd teased her with hints of passion and now he was letting the matter drop. She forced a smile to hide her disappointment. "See you tomorrow, then." As she turned away three high-school girls came running over, squealing and giggling, absorbing his attention. Determined not to be included in that kind of hero worship, she started up the path to the lodge.

OVER LUNCH Kathleen praised Sheila's innovative ideas for increasing business at the lodge. Kathleen was another example of how Edward Wocheck had utilized local talent in his organization. The Kelsey family was well-known in Tyler, and Kathleen was one of its classiest members. So far Sheila had really enjoyed working with her.

The briefing completed, Kathleen went back to her office to catch up on some paperwork, leaving Sheila to round up a few dining-room employees to help her organize the decorating for Sunday's brunch. She'd chosen a frontier and Native American theme to coordinate with the reenactors, who would attend in costume. In keeping with that theme, she'd asked Renata and Michael Youngthunder, owners of a regional Native American arts-and-crafts outlet near Tyler, to lend her some of their inventory. They'd been more than happy to give their business more exposure through decorations for the brunch.

As Sheila worked, the muffled sound of rifle fire erupted from the clearing near the encampment as the reenactors staged their mock battle. Finally she gave in to the temptation to walk out on the veranda and watch. Douglas figured prominently in the action as the designated leader of the Sauk nation, and although the battle was make-believe and the guns were filled with blanks, Sheila still felt a moment of fear as he charged a group of armed soldiers, swinging the butt of his rifle over his head.

Fascinated, she remained on the veranda until the Indians won the battle and stood over the "dead" bodies of soldiers. Then Douglas lifted his rifle, threw back his head and let out a bloodcurdling whoop of triumph. Sheila chuckled and shook her head at his dramatics, yet a chill skittered down her spine as a part of her reacted to the primitive note echoing in his cry.

The crowd of spectators applauded as the soldiers got to their feet, and everyone returned to the encampment. Sheila didn't realize until then that she was shivering from cold. Heavy gray clouds covered the sky, obscuring the sunlight that had graced the first part of the day. Maybe the weather report hadn't been so off base after all, she thought as she returned to the warmth of the lodge.

An hour later Kathleen came into the dining room where Sheila was putting the final touches on a dessert-table centerpiece of Native American pottery overflowing with beaded necklaces. "I don't want to second-guess you, but do you think we should consider a plan B for the encampment situation?" she asked.

Sheila glanced up at the dark-haired young woman. "What situation?"

"I take it you haven't looked outside recently?" Kathleen's blue eyes were grave.

"No."

"It's snowing."

Sheila closed her eyes and groaned. "Great. That could interfere with tomorrow's performance, which was supposed to swell the brunch crowd."

"I'm more worried about tonight's weather."

"Why? How much are we supposed to get?"

"I checked with the weather service fifteen minutes ago. Several inches by morning."

Sheila felt a stab of unease. She should have kept abreast of the situation. Her preoccupation with Douglas might already be causing her to forget her responsibilities. "We can't let them freeze out there in the snow, but sending them home wouldn't be very good public relations, either." She glanced at Kathleen. "Should we consider putting them up here? And if so, what should we charge? I'm not sure all of them have the resources to pay the regular rate."

Kathleen tapped a pen against her chin. "Technically I could authorize you to give them free rooms, I guess. But I need Mr. Wocheck's signature on a couple of things, anyway. As long as he's in town, let's get him out here and allow him to have a part in the decision."

"Fine." But Sheila didn't feel fine about any of it. She'd created this convention program so the lodge's profits would increase. Now it looked as if they might well take a loss on her very first group.

"I'll go call him." Kathleen returned to her office. A few minutes later she came back. "He's on his way. Says he needs some fresh air, anyway. Hey," she said, coming over to put a reassuring arm around Sheila, "don't look so glum. Stuff happens."

"I shouldn't have agreed to this encampment the first weekend in March. You never know what the weather will be like, but I was so excited about having such an interesting group that I—"

"Don't blame yourself," Kathleen interrupted, giving her a little shake. "Come on. Let's finish up this centerpiece while we're waiting for him."

Less than a half hour later Edward Wocheck, trim and distinguished-looking, came through the lodge's front door. Once snubbed by the reigning tycoon of Tyler, Judson Ingalls, Edward had left town as a young man, returning a few years ago a tycoon in his own right. After purchasing Timberlake Lodge from Judson, Edward had bought a controlling interest in Judson's plant, Ingalls Farm and Machinery, and in a final triumphant move had married Judson's daughter, Alyssa, a woman he'd loved since high school. Those dramatic events, coupled with Edward's mentoring behavior, had made Sheila a staunch admirer of her boss.

He strode into the dining room, unbuttoning his topcoat with one hand and brushing the snow from his hair with the other. He grinned at them. "So you two brilliant women can't control the weather, huh?"

"It sure looked like spring this morning," Sheila said.

"Well, it's not spring now, and I wouldn't want to spend the night in those tents down there, even if our ancestors started out that way. The reenactors are technically our guests. We can't have them out there getting frostbite on Addison Corporation property."

"I know, and I feel responsible for this mess."

"You didn't know we'd have a blizzard. Do we have enough vacancies to squeeze them in at the lodge?"

"Maybe just barely," Sheila said.

"Then I think you'd better go down there and offer them accommodations gratis."

"But we'll take a loss."

"Just on the utilities. We don't have the rooms rented anyway, and I'd rather give them free rooms than have somebody become ill because they stayed out in the snow. Lawsuits are expensive. Oh, and we might as well throw in a low-cost buffet dinner, too. I want their cooking fires out. Even if it is snowing, I'm not taking any chances with untended fires in the woods."

"I think we're all edgy about that after what happened out at Ingalls F and M," Kathleen said.

"You've got that right," Edward said. "Until the investigators decide how that fire started, I'm using caution with anything that burns. One major disaster in Tyler is enough."

"I'm sorry this encampment is causing so much trouble.'' Sheila's shoulders drooped. "I shouldn't have signed a contract with them once they said they weren't staying in the lodge.''

"Nonsense.'' Edward waved aside her guilt. "We all agreed it would bring us good publicity, and it has. A van from WTMJ out of Milwaukee was pulling out of the parking lot as I drove in. Now I hate to rush you, but the snow's coming down faster. We may be able to round up a snowmobile you can drive down there on if you want to.''

She lifted her chin. "Mr. Wocheck, I'm a Wisconsin girl. A little snow doesn't scare me.''

He laughed. "I'm a Wisconsin boy, and sometimes it scares the hell out of me. Be careful. I don't want to lose my top-notch manager in a snowbank.''

Sheila mustered a smile and headed off for her coat and boots. Moments later she crunched down the path, the hood of her wool coat pulled over her hair. As usual, Mr. Wocheck was taking this debacle with good grace, but she still felt responsible for the losses he'd incur by feeding and housing the reenactors. She hoped they would be properly grateful for their good fortune in dealing with a man like Mr. Wocheck.

Moist snow kissed her cheeks and calves, and was already sticking to bare patches on the ground. She glanced out toward the lake. Once this chore was completed she'd go down and whistle her father and Gus in. By this time in the season the shanty windows were so grimy that the men wouldn't be able to tell it was snowing outside.

As she neared the encampment she saw that some of the reenactors were huddled around the central bonfire, while others had retreated to their tents and wigwams. A quick glance through the crowd revealed Douglas wasn't there. Smoke curled from the roof of all the wigwams, including his, so he was probably inside with a fire going. She didn't see Charlie, either.

A couple of the reenactors recognized her and drew her over toward the fire with offers of hot coffee. Falling snow hissed as it fell onto the blaze.

"Actually, I need to speak to Mr. Ridenour," Sheila said. "Do you know where he is?"

"Having a powwow with some of the other men in Douglas's wigwam. They're deciding what we should do about this weather," a soldier said.

"Good. I think I can be of some help," Sheila said as she headed off toward Douglas's wigwam. Once there she wondered how one knocked on a flap. She decided one didn't, and pulled up the flap to go inside.

Four men looked up at her entrance. She stayed just inside the door so she wouldn't mash the fur mats with her boots. Douglas and Charlie sat on the far side of the wigwam on the buffalo robes, and two other men had taken positions on either side of the door.

Sheila pushed back her hood. It was toasty warm inside, just as Douglas had told her it would be with a fire going. Douglas started to get up, but she motioned him back down. "In view of the weather, Timberlake Lodge would like to put you all up at no charge and provide a low-cost buffet for dinner. You could leave everything set up, and maybe tomorrow the snow will clear enough for you to stage your battles and hatchet-throwing contests after all."

Charlie beamed. "That's a terrific offer, Miss Lawson. We'd just decided to double up in the wigwams, because the Army tents aren't designed to have fires inside them. But we'd be pretty darned crowded. We accept."

"Good." Sheila noticed that Douglas hadn't leaped at the suggestion as Charlie had. In fact, he was frowning. She'd probably spoiled his macho sense of adventure. Too bad. She pulled her hood up again. "Please make sure all your fires are completely extinguished. Then just come to the lobby, and I'll be there to direct you to your rooms."

BEFORE SHEILA RETURNED to the lodge, she trudged down to the lake and called her father and Gus in from the ice. Then she supervised the check-in procedure as the first few members of the reenactment group entered the lobby, looking like refugees from another era.

Eventually Charlie and his wife, Cathy, dark-haired and plump, appeared at the desk. "I thought you should know that Douglas won't be checking in," Charlie said.

Sheila glanced up from the computer screen. "That makes sense, since he lives in town. He can just go home."

Charlie mopped snow from his beard with a bandanna. "Oh, he's not going home. He decided to stay at the encampment."

"I don't understand."

"We tried to talk him out of it," Cathy said. "I should have known we were wasting our breath. He's been stubborn all the years we've known him."

Sheila frowned. Mr. Wocheck wasn't going to like this at all. "Stubbornness is one thing. Stupidity is another. Did he say why he insisted on this course of action?"

Charlie leaned toward her and lowered his voice. "Something about the fact that an arsonist could be on the loose in Tyler. He thought somebody should stay and guard our materials. I told him to forget about the stuff, but he won't."

Sheila's jaw clenched. She wasn't about to let Douglas Wagner stay down there by himself after Mr. Wocheck had made it clear he wanted everyone out of the encampment. "Thank you for letting me know," she said. "Perhaps he didn't fully understand our position. He must leave."

"Good luck in making him do it," Charlie said.

"Oh, he will do it," Sheila replied. She turned over the last of the check-in duties to her night manager, Ron Temple, and put on her coat and boots again. Kathleen and Mr.

Wocheck were gone. It was up to her to talk some sense into this crazy man.

By the time she'd started down the path toward the encampment, she'd worked up enough righteous indignation toward Douglas that she didn't notice the snow or the cold wind. He *would* have to mention potential arson in connection with the town, fueling a rumor that had the power to harm Tyler's tourist business and reduce reservations at Timberlake Lodge. And now, after doing the dirty deed, he was sitting in the encampment alone, defying the order to evacuate. Sheila vowed she would get Douglas out of that wigwam if she had to drag him out by the fringe of his sexy buckskins.

CHAPTER FOUR

WHEN SHEILA BURST through the flap of his wigwam, Douglas blinked and wondered if his recent fantasies had conjured her up. He'd just been thinking how perfect the setting could be with Sheila stretched on the buffalo robe beside him, her eyes filled with the lusty emotions he'd seen there when he'd turned from throwing the hatchet.

She folded back her hood and firelight touched her blond hair. He'd been in the act of pouring a cup of coffee, but he hung the pot on the hook over the fire and put the tin mug beside him as he prepared to enjoy this hallucination for as long as it lasted.

"You must either come up to the lodge or go home," she said.

That wasn't quite the speech he'd imagined in his fantasy. He'd conjured up something along the lines of *I can't resist you any longer. Take me now.* He gazed up into her resolute eyes. "I was having some coffee. Would you like a cup?"

"I'd like you to leave, please." The dulcet tones he remembered from that morning had been replaced by a no-nonsense finality. "You pose a liability to the Addison Corporation by staying here alone in a blizzard. Please put out your fire and go home."

He considered her deliberate stance for a moment. He'd suspected she had this sort of backbone, although in her high-school days she'd never displayed it in his presence. But much as he admired her spirit, he couldn't go along with her demands. "Is the Addison Corporation prepared to patrol the encampment throughout the night to ensure it won't be vandalized?" he countered.

Color tinged her cheeks, and he nearly lost his composure at the fierce beauty of it.

Her voice, though still controlled, rose a notch. "That's the other thing you've done. Do you realize how that arson story could damage Tyler's reputation and hurt the tourist business?"

"Yes, I do," he said quietly. The emotion flowing from her wasn't the one he wanted, but it was a start. At least she wasn't cowed at the moment by his image as a teacher. "Charlie and Cathy are the only ones I told, and I've asked them to keep it to themselves. I've known them both for fifteen years, and they can be trusted."

"Well, that's something, anyway. But you have to leave, Douglas. As the manager of Timberlake it's my responsibility to see that you do. I won't let friendship interfere with my duty."

He got to his feet. Matching wits with her promised to be a stimulating experience. "I'm sure you won't. And neither will I. As the only member of the encampment who really understands the threat to all these irreplaceable things, I have a duty to protect them."

"I doubt Mr. Wocheck would see it that way."

He skirted the ring of glowing coals and stood next to her. "I'm not leaving, Sheila. You're going to have to call the cops and have me thrown out."

"I will if that's what it takes." Her chin lifted.

If only she'd raised her face to his in anticipation instead of rebuttal, he thought. "I imagine it would be bad publicity for the lodge when people find out that Brick Bauer had to haul a guest away in handcuffs."

"Are you threatening me with bad publicity?"

"I wasn't threatening, just pointing out." What a shame,

he thought, that they had to argue, when all he wanted was to draw her close and explore her lips with his mouth while he unbuttoned her coat.... He forced himself to concentrate on the problem at hand. "I won't go peacefully, and unless you've been studying one of the martial arts since the last time I saw you, you'll need help getting me off the premises."

"Charlie was right about you." She crossed her arms as if defending herself against his unspoken desires. "You're stubborn as a Missouri mule."

And you're beautiful as a spring morning in Wisconsin. "I'm stubborn when I'm convinced a course of action is the right one." He glanced down into her face, tinged with firelight. "You and I both know there's a real chance the F and M was torched, and in a town this small it won't take long for word to get out that we abandoned the encampment to sleep in comfy beds at the lodge. If there is an arsonist in town, this camp would be an irresistible target. It would go up like a dry haystack."

The muscles in her jaw tightened. "If that were to happen, which it won't, you could go up with it. Had you considered the fact you might not hear an arsonist until it's too late?"

"No." He longed to smooth the tension from her jaw. "Ever since my wife...well, let's just say I'm a light sleeper these days."

Gradually her expression softened, as if he'd actually bestowed the soothing touch he'd wanted to give but dared not. She swallowed and glanced away. "That's something I've been meaning to apologize for. When we first talked, I—I didn't know about your wife. Otherwise I never would have said those things about scuba diving, and Indiana Jones."

"I know. No apology necessary. Your sensitivity was one of the things that...set you apart." *Be careful,* he thought. *She's probably not ready to hear that you wanted her even then, when she was a child of seventeen.* But something in his tone had brought her gaze back to his, and he couldn't stop looking into her eyes.

With her irritation gone, she became dreamily absorbed in him, and he watched the process in awed fascination. The passion he'd glimpsed in her expression earlier today developed slowly, and he watched it build, his heartbeat quickening in response. He hadn't been wrong. She wanted him, too. But now might be too soon to take advantage of that fact. He didn't want to ruin something with so much promise by rushing.

"So, what should we do about this?" he asked gently.

She looked startled, then embarrassed as she apparently realized he was talking about his presence at the camp. When she spoke, her voice had lost its commanding tone. "I want you to leave."

"I can't. Please try to understand."

"Not even to protect my job?"

He closed his eyes in dismay, then reopened them to gaze down at her. "The last thing I want to do is jeopardize your job." He thought hard, searching for a way out of this mess that would appeal to a businessman like Wocheck. Thinking wasn't easy when he'd much rather take her into his arms and forget everything but the pleasure of holding her at last. "Okay," he said finally. "I have a proposition." Bad choice of words, he chastised himself as her eyes widened. "Hire me as a security guard for the night. I worked my way through college doing that, so I know the routine."

She blinked. "A security guard."

"Sure. Make me a temp for tonight, when the encampment needs supervision. So if Wocheck asks if everyone's left, you can say, 'All except the man I hired to keep an eye on things.' Under the circumstances, if I were Wocheck I'd appreciate that kind of cautious thinking."

Her smooth brow creased as she considered his suggestion.

He'd always enjoyed watching her intelligent mind work through a problem. In the classroom she'd been his early-warning system to determine if he was getting through. If Sheila didn't fully grasp a concept, then none of his other students would have a clue. "It's a reasonable compromise," he said.

She cast an evaluating glance around the tent before focusing on the fire circle, where low flames wove themselves through chunks of blackened wood. "What if your fire goes out while you're asleep and you freeze to death during the night?"

"I'll get extra blankets from the other wigwams before I settle in for the night. And I don't plan to sleep much. Between keeping the fire going and listening for intruders, I'll be on watch most of the time." He smiled. "I promise not to freeze to death and cost you your job. I already have enough on my conscience where you're concerned."

Her attention swung back to him abruptly. "Excuse me?"

He sighed. The admission had slipped out, but they'd need to deal with that matter eventually. Maybe now was as good a time as any. "If we're going to get into that, you might want to sit down and have that cup of coffee."

"Get into what?" She regarded him warily.

"The essay."

Her glance skittered away.

"Coffee?"

"Okay." She still didn't look at him.

He moved to the opposite side of the tent and dropped to one knee. He heard her rustling about, and when he looked up from pouring the coffee, he was gratified to discover she'd slipped off her boots and chosen a spot to sit on a section of buffalo robe about three feet away from him. "How about some historically inaccurate powdered cream and sugar?"

She gave him a tentative smile. "Sure."

He doctored up both mugs and handed her one. "I smuggled the packets in. Never learned to drink the stuff black. I figure you can carry this historical-purity thing too far."

"Are you about to unveil your battery-powered television set?"

"Not yet." He winked at her and took a sip of his coffee.

She cradled her mug in both hands. "The fire does keep this place surprisingly warm."

"Want me to take your coat?"

"That's okay." She turned shy again. "I'll just unbutton it. I won't be here that long. I have to get home to my father pretty soon."

Something about the way she said it alerted him to the fact that her mother wasn't around anymore. He remembered Myrna Lawson from a couple of PTA meetings where she'd rabble-roused about something or other. She'd been an interesting woman. "Then your mother…?"

Sheila nodded. "She died seven months ago. My father was so dependent on her that I was worried about how he'd make it alone. Luckily, Mr. Wocheck needed a manager here."

So this new position was more important than he'd realized. No wonder she'd come after him with guns drawn when she thought he might louse things up for her. "How's your father doing?"

"Fine when he's out on the lake ice fishing with Gus Lemke. Terrible when he's at the farm. He and my mother sold the livestock years ago, but I've considered buying some dairy cows just to keep him interested in something."

Douglas nodded. How well he knew the need for activity and a connection with life. Without his teaching he would have gone crazy after Joanne died. "He's lucky to have you."

She looked at him over the rim of her cup. "You and your wife didn't have children?"

"No. We weren't able to." He gazed at the hypnotic dance of the flames. "We talked about adopting but never got around to starting the process. I didn't put much importance on it, but after she died, I would have given a lot for a child to help ease the pain."

A warm weight settled on his forearm, and he glanced up in surprise. Sheila had moved closer and laid her hand there, probably in an instinctive gesture of support. Her hazel eyes glowed with sympathy. He was astonished that he'd told her about wishing he and Joanne had completed the adoption process. It was something he'd never mentioned to anyone and had barely acknowledged to himself. He sat perfectly still and cherished the sweet touch on his arm, knowing that soon she would realize what she'd done and withdraw it. When she did, he couldn't suppress a sigh of regret.

"At least you had your students," she said.

"Yes, but I don't know how much they had me. I was a zombie for a long time."

"I'm sure you did a fine job."

He swallowed a mouthful of now-tepid coffee, then stared into the murky liquid. "I didn't do a fine job with you."

"I don't understand what you mean."

He turned his head to look at her. If he planned to make amends, he damned sure ought to do it right and face her like a man. "I shouldn't have let Beverly get away with taking credit for that essay."

She stared at him in silence for several seconds. "I had no idea you knew she copied from me," she said at last. "I assumed you thought of me as a cheater."

He shook his head and chuckled. "You? Never in a million years. You're probably the most honest student I've ever had, so that alone would have convinced me who was the cheat. But then there was the essay itself. The ideas in it could only have come from you. They represented your kind of analytical thinking."

She studied him. "You really thought about this, didn't you?"

"More than you know."

"It's nice to hear that you liked my ideas, but the truth is I probably wouldn't have won the scholarship, anyway. I couldn't write as well as Beverly. I'm sure she took my bare-bones wording and made it into something wonderful."

"Not at all." He was grateful for the chance to finally set the record straight. "You had twice Beverly's talent. She overwrote, adding so many embellishments the meaning was nearly lost. The ideas in that essay impressed the judges, not the writing. Your style was clean, spare. Beautiful." That last applied to more than her writing, he thought.

"Really?" Her eyes shone. Then she gave him a teasing smile. "You're not just saying that to soften me up about staying in camp tonight?"

"Nope."

"Because it wouldn't work. If I decide to let you stay, it will be for a logical reason."

"I wouldn't dream of trying to compromise your integrity."

Her gaze was thoughtful. "I know integrity's a big thing with you, which is why I hated to have you think I'd cheated."

"But I didn't think that."

"I'm glad." She smiled. "I remember lots of girls tried to bribe you with cookies and stuff, and it never worked.

They called you Eliot Ness, because you were so untouchable.''

He laughed. ''I didn't know that. I don't remember you ever trying that tactic.''

The way she squared her shoulders was quite endearing. ''I refused to act like some sort of groupie, just because all the other girls were drooling over you.'' Immediately she realized what she'd said and blushed. ''I mean—''

''Drooling? Seriously?''

''You didn't know? You had a fan club!''

''My God.'' He reached for a chunk of wood to feed the fire. He should have been strong enough not to ask, but he asked anyway. ''You didn't drool, I take it.''

Mischief danced in her eyes. ''Maybe a tiny trickle.''

''Thank you.'' How he would have loved to kiss her then, but still he held back. The moment would come when it would be the exact right thing to do. He picked up a small twig that had snapped off a larger piece of wood and nudged some coals closer to the blaze.

''You know,'' she said, ''letting Beverly have that scholarship was the right decision. She would never have escaped that family of hers if she hadn't gone to college. Last I heard, she was doing well in advertising.''

''Do you keep in touch?''

''No, not really. You know how it is once you leave high school and go your separate ways.''

Douglas could easily imagine how it would be with somebody like Beverly. Her dysfunctional upbringing had taught her to be a user. Once someone was of no value to her, she'd cast the person aside and move on to the next victim. ''Do you still write yourself?''

Sheila gave him a quick glance. ''Why do you ask?''

''I'd hate to think you gave it up.''

''I pretty much have.''

He snapped the twig in half. ''That's a shame.''

"No, it's not. The world doesn't need another writer. We waste enough trees as it is."

His patience evaporated. "To hell with what the world needs. To hell with what Beverly needed. What do you need, Sheila?"

She sat quietly without answering.

He knew he'd gone too far. He'd have been better off kissing her than making a comment like that. "Look, I only meant—"

"I know what you meant." Her gamine smile had a wistful tinge to it. "It's no use. I came down here as an adult in charge, ready to enforce the rules of the corporation I work for. Not only did I fail at that, but I end up feeling like a kid in school who isn't living up to her teacher's expectations. I think I'd better go." She started to rise.

He got to his feet, too. Dammit. Dammit to hell. "I'm sorry. It's just that I hate to see talent wasted. And for what it's worth, I don't think of you as a kid in school."

"No, in point of fact, I'm your boss," she said as she concentrated on buttoning her coat. "What do your services cost for tonight?"

He didn't have much left to lose, he decided. He'd tried to be so careful, and he'd still ruined the mood. Maybe he should throw caution to the winds and take a crack at erasing his schoolteacher persona, his blasted untouchable image from her mind. "The cost of my services depends on what you'd like me to include."

Her head snapped up.

"We've talked about a lot of things tonight, but not about what happened between us this morning when I turned around and saw you standing there in the crowd."

"I...don't know what you—"

"Oh, yes, you do." He stepped closer. "Come to think of it, we've spent too damned much time talking, Sheila."

"I really have to go." But she remained trapped by his gaze and made no move toward the tent flap.

"I've considered that it might not be me that attracts you," he continued. "It might be the buckskin." Slowly he reached for her hand and laid it against his chest. Her fingers quivered beneath his. He lowered his head as he pressed her palm against his pounding heart. "Tell me, is it the outfit or the man that puts that spark in your eyes?" He hovered above her mouth, savoring the sweetness of her breath as her eyes fluttered down in surrender. "Then again, maybe it doesn't matter," he whispered.

CHAPTER FIVE

SHEILA HELD HER BREATH. Mr. Wagner was going to kiss her. It felt dangerous...forbidden...and wonderful. A mouth soft as velvet became molded to hers. A perfect fit. Lips in firm command coaxed a sigh of delight from her, and she arched her neck in subtle invitation. He stroked her throat with the back of his hand, his touch so light it could have been his breath passing over her skin. Liquid fire sluiced through her, scorching away tension, leaving supple compliance in its wake.

With lazy pressure he urged her to slacken her jaw. He shifted the angle of the kiss, taking her deeper into it, sliding his hand beneath her hair and spreading his fingers to cradle her head. Her heartbeat thundered in her ears and she clutched the front of his shirt with both hands, gathering the soft buckskin in her trembling fingers. When he began to explore with his tongue, the fire within her fanned downward, creating an ache so strong she gasped at its power.

Slowly he lifted his head and gazed down at her, with an intensity that sent a fresh wave of heat through her. He released her and stepped away. "Go home to your father," he said in a voice rough with passion. "Before I beg you to stay."

She grasped for reason and found a snatch of it. Her car was still in the lodge parking lot, a bold advertisement that she was somewhere on the grounds. If it remained there much longer, people would likely start looking for her, and they would probably start here in Douglas's tent. And the snow continued to fall outside. She needed to start home now if she expected to get there at all. But to be snow-bound, in this tent, with Douglas... She reached for the hood of her coat and pulled it up over her hair.

"You see, I'm not as untouchable as you thought," he said softly.

She glanced at him standing in the shadows, drank in the imposing bulk of him clothed in tight buckskin. She fought the impulse to rush into those strong arms and forget the world outside. "You know what I wish?"

His low voice rumbled, mixing with the crackle of the fire. "What do you wish?"

"That I were really your white captive."

He took an unsteady breath. "If you stay another second, you might be. Now go."

She leaned down toward the tent flap. Then she straightened and turned back to him. "You never said what you'd charge for watching the camp."

A brief smile dimpled his cheek. "You just paid it."

With a soft moan she ducked out into the whirling snow. Propriety had never seemed so pointless.

THE SNOW STOPPED FALLING sometime during the night, and although the next morning was cold, the sun shone in a clear sky. Apparently the whole town had needed an ex-cuse for a party, Sheila thought as she surveyed the lodge grounds, which were packed with townspeople. Those who could afford it had come for Timberlake's Sunday brunch. Those who couldn't—mostly people thrown out of work by the F and M fire—had created tailgate parties in the parking lot.

The lodge maintenance crew had worked since early that morning to clear snow from a football-field-size area where the reenactors would once again stage their battle. Sheila felt good about providing a setting for people to let loose.

Joblessness and fear of a local arsonist had cast a pall over the town, but for today everyone could ignore modern-day problems as they watched a scene from the Black Hawk War unfold before their eyes.

Sheila looked forward to seeing Douglas. Although he'd been at the brunch, she'd been too busy to do more than catch a fleeting glimpse of him from across the room. That brief moment had been a potent one. He'd glanced up just as she looked over at him, and for a second she'd been aware of nothing but the power of those green eyes. Then someone else had claimed her attention, and the moment had ended.

But finally the last of the brunch customers had left, and the reenactors, all of them profuse in their gratitude, had checked out of their rooms. Sheila had donned her coat and boots to walk outside and view the mock battle. Edward Wocheck, his wife, Alyssa, and Kathleen Kelsey joined her.

"I take it you couldn't persuade your father to leave his fishing shack to come and watch," Edward said as they walked along a path cleared through the deep snow.

"Nope. He realizes his ice-fishing days are numbered, and he's using every second he has to try and beat Gus Lemke."

"You should get him off that ice pretty soon," Alyssa cautioned. A breeze lifted her silver-blond hair.

"Believe me, I know that," Sheila said. "Ever tried to budge a determined seventy-three-year-old man?"

Alyssa laughed. "Yes, my father. I sympathize."

"Mr. Ingalls couldn't make it today?" Sheila asked.

Edward shook his head. "He caught a cold. Blames it on staying around in this weather instead of going back to sunny Arizona. Personally I think he let the tension surrounding the fire investigation get to him. His resistance is down." His voice held genuine concern for the man who used to be his enemy.

"But he insisted we all come and report back to him about how everything went," Alyssa said. "I'm sure he's sorry to miss it."

"I see the soldiers drilling over there." Kathleen shaded her eyes from the sunlight, which was beginning to melt the snow. "But no warriors. My brother, Patrick, said Douglas Wagner had talked him into being a Sauk Indian for the afternoon. I'm dying to see how he looks."

"No wonder so many high-school kids are here," Edward said, turning up the collar of his coat against the wind. The rat-a-tat-tat of a snare drum issued from the marching soldiers. "How could any kid resist seeing Patrick Kelsey, alias their P.E. teacher, and Douglas Wagner, alias their history teacher, in war paint and feathers? I don't remember anybody getting that wild when we were at Tyler High, do you, Lyssa?"

"Back then I couldn't imagine teachers had a life." Alyssa tightened the belt on her navy wool trench coat. "For all I knew they slept on cots in the faculty lounge every night."

Sheila remembered having some of those same thoughts about her teachers, except for Douglas Wagner. Everyone knew he led a very romantic life when school let out. She used to picture him in a sleek wet suit diving for historical treasure in the South Seas, off the coast of Greece or in the Bahamas.

Kathleen chuckled and shook her head. "Teachers are pretty selfless, that's for sure. Between Pam coaching football and Patrick coaching basketball, their whole married life seems to revolve around school. And speaking of my talented and very happily pregnant sister-in-law, there she is now." Kathleen waved and called to Pam Kelsey, a radiant-looking young woman with shoulder-length brown hair. Pam waved back and started toward them.

Edward glanced over at the encampment. "The more I

think about it, the happier I am you decided to hire Douglas Wagner to keep an eye on the tents last night, Sheila.''

Sheila blessed the wind, which could be blamed for whipping the sudden color into her cheeks. ''It seemed like a good idea at the time.''

''It was a good idea,'' Edward said. ''I didn't think of the encampment as being a potential target for an arsonist. Thank God no one set fire to the tents last night. *If* we have an arsonist, of course,'' he added, tucking his wife's arm through his and glancing down at her.

Alyssa sighed. ''I know everybody considers me a Pollyanna, but I refuse to accept the idea that someone deliberately set the F and M on fire. I can't believe anyone would do something that vicious to the people of Tyler.''

''Let's hope not,'' Kathleen said, wrapping her wool scarf tighter around her neck. ''Even the suspicion that someone did is eroding community spirit, and I hate that. Thank goodness we had this event today, Sheila, so people could get together and remember what's special about living here.''

''And this is only the beginning of Sheila's campaign to liven up the place,'' Edward said, glancing at her. ''Seems to me the coming attraction is a convention of twins.''

''I heard about that,'' Pam Kelsey said as she joined the group. ''I'm going to find some excuse to come up here that week. I'm dying to find out if all the twins dress alike.''

''If they do it could be a nightmare for the staff,'' Sheila said with a laugh.

''I can hardly wait for the convention of astrologers,'' Kathleen said. ''I hope the stars are aligned while they're at the lodge. Just think—the Age of Aquarius right here in Tyler.''

Edward grinned. ''That's a good media hook, Kathleen. Let's use it. Looks like we'll have the Milwaukee television stations running out here on a regular basis.''

"I just hope we don't lose money again like we did this time," Sheila said.

"Don't give it another thought," Edward said. "I don't think you realize what a good idea you had booking these oddball conventions. I have a feeling we'll end up with national attention before long. Which can only mean more business. Whatever we lost this weekend is insignificant."

"It doesn't feel insignificant to me," Sheila said, frowning. "I had hoped we'd show a sizable—"

Alyssa laid a hand on Sheila's arm, silencing her. "You have to remember that Edward's outgrown some of that fiscal conservatism the rest of us learned growing up as Midwesterners. If he says not to worry about a loss, don't worry." She looked up at her husband. "Sometimes he scares me, but I've finally realized that he knows what he's doing."

Edward chuckled. "Can I get that on tape?"

"Look!" Kathleen cried. "Here come the warriors. There's Patrick! My God, Pam, he looks positively *fierce.*"

"I recognize that shade," Pam said, her eyes narrowing. "I'll bet he annihilated my tube of Kissable Red lipstick, and I just bought it last week. I should never have let him rummage through my cosmetic case this morning."

Sheila barely heard Pam's comment. Her entire focus was trained on the tall man striding next to Patrick, a rifle in one large hand. Yesterday, when she'd watched the battle from the veranda, she hadn't been close enough to see the black bands painted across his face. The slashes of war paint gave him a menacing air intensified by the grim set of his mouth—the same mouth that had captured hers so completely the night before. She could hardly believe it when the man who had trembled with passion now lifted his chin and glared at the crowd as if he needed no one, as if he had become, in fact, the proud warrior Black Hawk.

The contrast sent a thrill of sensual excitement down her spine.

The crowd that had gathered to witness the confrontation stilled, and for one crystal moment there was no sound but the cheerful song of a cardinal perched high in the branches of a snow-draped fir tree.

Douglas raised his rifle, threw back his head and issued a battle cry that shattered the quiet. His band rushed across the clearing toward the soldiers, who had dropped to one knee and raised their rifles to their shoulders. Gunfire exploded from both sides, and the acrid smoke from rifle barrels drifted toward the spectators.

The fight seemed so real that Sheila had to forcibly unclench her hands and tell herself that Douglas wasn't in danger. The rifles aimed at him were loaded with blanks, and Douglas would not suddenly fall to the frosty ground with blood spurting from his chest. In fact, he wouldn't fall to the ground at all. She knew the outcome of this battle: the Sauk Nation had won it. Yet she couldn't calm her racing heart, or dispel the fantasy of a Sauk chieftain demonstrating his prowess on the field of battle—for her.

At last it was over. Charlie Ridenour and his regiment lay crumpled on the ground, and Chief Black Hawk once again issued his cry of victory. The spectators applauded and spilled onto the field. Sheila started forward, too, but when a horde of teenagers descended on Douglas and Patrick, she turned away, unwilling to fight through a mob.

"I'm going over to hassle Patrick about that lipstick," Pam said. "Want to come along, Kathleen?"

"My pleasure," Kathleen said. "Besides, I see Mom and Dad heading over there, and I want to check what the plans are for Easter dinner this year." She hurried in pursuit of Anna and Johnny Kelsey.

"It's good to see Johnny out having a good time," Edward said after Pam and Kathleen left. "I sometimes think he still believes that, as the F and M foreman, he's somehow responsible for that fire.''

"You're probably right," Alyssa said. "He thinks of the people who work there as his extended family."

"Which is why he's so good at his job."

The mention of work reminded Sheila she couldn't stand out here all afternoon hoping for a chance to speak with Douglas. "I'd better head back to my office," she said to Edward and Alyssa. "I'm glad you were both able to come over for the performance this afternoon."

"Wouldn't have missed it," Edward said. "Why don't you suggest they come back and stage it every year? It could become a Tyler tradition. Maybe more local people besides Patrick Kelsey and Douglas Wagner would get involved if we made it an annual event."

"I'll talk to Charlie Ridenour about it. Well, I'll see you both later, then." With a smile, she started across the snowy ground toward the lodge.

"Sheila, wait!"

She turned at the sound of a deep masculine voice, one that made her skin tingle. Douglas came toward her, followed by Patrick, Pam, Kathleen and the senior Kelseys, who were teasing Patrick unmercifully. It didn't look as if Sheila would have a private conversation with Douglas, but at least she'd see him before he left.

"We all realized that nobody had taken time to thank you for setting all this up," Douglas said as he reached her. "So consider this the gratitude committee." It was a pleasant, uncomplicated little speech, but his gaze communicated something entirely different.

Sheila felt herself grow warm from his silent appraisal. "You're welcome."

"I had a great time!" Patrick said. "Until my family started in on me, that is."

Anna Kelsey's blue eyes twinkled behind her gold-rimmed glasses. "I just reminded him of the time he raided *my* cosmetics case for war paint when he was six years old. I can see he hasn't changed a lick."

"Boys will be boys," Kathleen said to her brother, laughing. "You and Douglas may pretend you're doing this for the educational value, but I know better. You're into the fantasy of it, pure and simple."

Douglas grinned and glanced at Sheila. "Fantasy has its place."

She gulped and swung her attention to Patrick, who had painted diagonal red stripes down his cheeks and horizontal ones on his forehead. "What did your basketball team think of your costume?"

"They think he should wear it for the donkey basketball game on Thursday, right, Patrick?" Johnny Kelsey said, nudging his son in the ribs.

"Which I would, but I don't know if Pam has enough of that red lipstick left."

Pam groaned. "He couldn't have used the cheap tube from the drugstore. No. It had to be the good department-store stuff."

"Donkey basketball," Sheila said with a smile. "I didn't know Tyler High still did that."

"We do," Douglas said. "Why don't you come?"

She barely had time to consider whether the casual invitation was a request for a date or an idle suggestion before Patrick jumped into the conversation. "You have to come," he said. "Any Tyler alum still in town is required to attend the donkey basketball game and watch Douglas, me and Clint make fools of ourselves."

"Clint?" Sheila asked.

"Clint Stanford, the new principal," Pam said. "He's from Texas, so we figure he should be able to ride a donkey."

Sheila laughed. "That's some trial by fire. Miss Mackie never had to ride a donkey."

"No, and she pointed that out to me when she called the other day from Florida, just to see if we're surviving without her," Patrick said. "She was ready to fly up here just to see the new principal on the court, but then I told her the temperature outside, and she reconsidered."

"Riding a donkey on the court's only half the problem," Johnny Kelsey said. "It's dribbling a basketball while riding a donkey that gets a bit dicey."

"I remember." Sheila looked at Douglas again. "I wouldn't miss it for the world."

"Good," he said.

She was relieved that he didn't follow that with an offer to pick her up. She wasn't quite ready to broadcast their status—whatever that was—to the rest of the town. From the corner of her eye she spotted Renata Youngthunder heading for the lodge. "I think Renata's ready to pick up the crafts she loaned me for the brunch decorations," she said. "I'd better go back to the lodge."

"And I have an appointment with a jar of makeup remover," Patrick said. "But thanks again, Sheila. This has given us all a real boost."

"Definitely," added Anna, looking at her husband's relaxed expression. "I think we all needed a dose of fantasy."

"And we'll see you Thursday," Pam Kelsey said.

"Yeah, Thursday. Seven sharp." Patrick clapped Douglas on the shoulder. "We'll give her a good show, right, Wagner?"

"Absolutely."

"I'm counting on it," Sheila said, backing away from the group. Douglas didn't say anything more, but she carried the memory of his smile with her as she turned and walked back to the lodge.

CHAPTER SIX

SPRING FEVER, Douglas decided as he struggled to keep his third-period class interested in the Civil War. He was having nearly as much trouble as they were, and he loved the nuances of U.S. history. But he was more interested in the nuances of Sheila Lawson at the moment. Today was only Monday, and Thursday seemed years away.

Yet he'd decided not to call her before then. They both needed time. If he followed the urges of his libido, he would arrange to be alone with her tonight, and the night after that, and the night after that. With the powerful physical attraction between them, they'd be lovers by Thursday. He knew that was too fast. The crazy basketball game would be a good way to start getting to know each other in the safety of a crowd.

With difficulty he brought his attention back to his classroom of juniors. He walked away from the chalkboard where he'd been diagramming the Battle of Bull Run and rested his hip against the front of his desk. "Robert E. Lee was a respected member of the United States Army, yet he turned his back on his government and aligned himself with the Confederacy." He tossed the chalk in the air and caught it. "Why?"

"Scarlett O'Hara," called out Matt Hansen, a forward on the basketball team. He grinned as several of his friends laughed.

"That's not as crazy an answer as you meant it to be, Matt," Douglas said. "Scarlett might be a fictional character, but she represents what many Confederate soldiers fought for—their homes and the honor of their women.''

"Women have had more to do with history than some people think," said Elaine Jenkins, one of the brightest students in the class and a budding feminist. "There was Cleopatra, and the Trojan War started because of Helen of Troy, and—"

"So *that's* where the brand name came from," cut in Andy LeBlanc, one of the more precocious kids. This time the boys laughed until they choked, and Elaine glared at him. The rest of the girls slid down in their seats and brought their open books up to shield their rosy faces.

"Yes, as a matter of fact," Douglas said, leveling a stern look at Andy, "but it wasn't very gentlemanly of you to embarrass half the class with that observation. I want you to apologize." He held the boy's gaze until Andy finally glanced away.

"I apologize," he said.

Matt turned in his seat to look at Andy. "Good move, LeBlanc. Did you see how this guy can throw a hatchet? I'd advise you not to mess with him."

Douglas tried not to think about what had happened after Saturday's practice for the hatchet-throwing contest, but it was no use. He couldn't block out the picture of Sheila's eyes glowing with undisguised desire.

"We're getting away from the topic," he said. "Which is Robert E. Lee's motivation for fighting for the Confederacy." He glanced toward the left side of the room, where Jon Weiss sat staring into space, his hazel eyes vacant. Jon was a nice kid, with a great smile when he chose to use it. But he'd just moved to Tyler at the beginning of the school year and was struggling to fit in, so he didn't smile all that often. "What do you think it was, Jon?"

Jon looked up in obvious panic. "I—I don't know."

Douglas considered pressing the point that Jon didn't

even know the question, let alone the answer. But something about the youth's frightened gaze elicited Douglas's sympathy and he backed off.

As he continued to direct the discussion, he watched Jon lapse back into his trance. He'd been daydreaming a lot recently. Douglas made a mental note to talk with him privately soon and find out if there was a problem aside from generally feeling like an outsider. He could be in love. At this age that could wreck your concentration. As a matter of fact, it could wreck your concentration at any age.

Douglas wondered what Sheila was doing at this very moment, and if she'd spent as much time thinking about him as he had about her. Maybe he'd go to Marge's for lunch. Not that there was much chance she'd be there. She was probably working hard at the lodge. But sooner or later, everyone seemed to turn up at the diner. Maybe today would be his lucky day.

SPRING FEVER, Sheila thought. That probably explained her restlessness despite having so many things to accomplish today, the only day she planned to take off this week. Monday was a good time to turn the operation of the lodge over to Abby, her assistant, because managerial duties were usually light.

Sheila had spent the morning dropping off dry cleaning, shopping at Olsen's Supermarket and buying her father a new shirt at Gates Department Store. Emil would say he didn't need the shirt, that he wouldn't live long enough to wear out the ones he had, but Sheila kept trying to reverse that attitude. Finally she stopped for lunch at Marge's Diner. She'd remembered that sometimes students and teachers from the high school came over to eat at the diner, but of course that had nothing to do with her decision. Like heck it didn't. She was looking for an excuse to run into Douglas Wagner.

Feeling like a teenager with a crush, she kept glancing up at the door of the restaurant every time it opened, but Douglas never appeared. Several friends stopped by to congratulate her on the success of the weekend reenactment, and a couple of other teachers came in, but not Douglas.

As Sheila finished her toasted cheese sandwich, Glenna Kelsey, another of Anna and Johnny's brood, elbowed her way through the door with her arms full of papers and books. Her last name wasn't Kelsey anymore, Sheila remembered. In fact, pretty soon it wouldn't even be McRoberts, the name of her ex-husband. She was engaged to Lee Nielsen, the investigator on the F and M arson case, and according to local scuttlebutt they were planning a summer wedding. Glenna had been only three years ahead of Sheila in school, yet she'd already been married and was the mother of two children. Now she was working on her degree in early-childhood education. In comparison, Sheila's life seemed uneventful.

Glenna paused at Sheila's booth. She'd inherited her mother's dark hair and the famous Kelsey blue eyes. "I heard the weekend turned out great," she said. "I'm sorry I missed it, but I've been so busy with classes and editing videos that I couldn't take the time."

"Those videos are a brainstorm," Sheila said, her creative instincts aroused by Glenna's idea. "It makes sense, though, that if you videotape preschoolers playing, other preschoolers will want to watch. Whatever happened to that offer you had to market them?"

Glenna looked as if she had a wonderful secret she was trying hard to keep. Her voice quivered a little as she tried to contain her excitement. "That didn't pan out, but I'm meeting Byron Forrester today to go over a contract from Pierce and Rothchilde. Apparently they're interested in distributing the videos."

"Why, Glenna, that's wonderful!" Sheila reached out

and squeezed her arm. "If you have a prestigious publisher like Pierce and Rothchilde behind you, you'll be on 'Oprah' before we know it."

"Oh, my God, I'd die! I want to be behind the camera, not in front of it."

"Fame has its price," Sheila warned with a chuckle. "Don't forget what happened to Britt Marshack when she started out with Yes! Yogurt. I still have a tape of the day she was on 'Oprah.'"

Glenna looked horrified. "You don't really think…oh, I just couldn't. Not in a million years."

"What couldn't you do, Glenna?" Byron asked, coming up beside her. His chiseled features and dark eyes and hair revealed his kinship to his brother, Cliff, Liza's husband. "Hi, Sheila," he said, glancing at her. "Great show yesterday."

"Thanks." Sheila thought about Glenna's good fortune in having this connection right in Tyler. Byron had come into town five years ago and swept Nora Gates, supposedly a confirmed spinster who wanted nothing more than to run her department store, right off her feet. Creative in his own right, Byron had opened a gallery in town where he displayed local art along with his own photographs. But he'd also kept his hand in the Forrester family publishing business in Boston. "I was just telling Glenna that with your company behind her videos, she's liable to be on 'Oprah' one of these days," Sheila said.

"Could happen," Byron said. "Finding ways to entertain very young children is a hot topic. Pierce and Rothchilde is excited about handling Glenna's work." He grinned. "Although I probably shouldn't say that and give her extra bargaining power."

Glenna looked pale. "Byron, I just couldn't appear on national television. Your company has to understand that I—"

"Let's not worry about that yet," Byron said as he took her arm. "Let's go talk about money. You *will* consider accepting money for your videos, I hope."

"Well, of course I expect to be compensated."

"I thought so." Byron winked at Sheila as he led Glenna away. "But I warn you, I'm a tough negotiator."

"So am I." Glenna was obviously relieved to forget the possibility of national exposure. "See you later, Sheila," she said over her shoulder.

"Hold his feet to the fire, Glenna," Sheila said. As she finished her coffee she wondered what it would be like to be signing a contract for something you'd created, a product of your imagination. She was happy for Glenna, and to be honest with herself, a little jealous. Douglas had awakened more than sensual desire on Saturday night; he'd also reminded her of long-repressed dreams.

With a sigh she picked up her purse along with her check, and headed for the cash register. As she stood waiting for her change, the door opened behind her and the hairs on the back of her neck prickled.

"Just leaving?" said a familiar male voice.

She turned and found Douglas standing there, his hands shoved casually in the pockets of his slacks, his black ski jacket unzipped.

Her heart started pumping so fast she grew a little dizzy. "Yes. I—I just stopped in for lunch." What a dumb remark. What else would she be doing at the cash register, collecting hush money for the mob?

His green gaze captured hers. "I thought you'd be at the lodge."

"I usually take Mondays off."

"Too bad I didn't know. We could have had lunch together."

You didn't know because you didn't ask, dammit. Although her attention kept drifting to his mouth, his wonderful, kissable mouth, she forced herself to act casual, so he wouldn't suspect she would have sacrificed a year of her life to have lunch with him today. "Oh, well. Maybe another time."

"Sure."

They couldn't stand there blocking traffic and collecting stares, she realized. "I'd better get going. Lots to do today."

"Right. See you Thursday night."

"I'll be there." Flashing her best smile, she walked past him and out the door. All the way home she replayed the scene and wondered why he hadn't used the opportunity to offer her a ride to the basketball game. And how he managed to look so darned sexy. After seeing him today she knew the answer to his question last Saturday night. It wasn't just the buckskin.

SEVERAL HOURS LATER she sat in the upstairs room her mother had designated as an office, with bits and pieces of her mother's life strewn around her. Sheila had set herself the chore of going through the desk today. Someone had to, and her father had refused.

Her makeup was smeared from alternate bouts of crying and laughing at the things her mother had chosen to save. An Easter card Sheila had made in second grade rested on top of a rather clever cartoon of a monster in an apron labeled My Ma—Tyler's Answer to Tyrannosaurus. Sheila remembered creating that when she'd been denied permission to go sledding at age twelve with a group of older boys.

Myrna had saved all the valentines and anniversary cards her husband had given her, including a few risqué ones Sheila had never seen. Apparently her parents had enjoyed a lustier marriage than she had imagined. Myrna had also preserved every one of Sheila's compositions, beginning in junior high and ending with the infamous essay that Beverly had copied. Douglas Wagner hadn't given it a grade, but Myrna had written across it, in print so bold it nearly tore through the paper, *Excellent!* Sheila hadn't credited that opinion, of course. After all, mothers were supposed to say things like that.

All the mementos had the musty odor of cigarette smoke. Sheila and her father had tried in vain to get Myrna to give up smoking, but she had insisted the cigarettes helped her think. Now, looking through her mother's scribbled-in notebooks, Sheila had a better idea of what she thought.

The notebooks were chock-full of witty observations and vignettes about Tyler residents, some long dead and others still around. None of it was mean-spirited, all of it fascinating to someone who'd lived for years in Tyler. Sheila's excitement grew at the thought of typing the contents of the notebooks and making them available for others to read. Elise Fairmont, the town librarian and self-appointed historian, might want a copy kept at the library, but Sheila could imagine the booklet becoming a bestseller in Tyler. It seemed like the perfect way to memorialize her mother.

At the bottom of the last desk drawer Sheila found a surprise—sixteen true-confession magazines. Apparently they'd been a secret passion, because Sheila had never seen her mother reading one. Here at last was something that could be thrown away. Everything else Sheila would keep as a precious reminder of the woman who had left such a gaping hole in the lives of her husband and daughter when she'd gone.

Glancing out the window at the growing twilight, Sheila stood and stretched. Time to drive to the lake and fetch her father.

"I CLEANED OUT Ma's desk, today," she announced as they sat at the oak table in the kitchen, eating the sloppy joes she'd prepared using her mother's recipe.

He glanced up, looked away again and nodded. Upon her insistence, he'd put on the new flannel shirt she'd bought him. The muted green-and-gray plaid brought out the color in his hazel eyes, which were still strong enough to look across the wide expanse of Timber Lake and spot a deer drinking on the far shore. Emil was proud of his good vision and only occasionally resorted to reading glasses.

"I know you don't want to look at anything now," Sheila continued, "but—"

"That's right. I don't," he interrupted.

"I just wanted you to know I'm not throwing anything away. I'll keep it, and if you change your mind, everything will be there."

Emil stared at the apple-print kitchen wallpaper and his throat worked.

Sheila's heart ached for him, but they had to discuss these things sometime. "The only thing I threw out were the confession magazines. I don't even know if you realized that she bought them."

His head snapped toward her. "You hafta keep them magazines," he said in a hoarse voice. "That's the most important thing." He pushed back his chair. "Where did you throw them? In here or—"

"I took them out to the garbage can," Sheila said, shoving her own chair back as her father leaped to his feet and headed for the kitchen door. "Pa, wait! I'll get them. It's cold out there!"

He paid no attention as he charged out the door. She ran after him, and the cold sliced through her turtleneck sweater and slacks. Emil threw off the metal garbage can lid with a clatter and leaned over to lift out the pile of magazines. He brushed away a crumpled paper towel, which fluttered to the ground and started to blow away. Her father, usually careful not to litter, didn't seem to notice as he examined the magazines for damage.

Sheila ran after the paper towel, grabbed it and threw it back in the garbage can. Then she replaced the lid. By the time she'd done that, her father was already striding back inside, the magazines held protectively against his chest. Sheila hurried to catch up, chastising herself the whole way for throwing away even this apparently unimportant part of her mother's past. From Emil's behavior with the magazines, Sheila was glad she'd decided to keep everything else, even if he didn't want to go through it now.

Inside the kitchen, Sheila rubbed her arms to restore warmth while her father set the magazines gently on the table. He went through the stack, issue by issue, brushing off a few small crumbs that had stuck to the covers.

Finally he sighed and patted the magazines. "That's okay, then. They're safe and sound. Safe and sound."

For six months Sheila had been watching her father for any signs of mental deterioration. She feared this could be the first indication that he was losing his grip. "Pa, can you tell me why these are important? I know they belonged to her and she probably read them, but she read the newspaper every day, too, and we haven't saved—"

"Her stories are in them magazines."

"Her…" Sheila felt as if he'd smacked her in the stomach with a very large pillow. "Are you saying she wrote for those magazines?"

He nodded. "They paid her. The only ones who would."

"She's published in these magazines?" Sheila still couldn't grasp it.

"Yep." He opened the first one very carefully and pointed to a story with the byline Miranda Leighton. "That's her. She used the same initials."

Sheila stared at the open magazine in disbelief.

He closed that one, laid it aside and opened the next to a piece written by Marilyn Lintz. "See? She always kept her initials. She couldn't use her real name, or the same name." He looked up at Sheila. "They're good," he said a trifle belligerently.

"I'm sure they are." Sheila held on to the edge of the table for support as she sat down. "It's just that I can't believe I didn't know. She was publishing stories and getting paid for it, and I didn't even know."

"She didn't think it would go over so good in Tyler. She figured you'd want to brag about it, you bein' that kind of loyal little kid, and the other kids would tease you."

Sheila gazed at the stack of magazines. "I guess I see what she was afraid of, but I wish I'd known. She was trying to break into the publishing world, and I didn't even realize she was writing anything except letters to the relatives. I didn't give her enough credit, Pa."

He walked around the table and put his hand on her shoulder. "Me neither, Sheilie. Me neither."

She reached up and covered his hand with hers while the tears spilled from her eyes. "Well, I'm going to fix that. I found all her notebooks, and I'm going to find a way to get them published. Maybe I'll have to pay to do it, and maybe the book won't get any farther than Tyler, but at least I want the people in this town to know that Myrna Lawson was a fine writer."

"She wouldn't like you to."

She swiveled around to look up at him. "Why not?"

"She never planned on anybody seeing them notebooks. She said she'd been spyin' on people for years, but only to get stuff for her stories. Most of the stories are about Tyler folks, but changed around so's they won't know themselves. Your ma loved the people here, and she wouldn't want them embarrassed."

"But the descriptions aren't embarrassing, Pa. They're

funny, and true, and touching, but I can't imagine why anyone would be embarrassed.''

He squeezed her shoulder. ''That's because you're still young. And times've changed some. Did you read the one about Judson Ingalls strippin' nekked and jumpin' in the lake one night, just because his wife, Margaret, dared him?''

''Yes.'' Sheila smiled, remembering that a fish had nibbled on Judson's private parts, and he'd come charging out of the lake yelling, ''Shark!''

''Margaret told that story to your ma. People was always telling her stories. But I doubt anybody else heard about it. He might be real embarrassed for people to read about that now.''

''But her writing is so *good.* I want people to know.''

''She wanted to write for the bigger magazines, *Redbook* and them, but she didn't make it. She wouldn't have minded being bragged about then.''

''Oh, Pa.'' Sheila let out a long sigh of sadness and frustration.

''She was hopin' *you'd* be a writer some day,'' he said softly.

CHAPTER SEVEN

WHEN SHEILA WALKED into the Tyler High School gym on Thursday night she felt as if she'd never left.

"Give me a T!" shouted the cheerleaders through blue-and-gold megaphones.

"*T!*" roared the crowd of students massed on the pull-down bleachers. The noise was deafening and so familiar that Sheila almost yelled with them. Except tonight she wouldn't be sitting on that side of the court and cheering for the student players. She breathed in the smell of damp wool and varnished wood.

"Give me an *I!*"

"*I!*"

Unbuttoning her coat, Sheila walked around the end of the court toward the marginally more sedate adults sitting on the opposite set of bleachers. Abby had promised to meet her there. About midway up in the stands someone waved a blue-and-gold pom-pom, and Sheila recognized Abby holding it.

"Give me another *T!*" cried the cheerleaders.

"Oh, no! What does *that* spell?" shouted the students.

Sheila chuckled. Apparently the same old gag was still in vogue. Spelling out T-I-T-A-N-S had always meant stopping in the middle for a little teenage humor.

"Nothing!" scolded the cheerleaders on cue. "Give me an *A!*"

"*A!*"

As Sheila climbed the varnished steps toward Abby, she

noticed that the town's two most prominent families, the
Kelseys and the Ingallses, were well represented. Even the
patriarch, Judson Ingalls, had made it to the game. Sheila
thought about the moonlight-swim story and wondered if
Judson had mellowed enough not to mind having his foi-
bles exposed. Maybe her father was wrong about how sensitive folks would be. Sheila wished she'd been able to talk
him into coming tonight, but as usual, once he was away
from the lake, he became a recluse who wanted no contact
with anyone except his daughter.

Sheila smiled at Jake and Britt Marshack, owners of Yes!
Yogurt. Britt was bouncing their two-year-old son on her
knee while she talked to Sandy Murphy, who had returned
to Tyler at Christmas to become the yogurt company's mar-
keting director—and had married Drew Stirling, the VP of
sales, on Valentine's Day. Partly because they'd both come
back to Tyler after an absence, Sandy and Sheila had struck
up a friendship.

"Call me!" she demanded. "We'll do lunch!"

"You bet!" Sheila called back. Most of the town had
turned out for the game, which benefited the school's athletic fund. Sheila had heard the basketball team needed new
uniforms, so perhaps with this kind of attendance they'd
get them for next year.

Abby scooted over as Sheila arrived. "Just in time for
the famous cheer," she said.

"Can you believe they're still doing that?" Sheila took
off her coat and folded it beside her. As usual, the packed
gym was warm.

"I think it's kind of cute. The way kids are exposed to
sex every five minutes these days, I would have figured
that joke was too tame for them. If they still get a kick out
of it, maybe they're not as jaded as I thought."

"I hope you're right." Sheila glanced at the bedraggled
pom-pom. "Dug that out of the closet, did you?"

"How do you know I don't still have it hanging on my wall, along with my Class of '83 pennant?"

Sheila laughed. "Let's hope not. High school was a while ago."

"Doesn't feel like it, though, does it?"

"Only when I glanced into the faces of those cheerleaders. They're babies, Abby. Mere babies."

"But when we were that age we thought we were so hot."

"Yeah, I guess we did."

"And speaking of that, you haven't given me a straight answer on how things went with Mr. Wagner on Saturday. Is there a chance you're here tonight to see him riding a donkey?"

"Sort of." Sheila knew there was a silly smile on her face. "Yes, actually."

"Then why didn't he pick you up?"

Good question. "It wasn't exactly a date sort of invitation." Sheila watched as Liza Forrester and her daughter, Margaret Alyssa, made their way down the bleachers and positioned themselves in front of the crowd. "I think Liza and Maggie are going to lead us in a cheer."

"You're changing the subject."

"It was really nothing significant. Douglas and I were standing around with Patrick and Pam Kelsey on Sunday after the reenactment battle, and the subject of the game came up. Douglas suggested I come, and Patrick said it was required of all Tyler alums. So I said I'd be here. That's all there was to it."

"I say he could have come by for you. Just suggesting you show up is kind of weak, don't you think?"

Sheila wasn't sure what to think. "Douglas and I need time to adjust to our new status," she temporized. "As two adults, not student-teacher," she added hastily. She had no intention of telling her friend about the kiss they'd shared.

She believed what she said intellectually, but waiting for tonight to arrive had been torture. She hoped Douglas had been tortured a bit, too.

"If you say so."

Liza made a megaphone of her hands. "All right! Give me an *F!*"

Little Margaret Alyssa, her blond ponytail bouncing, mimicked her mother. "Give me an *F!*"

The adults shouted out an F and Abby giggled. "An *F?* What are we going to spell?"

"Faculty," Sheila said. "Honestly, you're worse than the kids."

The adult side of the gym grew rowdier as Liza and Maggie coached them through F-A-C-U-L-T-Y and a few other impromptu cheers. Sheila joined in with gusto. It had been a long week, and it felt good to let off some steam. Then the pep band struck up the school fight song and the crowd surged to its feet as the locker-room doors swung open.

"Here they come." Sheila's voice quivered with excitement.

Abby gave her a questioning glance. "So it's no big deal, huh?"

"Not really." But Sheila realized she was holding her breath.

The students came first, three senior basketball players each holding the bridle of a less-than-enthusiastic donkey. The three faculty members followed, leading their own donkeys, and Sheila realized she wasn't psychologically prepared for the sight of Douglas, the man who had kissed her so well, clothed in a skimpy basketball uniform. The gold, scoop-necked jersey revealed the breadth of his shoulders and chest, and the shorts gave her a perfect view of powerful-looking legs. She couldn't decide whether to admire the dark swirls of chest hair that curled above the jersey or the flex of muscles in his thighs as he moved onto the court.

Abby glanced at her again, then waved a hand in front of her face.

She turned. "What?"

"Just checking to make sure you weren't catatonic or anything."

"Very funny."

Abby laughed. "You know, Sheila, I hate to see how you'd react to a *really* big deal."

FOR THE PAST FIVE YEARS of donkey basketball the Tyler High Future Farmers of America had provided Douglas with a cute little thing with long eyelashes named Daisy. He and Daisy had understood each other. Over the years the Daisy-Douglas combination had scored a total of six goals, which was a lot in donkey basketball. But Daisy wasn't feeling up to par this week, and so the FFA had substituted Esmerelda. Esmerelda had an attitude.

As Douglas trotted out on the court leading Esmerelda, he hazarded a glance into the stands to try and spot Sheila. Esmerelda executed a sideways hop and kicked him in the shins. She obviously wasn't used to the rubber bootees the donkeys wore to protect the basketball court from their hooves, and she was determined to get them off. Douglas gave up looking for Sheila and concentrated on the donkey, who managed to tag him twice more before the referee blew his whistle, signaling that it was time to mount up.

Douglas tightened his bandanna headband and slid one leg over Esmerelda's back, which was apparently her cue to head off toward the locker room. Douglas gripped with both thighs and wrestled her head back around. By the time he got her back on the court, the game was in progress.

If you could call it a game. Most people in Tyler called it a controlled disaster. The crowd's laughter drowned out the referee's attempts to enforce a few rules, and before long the contest turned into a free-for-all, as it did every year.

Patrick grabbed the ball away from Brad Schmidt, a big blond kid who was the star forward for the Titans. Patrick bounced the ball furiously in the middle of the floor as he urged his donkey forward. Trouble was, his donkey didn't want to move—in any direction.

"Wagner!" Patrick yelled. "I'm stalled! Take it down!" He heaved the ball half the length of the court, and the crowd hollered in approval.

Douglas managed to snag the ball out of the air, even dribble a couple of times before Esmerelda, with a loud bray, headed for the showers again. On his way off the court, Douglas chanced a hook shot that by some miracle went in. Just shy of the doors into the locker room, Douglas got Esmerelda turned, but by that time Danny Stevens had scored for the students' team. The game was tied.

Douglas headed down the court as fast as Esmerelda would agree to go, and nearly ran headfirst into the principal, Clint Stanford, whose donkey had decided to make a break for the basket, even though Clint wasn't in possession of the ball. Like Patrick and Douglas, Clint had agreed to wear a basketball jersey and shorts, but he'd also insisted on wearing his Stetson. After the near-miss with Douglas, he lifted his hat in apology, and the crowd responded with wild applause.

Patrick managed to hang on to the ball long enough to throw it in the general direction of the basket before his donkey reversed direction.

"Air ball!" shouted the students as Brad grabbed the rebound and rolled the ball down the floor to Titan guard Jack Patterson, who scored again for the students' team.

As if in protest, Clint's donkey deposited a steaming pile of manure mid-court. A cleanup crew hurried out, but Esmerelda was way ahead of them. Putting on an amazing burst of speed, she galloped forward and slid to a sideways halt, unseating Douglas. He tried to roll in the opposite direction, but it was no use. A second later he was covered with donkey doo-doo.

"Better hit the showers, teach!" called Brad as he spun the ball on the end of one finger. "The game's ours now!"

"I can stand it if you can!" Douglas shouted back. With a wicked grin he climbed on Esmerelda and headed her straight for Brad.

Being covered with manure had its strategic advantages, Douglas discovered. Brad elected to give up the ball rather than get dirty. "You win," he groaned, loosening his hold. "I have a date tonight."

"Me, too," Douglas said with a chuckle. Then he steered Esmerelda down the court, while everyone cleared a path and made a great show of holding their noses. Waves of laughter bounced against the gym walls as Douglas took his sweet time maneuvering into position, with no opposition from Brad, Danny or Jack. Esmerelda brayed as he sent the grimy ball in a graceful arc. A cheer erupted as it swished through the hoop. Nobody went for the rebound.

"That's the game!" a referee called out. "Faculty wins!"

As the pep band once again launched into the Titan fight song, Douglas dismounted and glanced over at Patrick. "Isn't this when we're all supposed to get together and hug?" he called.

"I think we might skip that tonight," Patrick called back. "In fact, you'd do us all a big favor if you'd leave. You notice our admiring fans haven't mobbed us on the court as usual."

Douglas had noticed that people seemed to be hanging back a bit. "But I'm your star! I should be nominated MVP!"

"I dub you the MVP! And for that you can have your own private dressing room!" Clint shouted over at him. "Now will you git?"

"Okay, okay. Esmerelda and I can take a hint." Douglas considered his options. He'd planned to hang around on the court until Sheila came down with the rest of the crowd. Then he'd have invited her to drive over to Marge's Diner with him after he changed clothes. Now she might slip away while he was in the shower. He couldn't leave it to chance, not after waiting four days to see her. He raised his voice. "Hey, Patrick, will you ask Sheila to wait for me?"

Several heads turned, and people regarded him with interest, but he couldn't help it. Once he walked into Marge's Diner with her, the gossip would start anyway.

"Will do," Patrick yelled back. "And use that heavy-duty soap!"

In the shower Douglas used every kind of soap he could find, scrubbing both his uniform and himself. After a while the other players, seniors and faculty members alike, came back to the locker room, and as Douglas got dressed he had to put up with a fair share of good-natured accusations about being a "dirty player."

He pulled a cable-knit sweater over his head and looked at Clint, who was easing a foot into a polished cowboy boot. "I think they've figured out our strategy, Clint. You might as well confess we planned the whole thing."

Clint looked up, a gleam in his eye. "Well, now, that's a fact. Used an old trick I learned down in Texas. That little pile of manure was our secret weapon, boys."

"You can call it little. You didn't roll in it," Douglas grumbled.

Brad grabbed his blue-and-gold letter jacket from the hook in his locker. "That reminds me, Wagner. Did I imagine it, or did you say something about having a date?"

"That was the plan," Douglas said. To preserve the mood, he decided not to make an issue of Brad leaving off the "mister" from his name, although it was typical of the cocky senior to take advantage of the camaraderie to be insolent.

Brad slammed his locker door and grinned at his history teacher. "You might want to stand downwind of her, then."

Douglas groaned and turned to Patrick. "Okay, tell me honestly. Do I still stink?"

Patrick seemed to be trying hard not laugh. "Not as bad."

"Did you talk to Sheila?"

Patrick's blue eyes twinkled. "She said she'd wait."

Douglas hesitated. "Maybe I should take another—"

"I don't think she'll wait that long," Patrick said. He clapped him on the shoulder. "It's not that bad. Were you going over to Marge's with the rest of us?"

"I thought we would."

"Then maybe Pam and I will go someplace else." Patrick laughed and held up both hands. "Just kidding! You're fine. Really. Listen, I gotta go. Half the Kelsey clan is out there waiting for me. See you at Marge's." He headed out the door, leaving only Clint and Douglas in the locker room.

"I'm taking off, too." Clint shoved his arms into a leather jacket and adjusted his Stetson.

Douglas reached for his ski jacket. "Maybe I'll just keep my jacket on," he muttered.

"You never know—" Clint started toward the door "—she might be the earthy type who likes the smell of animals on a man. I think that's a good sign, personally."

Douglas grinned. "Yeah, but you're from Texas."

"You bet your bluebonnets."

"Are you going to Marge's?"

"For a little while." Clint paused with one hand on the door. "Listen, don't you have Jon Weiss in your U.S. History class?"

"Yes." Douglas remembered that he hadn't yet created an opportunity to talk with Jon. He'd try tomorrow. "Why?"

"He and another kid got into a small scuffle after the game tonight. Fortunately I was able to separate them before it got out of hand, but the fact that it was Jon surprised me. I've never thought of him as the type to cause problems."

"He's been a little spaced out in class lately. I've been meaning to take him aside. Maybe I can do it tomorrow."

"Then why don't you come by my office after your last class and tell me what you found out? If a good kid's getting off track, I'd like to nip it in the bud."

"Okay."

"And now you'd better hustle out there to that little old gal of yours and find out how persnickety she is."

"I could cheerfully wring your donkey's neck for screwing up my evening, Clint."

"Look at it as a little test. You don't want one of those hothouse flowers who wrinkles her nose at every little thing. See you at Marge's."

"Right." He couldn't very well explain to his principal that he didn't want to test Sheila tonight. He just wanted to kiss her, and he didn't want that kiss tainted by the lingering smell of manure.

WHILE SHE WAITED for Douglas, Sheila stood with her coat folded over her arm and watched the maintenance staff clean the gym floor. The crew had finished with the mop and bucket at center court, and now they pushed wide dust mops up and down the polished floor. The game had been fun, and she'd laughed so hard her stomach hurt. When

Patrick had given her Douglas's message, she'd been thrilled, but the longer she stood in the empty gym waiting for him, the stronger her memories grew. Old memories seemed to widen the gulf between her and Douglas.

These days both the junior and senior proms were held at Timberlake Lodge; she'd just finalized the arrangements with both prom committees. But her senior prom had taken place in this gym, and Douglas had chaperoned. Sheila tried to remember if his girlfriend had been with him, but she couldn't picture anyone. He'd danced with Miss Mackie, the principal then, but nobody had considered that scandalous. Miss Mackie was old enough to be his mother.

Sheila had a clear image of Douglas, handsome as a prince in his tux, waltzing with the principal. Every girl in school would have ditched her date in a second to be asked out on that floor by Mr. Wagner. Sheila had been no exception. But it had been a safe fantasy then. Now a fantasy concerning Douglas Wagner no longer felt safe.

"Sheila?" Douglas walked toward her wearing jeans, a sage-colored sweater and his black ski jacket. His collar-length hair curled slightly, just after his recent shower.

No wonder each new crop of high school girls swooned over him, she thought. Just looking at him made her head spin. "You gave quite a performance," she said.

"By accident. You may be sorry you waited. I'm not sure I've gotten rid of the smell."

Her heartbeat quickened as he came closer. "Don't forget I was raised on a dairy farm."

"Sheila the milkmaid." He smiled and grasped her arms to draw her to him. "Now be honest." His green eyes sparkled. "Take a deep breath and tell me if I smell too bad to take you to Marge's for pie and coffee."

She had trouble managing any breath at all, let alone a deep one, with the imprint of his fingers burning through her cashmere sweater. Speechless, she looked into his eyes, and then her gaze drifted down to the curve of his smiling mouth. She remembered the velvet feel of that mouth as if he'd kissed her only seconds ago. She swallowed.

"Well?" His voice was husky.

Slowly she looked up. "You'll do," she murmured.

He drew in a sharp breath and his grip tightened. "Sometimes I wonder if you have the slightest idea…" He leaned toward her. Behind them a bucket clanged to the floor. He muttered a soft oath and released her. "Come on. We'll take my truck."

Her feet barely seemed to touch the floor as she walked with him to the door. She would have forgotten to put on her coat if he hadn't stopped and helped her into it. Even that, with the briefest of touches as he guided it over her shoulders, sent of jolt of desire through her. She had to get a grip on herself, she thought as they stepped into the cold night air. One look, one touch, and she became a hotbed of hormones. Perhaps this was a case of fantasy overload. The Indian chief in buckskin, the muscled basketball player and the former teenage crush were too much for her.

The truck was old but well kept, recently painted a dark blue. Sheila realized she'd seen it around town but hadn't known whom it belonged to. Now she'd have another thing to make her heart leap—catching sight of it. Douglas took her elbow to help her in. *It's only a ride to Marge's Diner,* she told herself as she settled into the upholstery and tried to regulate her breathing.

He climbed in behind the wheel and started the engine. Then he switched on the defroster to clear the already fogged-up windows. "How have you been?" he asked in a light tone as he shifted the truck into reverse.

"Fine." *Thinking of you.* Even in the confines of the truck she couldn't smell manure, but his woodsy aftershave took hold of her senses and created vivid memories of warm lips and a questing tongue.

"Charlie told me he agreed to bring the reenactment group back again next year." Douglas put his arm over the seat and turned his head to watch behind him as he backed the truck out of the parking space. His fingers touched her shoulder in the process of completing the maneuver. As Sheila held her breath, he returned both hands to the steering wheel.

Somehow she managed to retain the thread of conversation. "Charlie wants to include more people from Tyler next time. And schedule it a little later," she added with a smile.

"I thought the snow was kind of fun."

Sheila's brain short-circuited abruptly. The snow had been what had brought her to his wigwam Saturday night. Was that what he meant?

"Speaking of the weather, is your father still ice fishing?" he continued smoothly, as if he hadn't just exploded a conversational grenade.

"Yes." At least she could talk about this subject without having heart palpitations. "I wish I could bribe that fish into cooperating. Of course, once the ice fishing is over, I'm not sure what he'll do to pass the time until he can take the boat out and begin the summer fishing season."

"Does he play chess or checkers?"

"My mother used to play chess with him. I've tried, but I'm not the match for him that she was. Gus Lemke doesn't play, and I don't know anyone else who could give him a good game."

"I play," he said quietly.

"Oh." She wasn't sure what he meant by the statement. "I'm sure you're very busy, though, with papers to grade and—"

"Not that busy." He took his eyes away from the road for a moment. "Ask your father if he'd like to play. I'd make the time."

Her palms grew damp. He was suggesting an activity that would bring him to her house on a regular basis. Was the gesture meant for her or her father? "That's very generous of you."

"No, it's not. I love chess, especially if someone's good enough to challenge me."

"Okay. I'll ask him." She hesitated, and finally decided Douglas might be the perfect person to give her some ideas about the other subject that had been occupying her thoughts. "I cleaned out my mother's desk on Monday and discovered that she'd published several stories in true-confession magazines over the years."

"Really?" Douglas gave a little laugh of surprise. "Hey, that's great."

"I also found some of her journals, which are full of anecdotes about prominent citizens. Pa says she used the folks of Tyler for inspiration for her confessions, but she changed enough of the details so no one would be recognized. Of course, she didn't tell anyone she was publishing the stories, either."

"Now that's pretty fascinating." Douglas cruised along the street past Marge's Diner, searching for a parking spot. "I guess she could find a lot of material here."

"My first thought was to see about publishing her journals under her own name, just as something of interest for people in Tyler. But Pa doesn't want me to."

A sedan pulled out of a parking space, and Douglas backed up to take advantage of it. After he'd slid the truck effortlessly into the space and turned off the ignition, he glanced at her. "Doesn't he want people to know she was a writer?"

"I don't think it's that. He's afraid some of the people profiled in the journals wouldn't be thrilled to have some of their stories in print."

"Are they scandalous?"

"I don't think so, but Pa says I'm not being sensitive enough."

"Want me to take a look?"

Another link. "That would be wonderful."

He gazed at her and seemed about to say something else. Instead he opened his door. "Let's see if Marge has any cherry pie left. I'm a fool for cherry pie."

CHAPTER EIGHT

THE DINER WAS JAMMED, which was exactly how Douglas wanted it. Too much intimacy with Sheila and he'd be lost. Her cashmere sweater made her look as if she were wrapped in pink cotton candy, and he wanted to nibble it all away.

Patrick and Pam Kelsey called them over to the booth they were sharing with Patrick's sister Glenna and Lee Nielsen. While Douglas helped Sheila off with her coat and shrugged out of his ski jacket, everyone pushed aside coffee cups and dessert plates and scooted over to make room for two more. Douglas squeezed in next to Patrick, while Sheila sat across from him next to Lee. A big man with a confident manner, Lee was the perfect complement to shy, delicate Glenna.

A harried waitress brought two more glasses of water and promised to come back soon to take Douglas's and Sheila's order.

Douglas surveyed the remains of Patrick's pie. "I sure hope you didn't take the last piece of cherry."

"I didn't." Patrick pointed his fork at Pam's plate. "She did."

"No, it was Glenna," Pam said.

"Don't blame me. I'm positive Lee ordered the last piece they had."

"Will you look at that?" Douglas gestured around the table. "Every last one of you ordered cherry pie, which you know is my favorite, and with me being the MVP, too. Some friends.''

Patrick reached down and patted Douglas's stomach. "We don't want you getting fat, Mr. MVP. We have a title to uphold.''

"Hey," Pam said. "Enough about the MVP's pie. Have you two heard about the contract Glenna just signed with Pierce and Rothchilde? Her videos will now be distributed nationally.''

Sheila leaned past Lee and held out her hand to Glenna. "So you did it! Congratulations!''

"Thanks." Glenna's face glowed with triumph. "Sheila was having lunch in the diner on Monday when I met Byron to talk over terms," she explained to everyone at the table.

Patrick swallowed a bite of pie. "*Talk over terms.* You're sounding like a pro already, Sis.''

"She is." Lee put an arm around Glenna and gave her a hug. "Those videos of hers are amazing. They might even put Barney out of business.''

Glenna laughed. "I doubt it. That purple dinosaur is everywhere. But at least now there will be something besides Barney to entertain small children.''

"National distribution," Douglas said. "That's really something, Glenna. I was in Marge's on Monday and I saw you having some business discussion with Byron. I wondered if that was it. Congratulations.''

Pam raised her water glass. With a baby on the way, she was avoiding stimulants like coffee even more carefully than she usually did, Sheila knew. "To my sister-in-law, the film producer.''

"To Glenna," everyone else chorused, raising either coffee cups or water glasses in salute.

Douglas glanced over at Sheila and wondered if he was imagining the wistful look in her eyes as the group continued to speculate on Glenna's future in the video business. Sheila was every bit as creative as Glenna. He wasn't surprised to learn about her mother's writing talent, but he wished she'd concentrate on her own writing instead of trying to get her mother's journals published.

Sheila caught him studying her and quickly pretended to consult the menu as her cheeks turned the color of her sweater. She probably thought he was thinking about kissing her, when in fact, for a change, he wasn't. That was the intriguing thing about Sheila. She fascinated him on so many different levels. This level—the matter of her creative ability—was one he was impatient to explore, but she was so touchy on the subject he'd have to use caution.

"May I take your order now, Mr. Wagner?" Jane, the waitress, was one of his former students. He was pretty sure he'd given her a C in World History.

He glanced at Sheila. "What would you like?"

Mischief lurked in her hazel eyes. "Cherry pie, if there's any left."

"I think we have one piece back there," Jane said.

"Then I'll have that. À la mode." She grinned at Douglas. "And coffee with lots of cream and sugar."

Patrick glanced in her direction and lifted his eyebrows. "Well done, Sheila. Welcome to the group."

"It is a good choice," the waitress said, making a notation on her pad. "And what will you have, Mr. Wagner?"

He gazed up at her with a resigned expression. "No more cherry pie, I take it."

"Uh, no. Sorry. Except for the piece she ordered." She tilted her head toward Sheila.

"Then I guess we'll have to share that piece."

"What?" Sheila protested. "Wait a minute. You can't—"

"Please bring two forks, Jane," Douglas said. "And I'll take coffee with cream and sugar, too."

Jane hesitated, gave Sheila a look of sympathy and left with the order.

Patrick clapped Douglas on the back. "Way to alienate your date, Wagner. First you show up smelling like donkey poop and then you horn in on her dessert order." He leaned toward Sheila and spoke in a loud stage whisper. "You have to make allowances. Between being MVP and Chief Black Hawk, he thinks everybody should defer to him."

Sheila's eyes danced as she looked at Douglas. "Then he's in for a surprise. I'm pretty aggressive with a fork."

Douglas loved every minute of it, from the moment she'd preempted his pie order to her defiant reaction when he'd announced they would share. Teasing was good. A woman who could tease considered herself an equal.

Pam watched the interchange over the rim of her water glass. "This should be very interesting."

"I wish we could stay to see you two battle over the cherry pie," Lee said, "but I promised the baby-sitter I'd have Glenna home by ten."

Sheila slid from the booth to let Lee and Glenna out. She touched Glenna's shoulder. "Congratulations, again. I'd like to see one of your videos soon."

"They're more entrancing if you're two years old or have a child who is," Glenna said as Lee helped her into her coat. "If you ever become a mother, that's when you'll appreciate the videos, believe me."

Douglas had no trouble picturing Sheila as a mother. The poignancy of the image caught him off guard, and Charlie's words echoed in his mind. *If you still want to have kids...* He shook his head. That sort of speculation was getting way ahead of the game.

Sheila sat down again as Lee reached in his back pocket for his wallet.

"Anything new on the F and M fire?" Douglas asked him.

Lee tucked the money for Jane's tip under his saucer. "Not really. Whenever arson is suspected it's a long, slow process."

"Which really puts the F and M employees in a financial crunch," Glenna said. "In a way it's hard to celebrate my good fortune when so many people in town are trying to keep the wolf from the door."

"On the contrary," Douglas said. "I think your success can give people hope."

"I agree," Pam said. "Hug the kids for me, Glenna."

"Will do." With a wave, Glenna followed Lee up to the cash register.

"I guess we can spread out a little more," Douglas said, getting up and moving to Sheila's side of the booth with a sense of anticipation at being closer to her. She moved over some, but not to the far corner, which was encouraging.

"Here comes your point of contention, with ice cream melting down the sides," Pam said.

"I'm sure Sheila will be an adult about this," Douglas said as Jane placed the pie on the table midway between them.

"Look who's talking about being an adult," Patrick said. "The man who can't face life without cherry pie."

"It would be a difficult existence." Douglas picked up his fork and turned his head, noticing right away that a large chunk of pie was already gone and Sheila had sort of a chipmunk look to her cheeks. "No fair taking double bites!"

Patrick and Pam started to laugh, and so did Sheila, except she had a mouthful of cherry pie. She began to choke.

Fear hit Douglas like a jolt of electricity. In a flash he had both arms around her and his fists clenched at her breastbone, ready to perform the Heimlich maneuver. But she pushed at his hands and shook her head violently. "Can you breathe?" he asked.

She nodded, but kept coughing.

Keeping his right arm around her, he reached with his left for a glass of water. "Here."

She coughed again and took the water, tears streaming down her face.

"You're okay," he said, releasing his hold and stroking her back while she drank. "Take it easy. You're fine."

But *he* wasn't. He quivered from the adrenaline rush the crisis had brought, and the memories, as well. Reason told him Sheila wouldn't have died from choking on a piece of cherry pie, especially not when he was right there to dislodge anything stuck in her windpipe. He was overreacting. Still, the panicky feeling when he'd been afraid she couldn't breathe was sickeningly familiar, even after four years. He didn't like that feeling. Didn't like it at all.

Drained of energy, he sat back in the booth and let Pam and Patrick fuss over her for the next couple of minutes.

"I apologize," she said to the group in general when she could finally talk. "That was pretty stupid of me."

"No, I was the one who was stupid," Douglas said, glancing at her. "I shouldn't have made you laugh when you had a mouthful of food. I'm sorry."

"I was the one who stuffed my mouth, Douglas." Her voice was sweet but firm. "It's at least half my fault."

"Oh, I think Pam and I deserve some of the blame, if we're spreading it around," Patrick said. "We started Sheila laughing. In fact, we started the whole thing by deliberately trying to clean the kitchen out of cherry pie before you got here, Wagner. So you may want to take all the responsibility, but I won't let you have it."

Douglas reached deep and found a teasing smile. "First I can't have my pie, and now I can't have my guilt. What can I have?"

"The check," Patrick said, pushing it toward him. "I'm taking my lady home now. Moms-to-be need lots of sleep," he added, sliding out of the booth and offering his hand to Pam. "And tomorrow's a school day."

Douglas groaned. "Don't remind me. After tonight's little episode, I won't have any peace for weeks."

"And that's only counting the ribbing you'll take from the faculty," Pam said with a grin as she put her arms into the coat Patrick held for her. "The kids won't ever let you forget it."

"Tell me again why donkey basketball is such a good idea?"

"It's one of the biggest moneymakers of the school year," Patrick said. "We earned enough tonight, even in these tough financial times, to buy new basketball uniforms. And besides, you had so much fun." He gave Sheila a cocky salute. "Nice seeing you again. Don't let this turkey get away with anything."

"'Bye, Sheila," Pam said. "See you tomorrow, Douglas."

"I regret to say you will."

When they'd left, Douglas gave the pie plate a little push in Sheila's direction. "I think you've earned it. Eat up. I promise not to say anything funny. In fact, I'm completely out of funny."

"Actually, I'm not very hungry." She pushed it back toward him. "You have it."

"No, you." He shoved it in her direction.

"You." She nudged it back.

He sighed. "If I must, I must." The pie was now swimming in melted vanilla ice cream, turned pink with cherry juice. He loved pie that way, but it was better eaten with a spoon than a fork. Scooping a little onto his spoon, he glanced sideways at her.

She was watching him, her mouth open slightly. He started the spoon toward his mouth, and at the last minute changed his mind and eased it between her lips. Her eyes flew open in surprise, but she accepted the soupy mixture, except for a small bit of ice cream that dribbled from the corner of her mouth. He would have loved to catch that drip with his tongue, but they were in Marge's. He used the spoon.

Then he took a bite himself, using the same spoon. When he glanced back into her eyes, they were smoky with awareness. Silently he fed her another mouthful and took one for himself. Then he turned to her yet again. After he dipped the spoon into her mouth and eased it back out, a drop of pink-tinged ice cream quivered on her lower lip. He held his breath when her tongue stole out to lick it away. As he took another bite, his hand trembled.

He shoved the plate away and grabbed the check. "Let's go."

Marge Phelps herself was stationed at the cash register. She gave them both a friendly greeting, but Douglas could see the speculation in her eyes as she glanced from him to Sheila. "Looks like Patrick stuck you with the bill," she said, punching in the numbers.

"And me the MVP at the donkey basketball game," Douglas said.

Marge grinned. "I heard about your little tumble."

"I am surprised."

She handed him his change. "Don't worry. I can barely smell it. A few more days and it'll wear off."

Douglas rolled his eyes and guided Sheila into the frosty night. Once back in the truck he realized he was out of ideas to prolong their evening together. The weather was too cold for a drive, and he didn't dare invite her back to his house at this early stage. So he took the trip back to the high school parking lot at a slower pace than usual just to savor her presence a while longer.

"For the record, I think it's great that you played in the donkey basketball game," she said, breaking the momentary silence between them. "That's the sort of thing that shows a teacher's dedication to the school. And everyone wouldn't tease you so much if they didn't like you."

"Thank you," he said quietly.

"I was thinking tonight how much talent we have packed into such a small town. In our booth alone, we had you, an outstanding teacher, and two terrific coaches who win games and build character at the same time. Then there's Glenna, who's created those videos."

He couldn't have asked for a better opening. "And a talented writer."

"Don't be silly. Just because I had a flair for it in high school doesn't mean—"

"More than a flair," he interrupted as he swung the truck into the parking lot next to her car and switched off the ignition. He put the brakes on his impatience and lightened his tone. "And now that I know your mother was a writer, I can see that, with some encouragement, you might have been publishing bestsellers by now."

Her startled laughter told him how unlikely she considered that possibility.

He hesitated. "Sheila, what can I do to convince you to go back to writing?"

She faced him, her eyes bright in the glow from the parking lot security lamp. "This is sounding a lot like lecture time again."

He sighed and ran his finger along the curve of the steering wheel. "I suppose it is, but I can't help it. The idea that you're paying for my hang-ups is really bothering me."

She looked puzzled. "Your hang-ups?"

Here goes, he thought. "I never told you the whole reason I didn't dig into the truth about that essay." He gazed at her and saw a woman even more beautiful than the seventeen-year-old who had made his breath catch when he glimpsed her walking down the hall or laughing with her friends. "In order to investigate exactly what happened with that essay I would have had to talk with you alone, and I was terrified of that. You were far too great a temptation for me."

His implication gradually transformed her expression from confusion to disbelief. "But I was just a kid!"

Now it was his turn to laugh. "You underestimate yourself. Remember when I moved you to the front row?"

She nodded.

"I rationalized that you were my barometer of whether I was getting through to everyone else, because you had such an expressive face. The truth was, I wanted you close to me. I began to live in anticipation of that government class because you were in it. The night I fantasized about you while kissing my girlfriend, I knew I was in trouble."

Her eyes widened at that final confession. "I—I'm having trouble believing this."

"Teachers are sexual beings, too. If they're ethical, they suppress such feelings toward students. So I began to discipline myself to avoid any direct contact with you. I was a danger to you, and in total innocence you were jeopardizing my career. Unfortunately, my fears kept me from acting in your behalf when you needed me to."

She swallowed, and when she spoke her voice shook a little. "Considering everything, I don't think you should blame yourself."

"Oh, I could have done much worse. I could have seduced you and destroyed your trust and my life." He shook his head. "I'm beginning to realize that even after all these years, there's some residual guilt when I touch you, as if I can't quite accept that it's okay now. The encampment seemed to put us in a different world, but now, sitting in full view of the school where it all took place, I... It's difficult to admit this, but you're not the only one who's having trouble casting off the old roles.''

A metallic click indicated she'd unfastened her seat belt. He expected her to open her door, but instead she eased closer to him on the bench seat, her gaze never leaving his. She placed a hand on his arm. ''Do you still want to try?''

His chest tightened with emotion. ''Every time I look at you,'' he said in a husky voice.

''Then kiss me good-night, right here in front of that blasted school building.''

He opened his own seat belt and shifted toward her. As he gazed into her upturned face and reached to cup her cheek, his hand trembled. ''I used to hate myself for wanting this.''

''You can have what you want now.''

He took a deep breath of her flowery scent, hardly believing that the moment was real. For a split second as he lowered his mouth to hers she looked so young—almost as if she were seventeen again—and he hesitated.

''Kiss me,'' she whispered.

With a sigh he settled in…and was lost. The sweet pliancy of her mouth brought a soft moan from his throat. The seductive parting of her lips beneath his drove him wild with longing. He accepted her invitation, exploring her moist warmth with his tongue, tasting the promise of paradise.

She turned more fully in to him and slipped her hand behind his head. As her fingers tunneled through his hair, he reached inside her unbuttoned coat to gather her closer, just enough to feel the soft crush of her breasts. His throat ached from the wanting, but he kept his touch gentle, his explorations slow and erotic.

Her warmth reached through the cashmere, tantalizing him with thoughts of the soft skin beneath. He could easily slide his hand under the hem of her sweater, but he restrained himself. Once he touched that warm skin, he suspected he would lose all sense of where they were.

And they were, he remembered with regret, parked in front of the high school. Slowly he drew back. Her eyes drifted open, revealing the same dazed emotion he felt, and her lips remained parted, as if to coax him back inside.

As he fought that magnetic pull, he knew that he'd been right all those years ago. He'd been young and impetuous then, and one taste of her would have instantly replaced reason with desire. He was older now, more in control, and yet it took every bit of that learned control to release her.

"Good night," he murmured.

Holding his gaze, she reached blindly for the door handle and eventually found it. "Good night," she said. Then she stepped from the truck and slammed the door.

The truck windows were so fogged up he couldn't see out. He sat in the frosted silence and listened to the ignition on her car grind, grind again and catch. He let out his breath and realized he'd been hoping her car wouldn't start at all.

CHAPTER NINE

WHEN DOUGLAS WALKED into his U.S. History class, the kids all sat there with clothespins over their noses. He'd been the butt of jokes in his other two classes, but this was the first organized prank. Considering how many people in Tyler had clothes dryers, he was impressed that the students had rounded up so many clothespins on such short notice. None of them said a word or cracked a smile. Douglas figured the best response was no response, so he pretended not to notice the nose ornaments.

He also decided to change his lesson plan to fit the occasion. "Today let's discuss the effect of fashion on history," he began. As he described corsets that constricted women's rib cages until their ribs punctured their lungs and starched ruffs so wide they prevented the wearer from feeding himself, some of the students became so interested they didn't notice when the clothespins fell from their noses. But a classmate would nudge them and they'd replace the pins.

"Does anyone have any idea why these fashions continued to be popular, despite their obvious drawbacks?" Douglas asked.

Matt Hansen raised his hand. "Because nobody wanted to be different?" he said in a nasal tone, the clothespin firmly planted.

Douglas took his time glancing up and down the rows of pinched noses, letting the comment sink in. "That's right," he said, unable to hold back a grin. "Herd instinct."

Matt started laughing and took off his clothespin. Soon

Elaine followed suit, and finally the whole class was giggling and rubbing reddened noses. Everyone seemed to be having a good time, even Jon Weiss, who flashed one of his rare but spectacular smiles. Douglas reminded himself to speak with Jon after class and catch the boy in a good mood.

"You got us back, Mr. Wagner," Elaine admitted.

"Maybe so, but I have to tell you that this was by far the most creative gag of the day. Almost worth falling in a pile of manure for."

"Which reminds me. How was your date?" Matt asked.

Silence descended as the entire class leaned forward eagerly for his reply. He should have expected the question, he thought. First he'd mentioned the date to Brad Schmidt on the court and then he'd taken Sheila to the most public spot in town.

"Matt and me saw you with her at Marge's, sitting with Mr. and Mrs. Kelsey," said Andy.

Elaine turned around toward Andy. "That's not a *her,* that's Sheila Lawson, the new manager of Timberlake Lodge," she said in a superior tone. She turned back toward Douglas. "I think she's very pretty. You look good together."

A room full of clothespins was one thing, Douglas thought. This was quite another. He didn't want to discuss his personal life, but he didn't want to rebuke the kids for their understandable curiosity, either. At their age the dating game was of prime importance. Hell, it had become mighty important to him, too. He had absolutely no clue as to what to say.

"Hey, sometimes a guy needs his privacy, you know?" Jon Weiss said.

Douglas stared at him. He would never have expected help from that quarter. Jon wasn't one to make waves.

Something was definitely going on in the boy's life for him
to speak out in opposition to his classmates this way.

"I didn't mean it like that," Matt said, glaring at Jon.
"Shoot, nobody gets any privacy in Tyler, anyway. I guess
being a city boy, you haven't figured that out. You—"

"Easy, Matt." Douglas cut in. "Jon made a good point.
Remember when we studied life on the frontier and talked
about courtship rituals like bundling?"

Matt looked wary. "Yeah. I still can't picture that working out. Your whole family's in the cabin, and you and
your girlfriend sneak off in a corner and wrap up in a blanket to make out when the whole family's sitting not ten
feet away. How *gross*."

The rest of the class mumbled their agreement, several
stating out loud that they'd never do anything like that.

"But it worked," Douglas said, "because everyone
agreed to ignore the couple and give them privacy, even in
a restricted space. A small town like Tyler is sometimes
like that frontier cabin. People know things are going on,
but they pretend not to notice."

Matt shifted in his seat. "Yeah, but if everyone
knows..."

"It's a subtle distinction, but if no one brings up the
subject, then you've given people a measure of privacy,
even when everyone knows what's going on."

"So we're not supposed to mention that we saw your
truck and her car parked together in the high school parking
lot," Andy said slyly.

Douglas sighed. "Right." He waited for Andy to mention the fogged-up windows next. Miraculously, he didn't.

Elaine drew a finger across her mouth. "My lips are
sealed."

"Okay," Matt said with a grin of surrender. "I see your
point. No more bundling talk."

"And I'll return the favor," Douglas said.

Matt considered that for a moment. "Cool," he said at last.

Douglas glanced at the clock above the chalkboard and saw the bell was about to ring. So much for his lesson on the South during Reconstruction. "Have a great weekend, all of you. And read chapter twelve before you come to class on Monday."

A chorus of groans accompanied the shuffling of books and papers as everyone packed up.

"With all this homework, a guy barely has time for any decent bundling," Matt said, and winked at Douglas.

Moments like that, Douglas thought, were what kept him in the classroom.

As the bell rang he walked over to Jon's seat. "Could you come by the room after school today?" he asked, making the request casual.

Jon's friendly expression faded. "What about?"

Several students were dawdling at their desks in an attempt to overhear the exchange, so Douglas used the answer he'd prepared ahead of time. "Your answer to the essay question on the last test had some really interesting ideas in it. I thought you might want to clarify some of them and start thinking about the citizenship essay contest next fall." His reply was basically the truth, although it was still a little early to be preparing for the citizenship essay.

Jon didn't seem to buy the carefully prepared explanation, but he nodded and dashed out of the room. Douglas hated paying the kid back for his heroic behavior by embarrassing him in front of the other students, but he hadn't had a choice.

At the end of the day Jon returned, looking very much like a prisoner awaiting final lockdown.

"Hi, Jon," Douglas said, hoping a friendly smile would relieve his uneasiness. "Have a seat." While Jon took his normally assigned spot on the far left of the room, Douglas moved to the file cabinet, pulled out the drawer containing the tests he was in the process of grading and found Jon's.

Then he crossed the room, took the seat in front of Jon and turned to face him. "First of all, thanks for coming to my rescue today. I felt hung out to dry until you spoke up."

Jon looked at him and shrugged one broad shoulder. "I never did like nosy people."

"When I came here to teach thirteen years ago I thought Tyler residents were the nosiest people I'd ever met," Douglas said.

"You can say that again!"

"But I've learned something since then," Douglas continued. "They seem nosy, and maybe they are compared to the neighbors you and I had when we lived in a big city, but unlike big-city neighbors, they care about the people who live here. Their curiosity is good-hearted, not malicious."

"Did it take you thirteen years to get used to it?"

Douglas smiled. "I'm still not used to it. But knowing people mean well makes a big difference."

Jon wouldn't meet his gaze. "Maybe they mean well toward you. Try being practically the only kid who hasn't lived here all his life."

"That can be rough. That's why I was so impressed that you stood up for me today. You took a risk."

Jon looked at him and seemed to enjoy the praise, but the moment didn't hold. Soon his glance darted away again.

Douglas shifted to a discussion of Jon's essay answer, but the boy seemed uninterested and restless. Finally Douglas pushed the paper aside and cut to the heart of the matter. "I can see life isn't a bed of roses for you, moving in as a junior to a small school like Tyler High. But earlier this year I thought you were coping."

Jon gave him a swift sideways glance. "And now you think I'm not?"

"Are you?"

There was a long silence while Jon used his finger, the nail bitten to the quick, to trace a set of initials carved into the desktop many years ago. "I'm doing okay," he said at last.

"I used to tell people that, too, after my wife died. It wasn't true."

Jon's gaze lifted. "You had a wife?"

"See? Not everything is blabbed around in Tyler."

"Sure it is," Jon said bitterly. "Just not to me." His expression softened. "I'm sorry about your wife."

Douglas absorbed the boy's sincerity. He was really a good kid. "I must be getting like the Tyler folks. Here I am prying into your personal business, but it's because I want to help. Life can be tough, especially when we're trying to find all the answers by ourselves."

For a moment there was a glimmer in Jon's eyes, as if he might be thinking about confiding his problem, whatever it was. Then the light went out and the boy shook his head. "Thanks, Mr. Wagner, but I'm okay. Don't worry about me."

Douglas knew when it was time to stop probing. "All right." He stood, and Jon leaped to his feet as if he'd been poised to go the minute he was released. Douglas held out his hand. "Thanks again for sticking up for me today."

Jon shook his hand, his grip surprisingly firm. "Anytime. See ya." Then he was gone.

Douglas walked to the far side of the classroom and stared out at the leafless trees reaching up to the sky. Jon hadn't been ready to unburden himself yet, but maybe the groundwork had been laid for some future time when he trusted Douglas sufficiently to open up. Funny how some people thought teaching was all about imparting textbook knowledge. Douglas considered that the least important of his jobs.

AS SHEILA APPROACHED Douglas's classroom after school, the same one where he'd taught when she was a senior, she heard him talking to a student, so she paused outside the door. Ironically, the conversation was about the citizenship essay contest. Her wool coat draped over her arm, Sheila leaned against the wall of the deserted hallway to wait until Douglas and the boy were finished. If she left now she'd never find the courage to deliver what she held in her arms.

Remembering that Douglas had agreed to look at her mother's journals and wanting an excuse to see him, she'd stacked them in her car this morning before going to work. She'd decided to use her afternoon off to bring the material to Douglas at school. Sheila clutched the journals against her breasts as she thought about the contents of the manila envelope that rested on top. Prodded by his guilt over her abandoned writing career, she'd gathered up her most recent attempts and shoved them into the envelope.

Standing in the hall waiting for his student conference to end, she questioned the wisdom of showing him her work. After telling him she didn't write much anymore, she could have left it at that. The truth was she'd written more than she'd realized. The play and two short stories in the envelope were only the tip of the iceberg, but they'd been created for her own enjoyment, not for publication. Maybe Douglas would take solace in the knowledge that writing was a satisfying hobby for her. She would explain all that before giving him the envelope. He would understand perfectly that—

Her thoughts were interrupted as the conversation inside the classroom took a personal turn. Sheila hadn't meant to eavesdrop, but when Douglas mentioned the death of his wife, she listened shamelessly. Admiration swept over her at the gentle way he tried, by revealing his own pain, to draw the boy out. Obviously the essay had also been a tool for trying to get the student to discuss his problems.

Memories flooded back of the afternoon Douglas had spoken to her and Beverly in that same kind tone. How she'd longed to blurt out the truth! When silence fell in the classroom, she imagined the boy struggling with the same urge. But he didn't give in, just as she hadn't.

When he bolted from the room a second later, he glanced at her like a startled animal, and she saw the familiar emotions of guilt and fear in his eyes, just as she knew they must have been in hers years ago. She wondered what private demons he was fighting and wished him well. Then she took a deep breath and walked into the room.

Douglas stood with his back to her. Obviously he hadn't heard her come in. She took a moment to adjust to the bittersweet atmosphere of his special territory.

Chalk dust scented the air. Tyler High had kept its green slate boards and felt erasers, although Sheila knew many modern schools had replaced them with laminated surfaces and marking pens. The one-piece metal-and-wood desks with book holders under the seats looked like the same ones she'd sat in. She gazed at the maps rolled above the chalkboard, the travel posters on the walls, the globe in its stand in the corner and the assignments written on the board in Douglas's angular printing.

For the first time she realized how much she'd loved this room. Intellectual stimulation and erotic fantasies had been tucked into one tantalizing hour spent with Douglas Wagner. She'd felt safe to indulge both, yet all the while he'd had the power to destroy everything, and he'd been tempted. His restraint that year might be the greatest gift she'd ever received. He had known she couldn't have handled his adult passion at the age of seventeen. But now…

He turned and blinked. "Sheila!"

"Déjà vu?"

"Definitely." He walked toward her, his dark hair back-lit by the sunlight slanting in the windows. The added lines of maturity in his face and the hint of sadness in his eyes made him far more appealing than he had been at twenty-three, she thought, and he'd been quite appealing then. He wore an open-necked knit shirt of forest green that molded his torso and reminded her a little of how he'd looked in buckskin. The last time she'd set foot in this room she'd only imagined what it would be like to kiss him, to be held in his embrace. Now she knew.

"For a split second, when I saw you there with books in your arms, I thought I'd stepped into a time tunnel," he said.

"I know what you mean."

"I'm glad I haven't." His green eyes studied her with compelling intensity. "You know, you're much more beautiful than you were at seventeen."

Her heartbeat quickened as old images danced with new ones—the man who held sway in this room blending with the man who had kissed her so passionately. "I...brought my mother's journals. If you're still willing to look at them," she added quickly.

"Sure." He motioned toward the desks. "Do you have time to sit down?"

"For a little while." She consulted the black-and-white clock over the chalkboard. "I should be back at the lodge in about a half hour."

"That gives us a little time. Let's see if the janitors are headed this way yet." He walked toward the door.

Her breathing grew shallow at his implication that he'd like them to be alone. Out of habit she turned toward her old seat, folding her coat over the back and resting the stack of journals on the desk before sliding into it. She heard a click and glanced up. He'd locked the door.

"Douglas," she began, her heart hammering, "I really don't think we should…" Her protest trailed off at the look of speculation on his face.

"Why did you take that seat?" he asked, his voice husky.

"I'm…used to it."

"Not because it plays right into my fantasy?" He stood in front of the desk.

Her heart hammered. "Does it?"

"Yes, and I think you're well aware of that fact, you angel-faced temptress." He braced both hands on her desk.

Perhaps she was. But she wasn't sure she possessed the courage to finish what she'd started. "Maybe I should go."

Slowly he shook his head. "Too late. I just learned today that the whole town is already gossiping about us." He leaned closer. "So I think we should make use of an old frontier custom. Ever hear of bundling?"

Gazing into his eyes, she could barely remember her name, let alone some sociological term. "I don't…know."

He leaned closer still. "In crowded log cabins, a young couple would wrap in a blanket and pretend they were alone."

She ran her tongue over dry lips. "Then what?"

"I imagine they would do…something like this." He angled his head and nibbled gently at her lips.

She caught her breath.

"Or this." He changed the angle and brushed his mouth across hers. "Ah, Sheila." He took her fully at last, his clever tongue tightening a spiral of need that had been taunting her since the moment she'd left the steamy confines of his truck. So this had been what she'd sought when she looked for a reason to see him today.

To steady herself she grasped the muscled strength of his braced arms. She ran her hands up their length and felt him tremble beneath her fingertips. Then she gripped his biceps

as his kiss slid from her lips to the curve of her chin. Instinctively she arched her throat, baring it to him as he
discovered the sensitive spot where her pulse beat a mad
pattern of desire. And she wanted more. Much more.

A rap at the door brought her out of her sensual haze
with a jerk.

"Douglas?" called a male voice. "You in there?"

Douglas pushed himself away from the desk. "Yeah.
Just a second, Clint." He lowered his voice. "My principal.
I was supposed to go down to his office after school. For
some reason I forgot." Giving her a wink, he strode toward
the door.

Sheila got up from the desk and picked up her coat, the
journals and the envelope containing her manuscripts. She
tried to rid herself of the feeling that she'd been caught
doing something wrong, but she couldn't. Even if she and
Douglas were adults, they probably shouldn't be necking
in Douglas's classroom in the middle of the afternoon.

Douglas unlocked the door and opened it.

"Barricaded yourself in here to get some work done, I
suppose," Clint began. Then he looked past Douglas to
where Sheila stood. "Then again, that was just a wild
guess." He nodded to her. "Good afternoon, ma'am."

"Clint, I don't know if you've met Sheila Lawson,"
Douglas said. "Sheila, this is our new principal, Clint Stanford."

Sheila moved the journals and manuscripts to her left
arm and stepped forward to shake hands with the tall man,
who looked to be in his late forties. "Nice to meet you."
She forced herself to look him straight in the eye. Then she
released his hand. "Now if you'll both excuse me, I'd better get back to work." She was halfway out the door when
Douglas called her back.

"Aren't you leaving those notebooks with me?" he
asked.

"Oh." She'd entirely forgotten her original reason for coming to the school. "Yes. Yes, I am." She dumped everything in his arms and started out again.

"Did you mention the possibility of chess to your father?"

She turned back again. She was coming across as completely scatterbrained. "Yes, I did. He said that would be nice."

"Then why don't you tell him I'll come by tonight? And tell him to prepare for a drubbing. That should get his blood going."

The prospect of seeing Douglas again that night certainly heated hers. "Um, that would be great. I'll let him know." Then, with a totally juvenile-sounding "Bye," she dashed out into the hall, praying that she wouldn't trip or otherwise disgrace herself further. She didn't realize until she'd reached her car that she'd given Douglas her manuscripts without the pretty little speech she'd planned about what a delightful hobby writing had become. But wild horses couldn't have dragged her back into that building.

CHAPTER TEN

AFTER SHEILA LEFT, Douglas turned to Clint. "I apologize for not coming down to your office immediately. I did talk to Jon, but after he left Sheila dropped by and I was... distracted."

"No matter. I was in the neighborhood." Clint gave him a slow smile of apology. "And I'm truly sorry if I interrupted something."

"I needed to be interrupted." Douglas rubbed the back of his neck. "I'm behaving like a damn fool with that woman, to tell you the truth."

"According to the scuttlebutt, it's about time. The female segment of this faculty is dying to marry you off."

"Whoa." Douglas held up both hands. "Don't rush me into the wedding march, Clint, old boy."

Clint laughed. "I'd be the last one to do that. Once you're headed down the aisle, they'll probably start on me."

Douglas braced his hands loosely on his hips. "Come to think of it, I've already heard a few comments to that effect. In case you hadn't noticed, Tyler has a romantic streak a mile wide."

Clint grimaced. "Cute, ain't it?"

"Just darlin'."

"So, what did you find out from our boy Jon?"

"Not much I didn't already know. Most of the kids at Tyler High were born and raised here. That makes it tough for somebody moving in at his age, when all the alliances have been formed. He's probably frustrated with the lack of acceptance, and he's becoming a little belligerent."

"Did he mention anything more specific that's bothering him?"

Douglas shook his head. "I think he wanted to, but he doesn't trust me enough. That may be part of the problem. He doesn't have anyone to talk to, so little things fester and become a big deal. I left the door open for more conversation, so he may come to me later. I'll sure let you know if he does."

Clint nodded and wandered over toward the chalkboard, where he picked up an eraser from the metal tray. "I admire the relationship you have with your students," he said, turning the eraser over in his large hands. "If he'll open up to anyone on the faculty, it would be you."

"Thanks."

Clint replaced the eraser and picked up a stubby piece of chalk. "Jon would be better off if he'd become involved in some school activity, but he's obviously not into any of the major sports, and his records don't show any interest in music or drama. I thought being on the science team working at the F and M was perfect for him, but now that's no longer a possibility." He dropped the chalk into the tray before glancing at Douglas. "Jon's not the only student who could use a sport that's not competitive. I understand we used to have one."

Finally Douglas realized where this was leading. "If you want to revive the scuba club, you've come to the wrong place."

"I do want to revive it, and you're the only faculty member qualified to be the sponsor. I checked."

"Your information is old. I'm not qualified."

Clint didn't back down an inch. "So, you'd have to renew your certificate. No big deal for someone as skilled as you."

Clint had no idea what a big deal it was, Douglas thought. He hadn't had his equipment on since Joanne's death. He hadn't even had the fortitude to get it out of the closet long enough to sell it. "I'm sorry, Clint, but I have no interest in sponsoring the scuba club again. None."

"The thing is, activities like that provide a chance to reach students you can't connect with in the classroom."

"I'm aware of that." Had Douglas been out on a dive with Jon, the boy might have told him everything lodged so painfully in his heart. Douglas had found that if he could meet troubled kids on some neutral turf away from school, they lost much of their defensiveness. But he wasn't planning to take Jon or any other student out on a dive ever again. The potential gain wasn't worth it.

"It's not often you find a teacher with an unusual, intriguing skill and the empathy for teenagers that you have," Clint persisted, holding his position. "Apparently that scuba club of yours was known throughout Wisconsin, even in neighboring states. I heard tales of kids transferring from Sugar Creek just so they could be in it."

Douglas had thought of Clint as fairly easy to get along with, but he was seeing a thread of steel he hadn't noticed in the man before. Clint had decided that the students of Tyler High—his students—needed a scuba club, and he was going to get it for them or know the reason why. Douglas didn't want to discuss the reason why. "How about a chess club?" he suggested.

Clint waved his hand. "I have a half dozen teachers who could sponsor a chess club. It's okay, and we can do that, but it's more competition, and it lacks the benefit of physical exertion and unusual surroundings. When I heard about that scuba club, it captured my imagination. I want it back in the program, Douglas. Please. For the sake of kids like Jon."

Douglas met his gaze without flinching. "Sorry."

Clint absorbed the refusal in silence. Finally he drew in a breath. "This statement will probably make me about as popular as a skunk at a prayer meeting, but I'm going to risk it." His gaze was direct. "Everybody has a pretty good idea why you gave up scuba diving. But I've found that if you don't master your fears, they'll master you."

"Now, wait a—"

"I think you need this club as much as the kids do," Clint said quietly.

Douglas clenched his jaw. Unprofessional though it might be, he felt like telling Clint to go to hell. But he liked the tall Texan and understood his desire to create the best environment for the students. Douglas said nothing.

"I didn't expect you to like hearing that, but I respect you enough not to pull punches. Have a nice weekend." He left the room.

Douglas listened to the sound of Clint's boots thudding away along the hallway and wondered if the school board realized they'd hired Marshal Dillon to run Tyler High.

As SHEILA TRUDGED down to the lake to whistle her father and Gus in that evening, a blue jay squawked at her from the branches of a fir tree. Her mother had once compared her father to a blue jay—handsome to look at, noisily obnoxious and tough enough to survive a Wisconsin winter. Her father was still a nice-looking man at seventy-three, but he wasn't often noisily obnoxious anymore, and Sheila wondered if he was tough enough to survive this wintry grief he carried with him.

She hoped he'd really meant it when he'd agreed to play chess with Douglas. Of course, if Emil changed his mind she could always call Douglas and tell him not to come. That prospect depressed her more than a little, both for her father's sake and her own.

"I almosht got Jumbo!" her father yelled, his speech

strangely blurred as he whizzed toward her on his snow-mobile.

"Yeah, and the dang fool got so excited he lost his teeth down the hole!" Gus called as he zoomed along behind Emil. "Or maybe he tried to use his choppers as a new-fangled lure. With Emil you never know *what* he's thinkin'. Anyways, they're gone."

Sheila smothered her laughter. "Just as well. They needed to be fixed. Now you can get a new set, Pa."

Emil frowned at her. "A washte a' money."

"Now that's a fact," Gus said, gazing owlishly at Sheila. "On account of you won't be eating no victory dinner at Marge's."

Emil straightened and glared at his rival. "Oh, yesh I will!"

Sheila could have hugged Gus for knowing just what ornery thing to say. She'd always suspected Gus did it on purpose, but that one look told her for sure. "Then we'll call the dentist in the morning," she said. "And tonight Douglas Wagner's coming over for a game of chess. He said to tell you to prepare for a drubbing."

"Oh, yeah?"

Sheila shrugged. "That's what he said. I'm only the mes-senger. He seems to think he can beat you."

"Probably can, addlepated as you are," Gus interjected.

"Ha!" Emil thumbed his nose at Gus and patted the seat behind him for Sheila to climb on.

Just before she did, she turned and gave Gus a surrep-titious thumbs-up sign. Maybe with fishing during the day and chess at night, Emil would regain his old spark. Seeing Douglas tonight, and on any other night he came to play chess, wasn't a bad bonus, either.

TWO HOURS LATER, Sheila's heart wrenched as she watched her father lovingly unpack the old wooden chess set and arrange it on the kitchen table as he'd done on countless evenings when Myrna was alive. Belatedly she reconsidered the wisdom of stirring up old memories, but the wheels were in motion now. Douglas had called to say he was on his way. Sheila had warned him in a low voice that her father had lost his teeth down the ice-fishing hole today and his speech was a little difficult to understand without them. Douglas had laughed and said that chess players usually didn't talk much, anyway.

When Sheila heard his truck in the drive she took a last peek in the hall mirror to see if her hair and makeup looked okay. She'd changed into jeans, running shoes and a favorite old sweatshirt in royal blue with Tyler Titans emblazoned across the chest in gold. If her manner failed to indicate nonchalance, at least her clothes would.

Her father had stayed in the kitchen to practice a few opening moves, and she'd bustled around the rest of the house, straightening throw pillows and ruffled lampshades. She couldn't bear to stay in the kitchen watching her father's gray head bowed so intently over the chessboard, his pipe clamped firmly between his gums, and the seat opposite him, the one her mother always took, sitting empty. Maybe this chess game would banish a few of her own ghosts, she thought. She was so busy worrying about her father that sometimes she pushed aside her own grieving.

The truck motor sputtered to a stop and Sheila glanced around the room, trying to imagine how Douglas would see it. For several years while she was growing up, Sheila had longed for sleek modern furniture to replace the serviceable pine coffee and end tables and the couch slipcovered in blue gingham. Then the country look had come into vogue, and suddenly places decorated like the Lawson farmhouse had become the envy of urban sophisticates everywhere.

The craze had passed, but not the appreciation for heirloom pieces. Finally, Sheila had matured enough to appreciate them, too. When she'd left her Chicago apartment six months ago, she'd sold every stick of the Oriental furniture she'd once thought so glamorous.

The porch steps creaked, and Sheila's heartbeat accelerated. When two raps sounded, she walked to the door, knees trembling, and opened it. Then she unlatched the storm door, letting in a blast of cold air that she barely felt in her joy at seeing Douglas again. His dark hair shone in the light from the porch lamp, and his shoulders seemed incredibly broad as he came through the doorway.

He looked at her with the same startled expression he'd had when she'd appeared in his classroom that afternoon. "You keep doing that," he murmured.

"Doing what?"

"Rocketing me back thirteen years." He lowered his voice. "I'm beginning to feel like a dirty old man trying to despoil a virgin."

Chills of anticipation raced down her spine. "This sweatshirt is…comfortable."

"And makes you look seventeen. I swear you're teasing me, Sheila, messing with my head."

"Want me to change clothes?"

"No." His gaze flicked over her. "I'm beginning to like feeling like a dirty old man." He held out a square box with something in a paper sack balanced on top. "I stopped by Marge's after I left school and bought a whole cherry pie before the dinner rush wiped out the supply again. Vanilla ice cream's in the bag."

"Oh!" She'd been so absorbed in the warmth of his gaze she hadn't noticed he was carrying packages. "That's great!" She took the box, careful to keep the ice cream balanced on top. "Let's take this into the kitchen and—"

"Wait." His touch on her arm affected the balance of the ice-cream carton. She made a quick grab at the sack at the same time he did, and his hand closed around hers. He squeezed her hand and released it. "Steady."

Oh, sure, she thought. She couldn't get within ten feet of this man without salivating, and she was supposed to stay steady. She glanced at him and realized he was still wearing his black ski jacket. "Your coat..." she began, feeling as if she'd forgotten all her manners.

"Doesn't need to be hung up," he finished, shrugging out of it. "Listen," he continued, keeping his voice low. "I haven't finished the journals yet, but I read every last word of your stuff. I left it in the car. Maybe we'll have some time alone to talk about it."

"You read everything of mine?" A new sort of panic took hold of her.

"Couldn't help myself. And thank you for trusting me with it."

It sounded to Sheila like the sort of thing someone said to buy time, to evade bald truths. Cold shame washed over her. He probably didn't like her work. She'd been a fool to let it out of her grasp, a fool to invite comment on something so personal. She tasted the bitterness of regret, but forced herself to smile. "I just threw it in on an impulse. Some rough drafts of ideas, nothing important." Lies, all lies.

"I don't—"

"Are we playin' or not?" demanded her father from the kitchen doorway. He tapped the bowl of his pipe against his palm.

"We're playing." Douglas tossed his jacket on the sofa and crossed to Emil with his hand outstretched. "It's been a lot of years, Mr. Lawson. I think the last time we met was at Sheila's graduation."

"Thash right." Emil shook Douglas's hand and then pointed to his mouth. "No teef."

"So I heard." Douglas grinned at him. "And if you

think I'll feel sorry for you and give you a break, forget it. I'm out for blood.''

Emil looked at him in surprise, and for one horrible moment Sheila thought the evening would come to an abrupt end, with everyone's dreams in shambles. But after an interminable silence her father's face crinkled with amusement and finally he laughed outright, bare gums and all. Then he clamped an arm over Douglas's shoulders and guided him toward the kitchen. "Come on, shucker."

Sheila let out her breath. Carrying the pie and ice cream, she followed them into the kitchen. Emil gestured toward the far seat, and Douglas lowered himself into the chair, gazing at the chessboard as if already plotting his first move. Emil followed suit. They chose colors and Douglas won the first move. Within seconds the two men seemed to have forgotten Sheila existed.

"Let me know when you'd like pie and coffee," she said. "I'm going into the living room to read."

"Okay," her father said, although he remained focused on the chessboard.

Douglas didn't even speak.

Sheila vowed not to resent his complete attention to the game. That was the only way Emil liked to play, and the main reason she wasn't a good partner for him. She liked to chat and call breaks for snack time, and sometimes asked if she could take back stupid moves. She also liked games that lasted less than thirty minutes. From the opening gambits, she could tell this one might continue for hours. Douglas would be here, sitting in her kitchen, for that entire time. If only he weren't oblivious to her presence.

An hour later Sheila gave up on the novel she'd been forcing her way through. Every other sentence, she thought about her manuscripts waiting out in Douglas's truck. She even considered retrieving them and hiding them in her room upstairs in the hope Douglas would forget all about them. Yet she knew he wouldn't.

Finally she couldn't stand the inactivity another minute. She walked into the silent kitchen and started brewing coffee, just to hear the gurgle. Neither man took his attention from the game, which looked to be in a dead heat. Douglas must be pretty good, she thought. Emil had studied the game since he was a teenager and then taught Myrna, who was the only person Sheila knew who had ever beaten him.

She took out dessert plates and set them on the counter with a clatter, drawing no discernible reaction from the contestants. Figuring she could explode a bomb in the room and not disturb them, she began slicing the pie and popping individual pieces in the microwave to warm. When she'd placed pie à la mode and a mug of coffee next to each man, she served herself and sat down at the end of the table.

Her father picked up a fork and started to eat without taking his gaze from the chessboard, where Douglas had just captured one of his pawns. When Douglas's move was complete, he smiled at Emil before glancing back at the board. Watching as Emil's hand hovered over a knight, Douglas reached without looking, picked up his fork and cut himself a large bite of pie loaded with ice cream.

Feeling like the wallflower at the party, Sheila had just decided to take her pie and coffee into the living room when she felt the gentle nudge of Douglas's knee against hers. She sat perfectly still and wondered if the contact had been accidental. Apparently not, because now his knee moved against hers with deliberate pressure. She glanced at him, but he remained seemingly entranced by the game.

His knee retained contact with hers, however, and she was captured by the subtle caress, fascinated by his covert attention to her while he seemed to be focusing completely on the game. She ate her pie and drank her coffee without tasting either. The pace of the game no longer bothered her.

Life had been reduced to the warmth of Douglas's knee against hers, the curve of his fingers as he picked up a chess piece, the scent of his woodsy cologne, the shape of his eyebrows, the strength of his chin, the hollowing of his cheeks as he took a sip of coffee from his mug.

Realizing she was staring, she turned her attention to her father and was gratified at the liveliness of his expression. Gus had coaxed him out into the fresh air to ice fish, but no one had challenged him mentally in several months. This was just what he needed—a rigorous game of chess played with the intensity he loved. Filled with gratitude, she glanced back at Douglas and found him gazing at her with such fervency her pulse leaped. Then, with a half smile, he looked back at the board and put her father in checkmate.

"Misherable," Emil muttered, glaring first at the board and then at Douglas. "Absholutely misherable." At last he laid down his king in surrender.

"I don't suppose you'd be up to a rematch on Monday night," Douglas said casually.

"Absholutely!" Emil said, his hazel eyes snapping. "And I'll whip your assh!"

"Pa!" Sheila laughed despite herself.

"That's what you think," Douglas said, smiling at her father. "You've met your equal and you know it."

"We'll shee," Emil said cheerfully. He stood and held out his hand. "We'll shee on Monday. Now I need shleep."

Douglas stood and shook his hand across the table. "Better rest up for Monday. I'll be gunning for you."

"Ha!" Chuckling to himself, Emil left the kitchen and began climbing the stairs. For the first time in six months, his tread was noticeably lighter.

Sheila got out of her chair and began collecting dishes. "You've done something wonderful tonight," she said in a low tone.

''That's nice to know.'' Douglas started putting away the chess pieces with care.

Setting the dishes in the sink, she turned back to him. ''A less perceptive person would have let him win.''

Douglas laughed. ''Let him? He came damn close to beating me. He's a tournament-level player, Sheila.''

''I know he's good, but so are you. And when you had him on the ropes, you didn't give an inch. That was exactly the right thing to do. Now he has another challenge, which is what he desperately needs to keep him going. I appreciate that.''

He put the last chess piece in its green felt niche and closed up the box. ''Maybe I should have you testify on my behalf to my principal, so he won't think I'm such a heartless jerk.''

''Heartless?''

Douglas smoothed his palm over the inlaid wood design of the chess box. ''This afternoon he asked me to revive the scuba club, which would be a way to involve the kids who aren't into the major competitive sports like football and basketball.'' He looked up. ''And I refused.''

She crossed to him, wanting to erase the pain she saw in his expression. ''Does he know why you refused?''

He turned from the table and faced her. ''He's guessing that I'm afraid to get back into it after what happened to Joanne. That's not quite right, but maybe it's close enough.''

She rested her hands on his arms and felt the tension there. She sensed he was holding something inside that was doing him damage. ''Will you tell me why?''

He massaged her arms as he gazed down at her. ''This wasn't the topic I'd planned to discuss after your father went to bed.''

''But it's the topic on your mind, isn't it?''

He pulled her gently toward him. "Come here a minute."

"But—"

"Humor me. I just need to put my arms around you, teenager's sweatshirt and all. I really didn't mean to talk about this, but if we're going to, I think holding you will make it easier to deal with."

With a little sigh she nestled against him, as if she'd been doing it forever. Yet they'd never stood like this, arms wrapped around each other, her head laid against his chest.

He rested his cheek against her hair. "That's better."

"Now tell me."

He took a deep breath. "Joanne wasn't keen on scuba diving. I coaxed, urged and bribed her into it." He rubbed Sheila's back as he talked. "I taught her everything I knew, or thought I had."

When he didn't continue, she hugged him a little tighter. "Go on."

"Obviously I hadn't taught her well enough. When she ran out of air on a dive, instead of sharing some from my tank, she...shot right to the surface." He shuddered beneath her cheek. "Officially an air embolism killed her," he said tonelessly. "But—"

Sheila leaned away from him and grasped his face in both hands. "Don't you *dare* say it! Don't you dare!"

"Everything okay?" called her father from the top of the stairs.

Sheila kept her gaze fastened on Douglas's face. "Everything's just fine, Pa."

"I heard shouting."

"Oh, Douglas just said he didn't think the Brewers have a chance this year, and I got carried away defending them."

"Ha!" Emil said. "They'll win the World Sheries!"

"I told him that," Sheila called back. "Sorry if we disturbed you."

"Thash okay." A loose floorboard creaked as he made his way back to his room.

Douglas's green eyes were bleak, but he managed a wry smile. "Now you've done it. When I root for the Brewers, your father will think I have no convictions whatsoever."

Her heart squeezed at the implication that Douglas would be around during the baseball season, too.

She reached up and smoothed a thumb over his lower lip. "Well, he'll be wrong."

Douglas closed his eyes as she continued the soft caress. When she stood on tiptoe and kissed him, he groaned and gathered her close. What had begun as a gesture of comfort soon became something else entirely as his tongue sought entrance to her willing mouth and desire settled in with its sweet, persistent pressure. She arched against him and discovered that he was as aroused as she.

Aching with a ferocity that astounded her, she pulled his head closer and deepened the kiss. In response he made a sound low in his throat that was almost a growl as he cupped her bottom to bring her tight against him. Heat seared through denim and moist need poured from her.

He lifted his mouth. Breathing unsteadily, he leaned his forehead against hers. "One thing's for sure," he said. "I'm not the kind of guy who seduces his chess partner's daughter right under his nose."

Sheila was having trouble catching her breath, too. "You're not the one doing the seducing. I kissed you, remember?"

"I don't suppose I'll ever forget." With a sigh he released her and stepped away. "But I was more than glad to take it from there." His gaze was potent. "I'd better leave before we really disturb your father's rest."

"Now you're making *me* feel seventeen again, as if my parents are about to come down and find me necking on the sofa and ground me for a week."

The corner of his mouth lifted. ''Tyler has a way of freezing people in time, doesn't it?''

''Yes, it certainly does.'' She sounded as impatient and frustrated as she felt.

''I'll see myself out,'' he said, backing out of the kitchen. ''If you come to the door I'll be tempted to kidnap you and take you home with me.''

It sounded like a perfectly wonderful idea to Sheila. She was thirty years old, for heaven's sake. It wasn't as if she'd never spent the night with a man. But she'd never spent the night with a man in Tyler. And if she were honest with herself, that would take more courage than she possessed at the moment. So she stayed in the kitchen until she heard Douglas drive away.

It wasn't until she started getting ready for bed that she remembered they hadn't discussed her writing.

CHAPTER ELEVEN

WHEN SHE GOT to her office at the lodge the next morning, Sheila decided to put in a call to her aunt Gracie, her father's stepsister. The child of a late second marriage for Emil's father, Gracie was thirty-three years younger than her stepbrother and more of a sister than an aunt to Sheila. She lived in a rural area some distance outside of Tyler and kept extremely busy raising toy poodles. Although she had limited time to visit and didn't want to appear to hover, she was worried about Emil and had asked Sheila to keep her informed about his mental health. At last Sheila had something good to report.

She could tell her aunt had answered from the kennel extension by the constant barking in the background. "Hey, sweetheart!" Gracie said, effervescent as always. "I've been thinking about you. That was great coverage on television for the reenactment group you had at the lodge."

"Unfortunately we lost money when it snowed and we had to put them up at the lodge gratis," Sheila said. "But Mr. Wocheck didn't seem to mind about that. He kept emphasizing all the free publicity."

"Edward Wocheck's a smart man. Always has been," Gracie said. "For one thing, he hired you."

"And you're prejudiced." Sheila fought a lump in her throat. Now that her mother was gone, Gracie was the only close female relative she had, and she cherished her aunt's loyal devotion more than ever.

"I am not prejudiced," Gracie said. "I'm a professional breeder, and I know quality when I see it."

Sheila laughed. "Next you'll be praising my conformation."

"Which is pretty good, now that you mention it. What other groups have you lined up besides the reenactors?"

"Next we have a convention of twins," Sheila said, ticking them off on her fingers, "and then fly fishermen, and—let's see—oh, jingle writers."

"Where on earth did you get all those ideas?"

"There's a great directory of organizations I found. So I'm sending brochures to the most interesting ones."

"How about dog breeders?" Gracie asked. "We're a pretty crazy bunch."

"You'd, ah, bring dogs?" Sheila had visions of issuing pooper-scoopers to the entire staff.

"Of course we'd bring dogs! We're never without dogs. But you're a clever girl. You could work out the logistics."

"Well, maybe." Sheila decided it was time to change the subject. "Listen, I called with some good news about Pa."

"Really?"

Now that she was at the point of explaining, Sheila realized she wasn't quite sure how to describe her relationship with Douglas. "You know how he and Ma used to play chess," she began.

"Lord, yes! Used to drive me crazy, the two of them sitting there for hours. When I visited them as a kid I'd run through the kitchen pretending to be a fire engine. They wouldn't even look up."

"I used to roar like a jet taking off," Sheila said, chuckling. "Same response. Anyway, I've found Pa a chess partner who's a real match for him."

"Sheilie, that's inspired! Who is he, some old geezer from Worthington House?"

Sheila thought of Douglas in his tight buckskin outfit and smiled. "Not exactly. He's my old history teacher, Douglas Wagner."

"Can't say I remember, but I'd moved out of Tyler by the time you hit high school. A teacher, huh? I always think of teachers as being mild-mannered. Is he feisty enough for Emil?"

"I guess he is. He won the first game and Pa agreed to a rematch."

"That's terrific. Probably puts some spice into both their lives, bless their hearts. You're a miracle worker, Sheilie. I know, even if Emil doesn't, that you moved back to Tyler just to keep tabs on him. Do you miss the big city horribly?"

"Actually, no." Especially not since Douglas Wagner had come into her life, Sheila thought. "I may stay here indefinitely."

"Just so you don't devote your life to taking care of your aging father and put your own happiness on hold. I won't have that sort of self-sacrifice from my favorite niece."

"I'm your only niece."

"Which makes your welfare doubly important to me. Whoops, one of the puppies just upchucked in his water bowl. Gotta go. Hang in there. I'll try to pop over for a visit soon."

"Do that," Sheila said as a longing for family swept over her.

"I will. Bye."

Sheila hung up the phone with a soft smile on her face. Explaining Douglas's presence in her life and Emil's hadn't been so difficult, after all. Of course, Gracie had a slightly skewed image of what this "old history teacher" of hers was like, but that was okay. If Sheila had been more specific, Gracie would have sailed in for an immediate inspection, despite her busy schedule. Sheila didn't think either she or Douglas were up to that kind of scrutiny yet.

"I hope that smile has something to do with me."

She glanced up and saw Douglas leaning in the doorway of her office. His black ski jacket was unzipped, revealing a white pocket T-shirt that looked as if it had been worn and laundered until it remembered the exact shape of its owner when he pulled it over his head.

"Hello, Douglas," she said, straightening in her chair. No matter how glad she was to see him, she needed to remember to behave professionally.

"Abby said it would be okay if I just dropped in."

"Sure. We're not all that formal around here." She motioned to one of two leather chairs positioned in front of her heavy oak desk. "Have a seat."

He sat across from her and looked around at the rough-cut paneling and woodland prints on the walls. An unadorned, multipaned window presented a view of fir trees and a tiny glimpse of the frozen lake. Unfortunately for Sheila, it wasn't the section where her father and Gus fished, or she could have kept an eye on the fishing shelters from her office. Against her advice, Gus and Emil had replaced the wooden structures with portable canvas ones.

"Nice office," Douglas said.

"Kathleen and I thought it should have the same rustic feel as the rest of the lodge."

"You achieved it." He relaxed into the chair, looking sexier than any man had a right to, and studied her. "Is this the realization of your dreams, then? This office and this position?"

She grew wary. "What do you mean?"

"This job has *career* written all over it. We're not talking a forty-hour work week, are we?"

"No. I work whatever hours the job requires."

"So there are lots of demands, not to mention a certain amount of power and prestige. Is it what you want?"

"For now." Something about his attitude was getting under her skin. She probably shouldn't ask the next question, but she did anyway. "Why?"

"Because we didn't get around to discussing your writing last night—"

"Maybe we should just let that go," she said hastily, her stomach clenching. He was probably about to suggest she keep her day job. "I shouldn't have brought it to you in the first place."

"On the contrary. It would be a crime to keep it hidden away in a drawer. You have a future as a writer."

She'd been so prepared for criticism she had to blink to clear her head for praise.

"Now don't start contradicting me, Sheila. You're good. That play, for instance. I think you should show it to Jan Redman in the drama department. They're putting on a selection of one-acts in May, and if we move quickly they could still produce—"

"Hold on a minute, Douglas." She studied him while trying to assimilate his comments. It was nice that he liked her work, but he was already planning how to get it before the public, and that bothered her. She remembered how guilty he'd felt about letting Beverly enter the essay that should have been Sheila's. This could be his way of making amends, by arranging for the drama teacher to produce her play. The drama teacher might agree to present the play regardless of its merit, and Douglas might be so guilt-ridden he couldn't tell whether Sheila's writing was worth anything or not.

"I take it from the skepticism in your expression you're not ready to fall in with this plan," he said, his tone dry.

"To evaluate anyone's writing is a very subjective

thing," she began slowly. "My mother used to say I was good, but let's face it—she was my mother."

His mouth quirked. "Something you can't accuse me of being."

"No, but you…probably aren't any more objective than she was."

He gazed at her silently for a moment and then swore softly under his breath.

"What?"

He stared out the window. "Never mind."

"You might as well say it, Douglas."

He faced her again. "All right. I can't help thinking that if I'd validated your ability thirteen years ago, we wouldn't have to have this conversation. Not getting a boost at that time was like leaving out a step in your development."

Thoroughly irritated, she pushed out of her chair with more force than she'd intended. The chair sailed backward off its plastic mat and banged into an oak filing cabinet behind her.

He glanced from the chair to her face. "I knew I shouldn't have said it," he muttered.

"No, I'm glad you did. We need to get this straight." She flattened both palms on her desk blotter and leaned forward. "I may have been your student once, but I am not any longer. I am a grown woman capable of making intelligent decisions about my life, and I highly resent being referred to as if I were some failed experiment!"

He rose and placed his hands opposite hers, so their fingers nearly touched. When he leaned forward, they were close enough to kiss, but he obviously didn't have kissing in mind. His eyes blazed with anger. "Then why in the devil did you give me those manuscripts?"

"I wish to God I hadn't." She met his anger defiantly. "I had some idea that you were suffering because you thought I'd given up writing completely. I thought if you knew that I'd kept it as a hobby, you'd—"

"A *hobby?*" He said it as if it were a disease. "You must be joking."

"Listen, *Mr. Wagner,* there is nothing wrong with having a career in hotel management and a fulfilling hobby writing stories. I don't recall anyone putting you in charge of the universe, so stop pushing me!"

His jaw clenched and his gaze smoldered as he looked into her eyes a moment longer. Then he turned and left the office without a word.

She gazed sightlessly out the door long after he'd departed. Then she allowed her head to fall forward between her outstretched arms. She'd brought this on herself, giving him the manuscripts as if she were still his student awaiting his judgment. No wonder he'd reacted like the teacher he was, the teacher he'd been. But a teacher-pupil relationship was at the opposite extreme of what she wanted with Douglas. Perhaps, through her own stupidity, she'd just destroyed all hope of having any relationship at all.

SHEILA HAD TRIED to prepare Emil for a day without ice fishing so they could drive in to Sugar Creek on Monday for his dental appointment, but still he complained the entire trip, saying he could go without teeth.

"Don't you want to be able to eat corn on the cob this summer?" she asked as she drove along the wintry highway to Sugar Creek. Although Emil could still drive, he preferred not to except around Tyler, where he knew the roads.

"Could be dead by shummer," he muttered.

If she'd imagined that one chess game with Douglas would completely change her father's attitude, she'd been mistaken. She only hoped Douglas would show up again tonight despite their quarrel on Saturday morning. Without his bout of ice fishing to perk him up, her father would need the chess game even more. But she didn't really doubt that Douglas would show up. He had appointed himself to help Emil through his grief, and he'd follow through. Too bad he'd also appointed himself to organize her life.

A flash of rusty orange shot across a snowy meadow and bounded through the trees on the left side of the road.

"Did you see the red fox, Pa?"

"Shaw it," he said without enthusiasm.

"Just think, in another month we'll have daffodils. And I can hardly wait for the tulips and hyacinths."

Her father sat stoically in the passenger seat, saying nothing.

"Ma would want us to enjoy the flowers, you know," she said gently.

There was an audible swallow from the passenger side of the car, and when she glanced at him, his eyes were shiny with unshed tears.

She reached over and squeezed his arm. "I want you to enjoy the flowers, Pa," she said around the lump in her throat. "I want us to enjoy them together. Please don't give up. I need you."

Emil didn't look at her, but he gave a slight nod. She knew it was the best he could do, and she was grateful for even that much show of resolve.

Two hours later her father's spirit returned in force when he found out how much his new dentures would cost. "Highway robbery!" he harangued as Sheila drove him home. He could talk more clearly with the set of temporary plates the dentist had provided.

Sheila almost wished the dentist had taped her father's mouth shut. "Those dentures you had were twenty years old," she said. "Everything costs three or four times what it did back then. It's not as if you can't afford it."

"I can't, dang it!"

Sheila had gone over her father's finances with him after they'd settled all the medical and funeral expenses for her mother. He wasn't wealthy, but Sheila estimated he should be able to live out his life in comfort and pay for a new set of teeth when he needed them, for heaven's sake. "You have plenty of money, Pa. The cost of these teeth will take a very small bite out of your budget, if you'll pardon the pun."

"Ha, ha." He fiddled with his seat belt. "I think I'll just call that horse thief and cancel the order."

"Pa! You'd better not, considering we spent the whole day getting this taken care of. Trust me, you won't miss this money."

"I need it," he insisted stubbornly.

"What for? You never go anywhere except to the lake to fish. Your house is paid for and so's this car. Unless you've booked a cruise around the world that I don't know about, you're in fine shape."

"It's...for college."

She thought she must have misunderstood. "What?"

"For college," he said again.

"Oh, Pa." Her throat tightened. "I really don't want to go now. I have a great job, and I—"

"Not for you. For my grandkids. That's what my will says. And that's what it's going for. And I don't want some dentist with a Cadillac and a danged summer home on Lake Geneva piddlin' away my college fund! I'm canceling the teeth, Sheilie."

Her heart ached for him. He still regretted not providing for her education, and he would remedy it by making sure there was money for the next generation. But there was a major flaw in his logic. "You don't have any grandkids," she said gently.

"I will." He nodded confidently. "Might not be around to see them, but somebody'll talk you into gettin' married and having babies. Might even be this here history teacher.''

Sheila gripped the wheel. ''I doubt that.''

''You could do worse.''

That was high praise coming from her father, but Sheila wasn't surprised that Emil liked Douglas. He only saw the compassion, the intelligence and the good humor, traits Sheila could grudgingly acknowledge. But Douglas didn't try to boss Emil around.

''Saw you kissing,'' her father said.

''Pa!'' Heat swept her cheeks.

He chuckled. ''After all those nights when you was a teenager, I know what's going on when it gets real quiet downstairs and nobody's drove away yet. Just thought I'd take a peek, and sure enough, he had you in a lip lock. Seemed like you was enjoying it, too.''

Totally embarrassed, Sheila said nothing.

Her father's tone was contrite. ''I won't do no peeking tonight.''

''Peek away,'' Sheila said. ''I can guarantee we won't be kissing.''

''Have a little spat?''

''You could say that.''

''Spats is the most normal thing about this courtin' business. If you don't have no spats, you'll never get to know each other.''

Sheila thought about that. ''I don't remember you and Ma fighting.''

''That's because we was both raised not to fight in front of the kids. When we really had to go at each other, we'd head out to the barn.''

Sheila gasped. ''You don't mean you hit each other?''

''No.'' Emil chuckled at her indignation. ''Your ma woulda liked to smack me a few times, I bet. But we didn't believe in hittin'. We'd just yell at each other till one of us ran out of breath or started to laugh.''

Sheila smiled wistfully. Here she'd imagined she knew her parents so well, and in the past week she'd discovered all sorts of new things.

"I even miss them fights," Emil said softly.

"I'll bet you do."

"With me bein' older, I just naturally thought I'd go first. Never figured on this."

"No." Sheila glanced at him. "Ma would have argued with you until you paid for those new teeth and used them."

"I s'pose she would."

"And you will need them for the victory dinner at Marge's, don't forget."

"Old Gus-Gus better not have caught my fish today," he muttered darkly as they turned off the highway and headed down the lane leading to the Lawson farm.

"He promised not to fish while you were in Sugar Creek."

"That's what he *said,* but how do I know he didn't sneak out there, anyway?"

Sheila knew Gus would never cheat, and so did her father, she suspected. But she played along because it was a safe subject. "If you want, I'll drive past our house and on up to Gus's so you can see if his snowmobile's in the drive."

"I hate to waste the extra gas on the old buzzard, but I gotta keep an eye on him. Go on up there."

Sheila drove past her parents' white frame house and the dull red barn several yards away. Now whenever she looked at that barn she'd have the bittersweet memory of her mother and father charging into its hay-scented confines to hash out their differences in front of the milk cows. Until somebody started laughing. That was her favorite part of the story.

The Lemke farmhouse was similar in construction to the Lawsons', except that the small front porch had been glassed in and a tattered blue-and-gold flag hung from a bracket by the door. Last summer Faye had talked Gus into painting the house buttercup yellow. Emil had commented, in Gus's presence, that the color matched the streak down Gus's back. Gus had responded that a white house was perfect for somebody as lily-livered as Emil Lawson. They'd carried on like that for years, and Sheila suspected it had turned into a ritual that expressed deep affection far more than disdain.

"Well, his danged snowmobile is there, but he coulda come in early," Emil said as Sheila cruised past the Lemke driveway. "Stop here. I'm gonna go feel the hood and see if that engine's been running today."

"You're not!"

"I am." He snapped off his seat belt and reached for the door handle. "Stop the car."

"Oh, for heaven's sake." Sheila pulled to the side of the road where the footing didn't look too mushy and applied the brakes.

"Keep 'er running," her father instructed as he climbed out of the car. "I want a clean getaway."

"I don't know why I—" But there was no reason to finish her protest. Crouching low, as if that would make his tall, gangly frame less visible in the stark landscape, Emil crossed the road and crept up the Lemke driveway.

Sheila shook her head. At least he'd forgotten about canceling his order for dentures. Maybe she'd call the dentist and ask him to contact her if he got a cancellation notice from Emil. She wanted her father to have the teeth, not only in order to eat better, but for the psychological boost.

He looked as if he were acting out a scene from "Mission Impossible'' as he paused in the driveway and peered around. Then he hunched lower and continued toward the snowmobile. Sheila prayed his back wouldn't go out on him while he was all bent over like that. He reached the snowmobile and took a 360-degree survey before laying a hand on the hood.

At that moment Faye's Pekingese must have scented him, because the dog began to yap and throw herself at the porch's storm door. Emil whirled and started to run, still bent over, so that he looked a lot like a chimpanzee as he charged down the drive. Sheila covered her eyes. If he fell in the middle of this crazy stunt...

The storm door banged open and Gus boiled out, still buttoning his coat. "Lawson, get back here, you piece of crow bait! I know what you was doin'! Feeling my motor, wasn't ya?'' He came down the steps too fast, and his arms pinwheeled as he tried to keep his balance. Somehow he avoided falling in the snowdrift he'd created when he'd shoveled the steps a week ago. "Lawson!'' he bellowed, starting down the drive.

Emil reached the car and jerked open the door. "Peel out!'' he said, panting.

Sheila waited until he was seated with the door closed before she swung the car around and started back down the road. Fortunately, Gus's added bulk made him a lot slower than Emil, and he'd barely reached the end of the drive as Sheila and Emil cruised past. He raised his fist and shook it in Emil's direction.

Emil cackled and made an obscene gesture back.

"Honestly, Pa,'' Sheila said with a sigh. She'd thought she wanted her father to regain his old spunk, but now she was wondering if there couldn't be a happy medium somewhere.

"Motor was cold,'' Emil announced smugly. "But it's good I checked. Keep that old buzzard honest.'' He rubbed his hands together. "That was fun. Got my blood up for the game tonight."

The game. For a few minutes, as she'd worried about her father and Gus and their endless pranks, she'd forgotten about the evening ahead. She hadn't heard from Douglas since that morning, but why should she? She'd told him off in no uncertain terms. Just because he came to see her father didn't mean he planned to have anything more to do with her. All things considered, maybe that was just as well.

CHAPTER TWELVE

DOUGLAS HAD BEEN in more awkward positions in his life than this, but he couldn't remember many. He slammed the door of his truck and mounted the steps to the Lawson porch empty-handed. He'd even left the journals and Sheila's manuscripts in the truck, because he couldn't be sure she would answer the door, and Emil wasn't supposed to know he had Myrna's journals. He hoped sometime during the evening he'd be able to return both the journals and the manuscripts, but in order to do that he'd have to see Sheila alone. She might not be in favor of that.

As it turned out, she did answer the door, and it looked as if she'd taken great pains to dress down for the occasion. The bib overalls had to be Emil's—the cuffs were rolled up several times and the straps on the bib were hitched up as far as possible to approximate a decent fit. Describing them as baggy would have been an understatement. Beneath the overalls she wore a long-sleeved knit shirt that fastened down the front with a row of tiny buttons. Its indistinguishable color hinted at involvement in several laundry accidents.

She lifted an unsmiling face scrubbed free of all makeup and pushed back tousled hair. "Come in."

He shouldn't have laughed. The minute he started he knew it was the wrong response, but he'd never seen anyone work so hard at demonstrating that she didn't give a damn.

Her eyes narrowed and she shoved her fists against her

hips, which finally defined for him where they were inside all that denim. "When you've collected yourself, you can go into the kitchen. My father's waiting." Then she turned, flounced out of the room and headed up the stairs.

He watched her go through swimming eyes. "Sheila," he called, his voice choked with laughter. "Don't leave. I..." But she'd topped the stairs and barreled inside what he assumed was her bedroom. The door slammed. He'd blown it again. With a sigh he walked toward the kitchen.

Emil looked up with such delight and anticipation that he was glad he'd come, after all. The older man took his pipe from his mouth. "Havin' a spat, aren'tcha?" he said.

"I guess so." Douglas took his seat and gazed down at the board, which the older man had set out so carefully for the match. Emil's devotion to the game was touching.

"She'll have time to stew while we play, and then you can mosey up there," Emil advised.

Douglas lifted his head in surprise.

"It's all right. When she was a teenager I didn't allow no boys up there, but she's not a teenager anymore."

"She didn't look much older than that tonight," Douglas said with a wry smile.

"Didn't act much older than one, neither." Emil chuckled. "'Course, I can't blame her none. I know exactly where she gets it." He studied Douglas with his still startlingly clear hazel eyes. "Heard you laughing in there."

"Yeah." Douglas rubbed his neck. "I shouldn't have done that. Really ticked her off."

"Sure you should have done that," Emil said.

Douglas gazed at him in puzzlement.

"It's the best thing for spats—laughing. Don't give up on her yet."

"I hadn't planned on it. She's...well, I don't have to tell you what a wonderful person she is."

Emil nodded. "She's got a lot of her mother's spirit in

her. Sometimes that's fun, but sometimes it's just plain infuriatin'.''

Douglas understood completely. "But never dull," he added.

"Nope. Want some coffee?"

"Sure."

Emil pushed himself away from the table. "Sheilie didn't make any, but I know my way around a coffeepot." His eyes twinkled. "'Fraid she dumped the rest of your pie in the garbage, though. We got Girl Scout cookies."

"Caramel pecan?" Douglas asked hopefully.

Emil turned from his work with the coffeepot. "Of course."

"Can I help do anything?"

"Cookies are in the freezer. Plates are in that there cupboard, if you want to get fancy." He pointed to a glass-fronted cabinet to the left of the sink.

"I can eat them out of the box."

Emil nodded. "Figured you could."

It occurred to Douglas as he opened the freezer and rummaged around as if he lived in the house that he was getting along better with Sheila's father than with her, which wasn't the way he'd have ordered things if he could have chosen which Lawson to impress.

Within a few minutes they'd started the game, with mugs of fresh coffee and an open box of cookies on the table beside them. At that point the friendly conversation stopped, as if both men were mentally rolling back their sleeves and setting to work. Douglas realized from Emil's response to his opening moves that the older man had reviewed Friday night's game, including any mistakes he'd made. Emil's grammar might not be correct, and anyone meeting him for the first time might dismiss him as an ignorant farmer, but Douglas recognized a superior intellect in action. This second game would be a far greater challenge than the first.

Three hours later the coffeepot and the cookie box were empty, and Douglas was staring at checkmate. He'd lost, and not because he hadn't given the game all his concentration. Emil had won when Douglas was at the top of his game, and that was a sobering thought. He'd have to do some studying himself before the next confrontation.

He glanced up and caught the gleam of triumph in Emil's eyes. "Wednesday night?"

"Sure thing."

Douglas stood and held out his hand. "I'd better be on my way."

"Aren't you going up to see her?" Emil pointed the stem of his pipe upward, toward the ceiling.

"I'm sure she's asleep by now."

"Not likely. Wouldn't put it past her to be lying on the rug with a glass to the floor, trying to hear what we're saying down here."

A scrambling noise above their heads made Douglas grin and look upward. "Mice?" he said softly, glancing at Emil.

"We don't have no mice," Emil said. "There's a magazine I've been meanin' to look at. Believe I'll go into the living room and read a bit before I turn in. Reckon I'll read about twenty minutes. How does that sound?"

Douglas nodded. "Fair enough."

Emil left the kitchen, and Douglas passed a hand over his face. He had twenty minutes to convince a very angry Sheila that he hadn't meant to treat her as a failed experiment. That he thought she'd done a fine job with her life, and he hadn't intended his comments as criticism of her choices. That if she didn't want to show anyone her writing, that was her prerogative. The last part bothered him, but she'd been pretty clear about the ground rules. He'd do his best to live by them, if he could wangle a second chance to try.

He walked out of the kitchen and started up the stairs.

SHEILA HEARD HIM coming. There was no mistaking his determined tread for her father's slower, more tentative one. She moved to the door, her hand on the lock. No doubt he had too much respect for property to break down the door in her father's house. She could choose not to see him. What happened now was totally up to her.

He rapped on the door. "Sheila?"

She pressed her forehead against the door and tried to work up her fury at him for laughing at the way she was dressed. But she kept thinking of what her father had said that afternoon. *Till one of us ran out of breath or started to laugh.* "What?"

"Will you open the door so we can talk like reasonable adults?"

She really wasn't behaving much better with Douglas than her father behaved toward Gus, she thought. She stepped back from the door and opened it.

His gaze encompassed her outfit, which she hadn't changed. He didn't laugh, but he smiled. "It didn't work, you know," he said.

She held on to the door for support. Just looking at him standing outside her bedroom door made her knees weak. "I don't know what you're talking about."

"Sure you do. You did your best to appear unattractive just to snub me and let me know you weren't about to fix yourself up for the likes of me."

The corners of her mouth twitched as his accurate assessment nearly made her smile in return.

"But I have to tell you, you look cute as hell with no makeup and that baggy outfit on. And when you muss your hair like that all I can think of is what you'd look like after you'd been rolling around in bed…with me.''

She gasped. ''Douglas…my father—''

''Is in the living room reading. He can't hear me. We have—'' he paused to consult his watch ''—seventeen minutes before he starts upstairs. May I come in?''

She stood back from the door and held her arm out to encompass the room, which held a single bed littered with reading material, a dresser and a desk—a serviceable pine set her parents had bought her for her sixth birthday. ''There's not much space.''

''I don't need much.''

She watched him uneasily as he walked in and nudged the door shut behind him with his foot. Then, before she had assimilated his presence here in her girlhood bedroom, he swept her into his arms. ''I'm sorry, so very sorry.'' He feathered her lips with soft kisses. ''Forgive me for presuming to know what you want.''

This. So quickly as to be embarrassing, she abandoned her anger and reveled in his ardent attention to her mouth. He tasted of coffee and caramel pecan. ''You've been into the Girl Scout cookies,'' she murmured between kisses.

''I ate every last one,'' he said against hers lips.

She nibbled at his. ''Greedy, aren't you?''

''You don't know the half of it.''

She was beginning to suspect the half of it, however, even through the thick denim of her father's bib overalls. The deeper his kisses, the more obviously aroused he became. A responding ache settled between her thighs and she pressed closer, her heart pounding with unfulfilled needs, needs he seemed quite ready to satisfy.

Breathing hard, he leaned away from her. His hand trembled as he stroked the back of his knuckles down the column of her throat to the first button on her knit shirt. His voice was husky. ''You're driving me crazy.''

"That can be…a two-way street."

"I'm counting on it." He unfastened the top button, but there were at least thirty down the front of the shirt, not to mention the barrier of the bib overalls.

And her father was downstairs, Sheila managed to remember, and he would come up in a few minutes. The second button gave way, and her pulse skittered in response.

"I want to touch you…everywhere." He slipped the third button from its hole as his gaze burned into hers. "I want to make love to you until neither of us can move." Another button.

She could barely breathe as a fifth button came undone, and a sixth.

"But it never seems to be the right time." His voice rasped with tension, and a seventh button eased open beneath his fingers. "Or the right place." With eight buttons unfastened, he leaned down and pressed his mouth slowly and deliberately against her heated skin.

She closed her eyes and thought she might burst into flame. Her imagination brought his mouth to her breasts, her inner thighs, and all the secret places longing for his caress. But that wouldn't happen now. She whimpered in distress.

He lifted his head and stepped away from her, leaving her shaking with desire. "You're a creative woman," he said. "The next step is up to you." He walked past her, opened the door and left the room.

DOUGLAS PAUSED on the landing to pull himself together. The pursuit of Sheila would be a wonderful challenge if it didn't kill him. He hadn't lusted after a woman this much and denied himself satisfaction since…since the day he'd first seen Sheila Lawson sitting in his classroom thirteen years ago. He had more hope for the outcome now than he had before, but there was no denying the psychology was tricky. In order to win Sheila he had to turn off all his teaching instincts. It would be hard work. A truly smart man would say to hell with it and look for someone less difficult to please. But he wanted Sheila. God, how he wanted her.

He glanced down at his jeans and decided he was finally presentable. Taking a deep breath, he looked at his watch. Three minutes to spare. Damn. He would have had time for another button.

DOUGLAS HAD HANDED her an impossible situation, Sheila decided as she listened for his truck in the drive on Wednesday night. She'd interpreted his final remark to mean that she was supposed to find an appropriate time and place for them to be alone together, a place to make love. Her house was out of the question with her father living here. Douglas's house was located too close to the high school—both students and faculty would notice her car parked out in front. They were both consenting adults, of course, but Sheila still didn't like the idea of advertising their first night together like that. The experience should belong to them, not half the town.

She'd considered making reservations out of town, in Chicago or Milwaukee, but checking into a hotel seemed like such a cold and calculating, singularly unromantic thing to do. Therefore, as Douglas's knock came on the storm door, she was no further along toward their rendezvous plans than she'd been when he'd walked out of her room and left her nearly blinded with passion.

Tonight she'd worn soft wool slacks and a V-necked sweater of sage green. When she wanted to look demure, she wore a cotton turtleneck under the sweater. She wasn't interested in being demure tonight. When she opened the door she took satisfaction in his quick intake of breath.

He stepped inside and pulled her close. He smelled of cold night air and chocolate. Something rectangular pressed against her back as he held her for his kiss.

"What are you holding?" she whispered as he lifted his lips from hers.

"You."

"No. Behind my back."

"Girl Scout cookies. Two boxes from my freezer." His glance drifted down to the neckline of her sweater. "What happened to the bib overalls?"

"In the laundry hamper."

His smile was predatory. "Sure they are." He traced the neckline with one finger, making her shiver with need. He lowered his voice. "How am I supposed to beat your father at chess when I'm fantasizing about you in this very approachable outfit?"

"I—"

"Never mind. I can be strong." He dropped another quick kiss on her lips and released her. "And I'm not leaving again with your mother's journals still in my truck," he said in an undertone as he handed her the boxes of cookies and took off his jacket.

Tonight he wore a long-sleeved cotton shirt unbuttoned at the neck, and she nearly dented the cookie boxes as she gazed at the sexy way his dark chest hair was revealed by the casual opening of that top button.

He took the boxes from her unresisting hands with a faint smile. "Whatever else happens after the chess game, I'm bringing them in so we can talk about them."

"Talk about what?"

He took her chin between his thumb and forefinger. "Your mother's journals." He gazed into her eyes. "But if you keep looking at me like that, I'll probably forget all about them, too." He drew in a ragged breath. "Maybe you'd better stay in here and read tonight."

"I thought nothing could break your concentration when you were playing chess."

"I didn't think anything could, either." He withdrew his hand. "He won the last game, and if he wins this one he'll probably start losing interest in playing me."

"I don't want that."

He winked. "Then stay out of the kitchen."

She did, but with every noise from that room she abandoned her book and listened intently. She knew exactly when they brewed coffee and opened the first box of cookies. She heard someone put the second box in the freezer. After two excruciatingly long hours, she heard her father say "Friday?" and decided the game must be over. There was no indication who had won, but at least her father was suggesting another game.

"Can't make it Friday," Douglas said. "The reenactment group is going on a weekend retreat to plan the summer's activities. I said I'd be there. I'll be available Sunday night, though."

"Sunday it is," Emil said. "That'll give me more time to study up."

Sheila heard them moving around the kitchen, picking up mugs and putting away the chess set. She decided to stay where she was and let their friendship have a chance to grow without her interfering presence. She enjoyed listening to Douglas talk to her father, and this time the conversation was much clearer than it had been with a glass pressed to the floorboards.

"Where'd you learn to play, anyway?" Emil asked.

"My dad."

"Is he as good as you?"

"He was better. He died two years ago."

The information shed new light on Douglas's offer to play chess with Emil, Sheila thought. He probably missed his own father. She suddenly realized she was flirting with disaster by encouraging Douglas and Emil to become friends, considering the uncertain nature of her relationship with Douglas. It reminded her of a working associate in Chicago who'd been cautious about dating because her three-year-old became attached to every man she brought home. Emil wasn't a child, but he was needy right now.

Then again, maybe Emil and Douglas would go right on being friends, whether she and Douglas continued to see each other or not. That was an unsettling thought. She heard the two men start into the living room and grabbed her book.

"He whipped me," Emil announced.

She glanced up from the book and focused on her father. She was a little afraid to look at Douglas, for fear her yearning might show. "Is that right?"

"But Sunday will be a different story. Yep, sir. A different story altogether." Emil turned and held out his hand to Douglas. "I'm turning in. See you Sunday, then."

"I'll be here," Douglas said, giving him a firm handshake. "Thanks for the game."

"You won't be thanking me on Sunday. You'll be lickin' your wounds."

"We'll see about that, won't we?"

Emil chuckled. "Yep, we will. Good night, you two lovebirds." He turned and headed upstairs.

With apparent nonchalance, Douglas wandered toward the sofa. "Good book?"

"Excellent." She held his gaze. "It's kept me totally absorbed."

"Really?" He eased down on the sofa next to her and stretched his arm along the back.

A pulse beat erratically in her throat and her skin began to tingle even though he hadn't touched her. "You know how it is with a well-written story," she said. "You can't put it down."

"I can see how it would take all your concentration." He looked deep into her eyes.

"You've read it?"

"No. But anything would be a challenge if you're reading it upside down." Still holding her gaze, he reached for the book and repositioned it right side up in her hands. "Try not to get bored doing it this way while I'm outside getting your mother's journals." He stood up and started toward the door without retrieving his jacket from the back of the easy chair where he'd tossed it earlier.

"Your jacket," she called to him.

"Don't need it. I'm already hot," he said, and was gone.

Amen. Sheila smiled ruefully as she closed the book and laid it aside on the table. No point in pretending that she was in full possession of her faculties when Douglas was around. Might as well get comfortable and enjoy the trip. She kicked off her shoes and drew her stocking feet up under her.

He came through the door holding the journals and the envelope containing her writing. She had an instant of foreshadowing as to how it would feel to have him come home to her every night. The thought was disturbingly wonderful, considering how shaky she felt about their future.

Crossing to the sofa, he placed the pile of materials between them. "Maybe if I have to go around these to get to you I'll remember to discuss them," he said as he sat down and rubbed his hands together.

"Here." She caught his wrists and brought his chilled hands to her warm cheeks. "Let me."

"Let you what?" he said softly, his hands very still against her skin. "I'll tell you right now, whatever it is, you don't have to ask permission."

The need in his eyes threatened to overwhelm her. To give herself a foothold on reality, she turned her head and placed a kiss against his cool palm. He slid his hand down until the pad of his thumb caressed her upper lip, then downward coaxing her mouth open. She slid the tip of her tongue out to flick against his caressing thumb and heard his breathing quicken.

With the heel of his other hand he guided her back around to face him as he leaned forward across the pile of journals. Teasing her mouth open further, he gradually closed in, replacing his probing thumb with the demanding thrust of his tongue. It was a blatant invitation, and her stomach cartwheeled as he launched her into sensuous overload.

After several moments of whirling her in the maelstrom he created with his suggestive mouth, he drew back. "When, Sheila?" he murmured, his eyes heavy-lidded and dark with passion.

"Not here," she managed to whisper.

"No. Not with your father—"

"Not in Tyler at all." Ever since she'd heard him mention the reenactment group an idea had been forming. "Do you know what I want?"

"Tell me."

"Would it be historically accurate if…Black Hawk had a…squaw?"

Dark fire burned in his eyes. "Do you really imagine I'd care about historical accuracy if you'd agree to spend the weekend with me?"

"I can't spend the whole weekend. Too many things are going on Friday for me to get away. But if you'll give me directions, I should be able to get someone to cover so I can drive out Saturday afternoon—" she paused and licked dry lips "—and stay until Sunday."

His grip tightened along the curve of her jaw. "Saturday. I may be a madman by Saturday."

"This is the right way, Douglas. Away from Tyler, away from all the baggage that seems to come between us."

"Speaking of that..." He released her and scooped up the journals and envelope and set them behind him. "Excuse me, Myrna," he said to the stack of notebooks, "but a guy has his priorities, you know." He turned back and reached past Sheila to turn off the lamp beside the sofa. "Now, about that sweater..."

Her heart pounded as he guided her around until he cradled her in his arms and leaned her against his bent knee. She looped her own arms around his neck and rested against his knee while she studied the perfection of his intelligent forehead, the intensity of his green eyes, the decadent fullness of his lower lip. He gazed at her with the same steady absorption. Then her breathing grew shallow as he slid one hand up her back beneath the sweater. In a move that separated boys from men, he flicked open the back catch of her bra.

She lay in his arms, her nipples tight with anticipation, while he took his own sweet time claiming the prize he sought. Her longing grew with every second that ticked by. Almost casually he rested his hand at the neckline of her sweater. Gradually he eased the soft knit off the curve of her shoulder and lowered his head to kiss her there. A nudge from his finger and her bra strap slipped down, too. She trembled as he lifted his head and pushed the sweater down slowly, stretching the moment to its fullest. When the edge of the neckline grazed her nipple, he paused, then guided the material away from the puckered areola.

"So beautiful," he murmured, gazing at her unfettered breast. Cupping its weight, he leaned down and circled the tip with his tongue. She pressed the back of her hand to her mouth to keep from moaning out loud. He drew her more fully into his mouth and she closed her eyes in ecstasy. As he dispensed sweet torture with his lips, tongue and teeth, she lost track of where she was. Had he slipped off the rest of her clothes and made love to her on that sofa, she wouldn't have stopped him.

But apparently Douglas hadn't forgotten where they were. With a soft groan he released her breast and eased her sweater back in place. "If I don't stop now, I won't be able to," he murmured, combing his fingers through her hair and gazing with regret into her eyes. "I won't sleep tonight as it is, and I hope to hell you won't, either."

"I haven't slept well for days," she admitted softly.

He lifted her face to his and nuzzled her lips. "Don't expect to catch up on Saturday night."

"No." She matched him kiss for kiss, breath for breath, as their tongues parried and their mouths opened, deepening the caress until they were once again locked in each other's arms, and Douglas was reaching beneath her sweater to stroke her aching breasts.

"I have to go," he gasped, tearing his lips away. "I would never forgive myself if I—"

"Douglas," she whispered, pulling him down for one last kiss.

"Now. I'm leaving now." He set her firmly away from him and staggered up from the sofa. He nearly tripped over the journals. "Next time, Myrna," he said.

"Douglas, wait. What am I supposed to wear?"

He turned, his chest heaving. "As little as possible."

"No, really. Shouldn't I be in costume?"

His heated gaze moved over her. "I'll take care of it." He shook his head. "And if I don't want to be the laughingstock of the encampment, I'll dress you in a gunnysack." With that he grabbed his jacket and hobbled out the door.

CHAPTER THIRTEEN

SHEILA TOLD four people her destination for Saturday night. Emil didn't seem particularly shocked and said he was glad the "spat" was over. Abby hugged her and said of course she'd cover Sheila's duties at the lodge. Informing the third and fourth person required some subterfuge on Sheila's part. Thursday evening she told her father she needed to drive into town to pick up a few groceries, which was true. She didn't mention that she planned to drive to Gus and Faye's house first.

That afternoon after school Douglas had stopped by the lodge to bring her a map and directions to the encampment. She had a photocopy of the information in her purse.

As she parked in the drive, she noticed that Gus had trained a spotlight on the bedraggled blue-and-gold flag hanging from the glassed-in front porch. Just wait until Emil saw that, she thought. Bitsy, the Pekingese, yapped and hurled herself against the storm door when Sheila started up the walk.

The barking dog reminded her that she had to finalize plans for the toy-dog breeders' convention and dog show she'd scheduled in the fall. To her surprise, Mr. Wocheck had approved the idea, and Aunt Gracie was proud of herself for contributing to Sheila's master plan. Sheila had misgivings about bringing that many dogs onto the grounds, but at least the dogs would be small and she'd be able to see Aunt Gracie again. More important, the event should attract media attention.

Gus came to the door and shouted something at Bitsy, which had no effect on the yapping dog. He grinned when he glimpsed Sheila through the glass of the storm door. With his rounded features, he reminded Sheila of the smiley faces that encouraged people to Have A Nice Day.

Picking up the dog, he opened the door. "You got that ornery old cuss with you?" he asked.

"No, I left Pa at home on purpose," she said. "I didn't want any shenanigans between you two while I was trying to talk."

"Shenanigans?" Gus said in shocked surprise. "Did you hear that, Bitsy? Shenanigans from an old codger like me. She must be thinking of somebody else."

"The same person who's trained a spotlight on the flag, no doubt," Sheila said.

"Who's here?" Faye came out from the kitchen, drying her hands on a towel. "Why, hello, Sheila. What a nice surprise." A stout woman of medium height, Faye hadn't changed her mind or her hairstyle for thirty years.

Glancing at her tight gray curls, Sheila wondered how Faye would react to news that Sheila was spending the weekend with a man. But her neighbors needed to know exactly where she was, and with whom, in case of an emergency. At least Faye wasn't a gossip.

"Let me take your coat," Gus said, setting Bitsy back on the floor.

"And how about something to eat or drink?" Faye added. "There's coffee yet from supper, and a piece of lemon icebox cake to go with it."

"Oh, no, thank you." Sheila handed Gus her coat. "I'll only stay a minute."

"Well, you have to stay long enough to see the newest pictures of the grandkids," Faye said. "We have one graduating from high school this spring, if you can believe it. With honors, of course."

"Of course." Sheila figured exclaiming over Gus and Faye's grandchildren was the least she could do. Their two married sons were ten and twelve years older than Sheila, and she hadn't known them very well, but they seemed like good guys. Both Faye and Gus puffed up with pride whenever they talked about either son, and the grandchildren were all geniuses, according to Gus.

Sheila had been around many times when Gus was sounding off about them, and she'd watched Emil struggle with his jealousy. Yet her father had never prodded her to get married and produce grandchildren he could boast about. Instead he'd quietly expressed his yearnings by squirreling away money for a college fund.

The snapshots appeared, and Sheila settled into the rocker at right angles to the sofa where Faye and Gus sat with Bitsy. The older couple glowed as Sheila looked through the photographs and praised the attractiveness of everyone pictured in them. Then, as Faye tucked them back into an envelope, Sheila broached the subject she'd come for. "I have a favor to ask of both of you," she said. "I'll be gone from about noon on Saturday until noon on Sunday, and I want to leave you a map of where I'm going so you can find me if there's any problem with Pa."

"A map?" Faye asked with a chuckle as she settled Bitsy on her lap. "Where on earth are you going that we'd need a map to find you?"

Sheila told them and braved the skeptical looks they gave her during the explanation. She took the map from her purse and spread it out on the coffee table next to a stack of crocheted coasters. "We'll be here, on the Rock River, and the turnoff is right after a big red barn on the right side of the road, according to Douglas. It should be only about an hour-and-a-half drive from here."

Gus smoothed the map with one age-spotted hand and studied it. "Yeah, I know about where this is. Pretty spot.

Kinda out of the way, though. Don't know why some-body'd want to camp there in the wintertime.''

Sheila accepted the hint of disapproval without comment.

Gus looked up from the map. ''You joinin' up with this history group, then?''

''No. I'm just a guest for the weekend.'' She rushed past the censure in Faye's expression. ''Pa hasn't been alone overnight since Ma died, and with the ice fishing, I worry there could be some sort of accident.''

''So do I,'' Faye said, glancing at her husband. ''But he says they're safe out there.''

''Like I keep sayin', you have to know the ice.'' Gus turned Sheila's map over and picked up a stubby pencil from where it lay next to a half-worked crossword puzzle on an end table. ''Here's Timber Lake.'' He sketched in a rough outline. ''Now this spot where me and Emil fish every year—'' he marked it with a big X ''—is always solid long after other parts get rotten.''

''And one of these days, you'll be floating on it like a couple of Eskimos and we'll have to hire a helicopter to get you off!'' Faye said.

''No, you won't.'' Gus spoke with exaggerated patience. ''Because we have our path figured out, and we don't go over no rotten ice on the way out and back.'' He drew a zigzag line from the shore to the X. ''Like that. Me and Emil've been fishing that lake for better'n sixty years. We know what we're doin'.''

Sheila decided that as long as she had this golden op-portunity, she wouldn't waste it. ''I believe you,'' she said. ''But Pa seems more determined to win this year than in other years, probably because of not having Ma and every-thing. I worry that he won't exercise good judgment, and I've been counting on you to be the rational one out there, Gus-Gus.''

''Ha!'' Faye said.

Gus gave his wife a scornful look. "Don't worry none, Sheilie." He reached over and patted her arm. "I'll be careful. But it seems like it does him good to get riled up."

"You're right. And now Douglas comes over several nights a week to play chess with him. I think between the two of you he might begin to feel life is still worth living."

"What does Emil think of you taking part in this encampment business?" Faye asked.

"He thinks it's fine."

Faye nodded. "Guess he would. He and Myrna always were a bit radical that way. Especially Myrna, with her smoking and martinis and all."

Gus gave her a warning glance. "Now, Mother. Don't be speakin' ill of the dead."

Faye sniffed. "Just stating the facts, is all. Myrna didn't try to hide it. She seemed proud to be different. Remember the time she sat right in this room and told us about sneaking up to the hayloft with Emil so they could—"

"Mother," Gus interrupted firmly. "That's not a story for Sheilie to hear."

"I don't know why not," Faye said. "After all, Sheila and the history teacher are going off for the weekend, aren't they?"

"That's not the same as thinkin' about your folks...doin' it. Besides, times are changin', Mother."

Faye scowled. "For the worse, I say. Look at what we have now—AIDS, women hired to have other women's babies, drugs—"

"I promise not to do any drugs on this trip," Sheila said with a tiny smile.

Faye looked startled. "That's just the sort of...thing Myrna would have said."

Sheila suspected Faye had edited out the phrase "smart-aleck" from the comment. "Thank you," she said, standing. "And thank you both for watching out for Pa while I'm gone. I don't know what I'd do without you."

"Hey, that's what neighbors are for." Gus stood and held out his arms. "Take care of yourself, Sheilie."

Sheila hugged him and unexpected tears pooled in her eyes. "Thanks, Gus-Gus." She emerged from his bear hug to discover Faye standing, too, her expression softened.

"I've always thought of you as the daughter we never had," she said, giving Sheila a hug, too. "We just want you to be happy. I'm sure you miss your mother somethin' terrible."

"I do, Faye." Sheila stepped back and wiped at her damp eyes.

"If you ever need another woman to talk to, I'm here."

Sheila almost giggled through her tears, but she managed to keep from doing so, because the offer was sincerely meant and she didn't want to hurt her neighbor's feelings. Yet the idea of telling Faye her fantasy of stripping the buckskin from Douglas's virile body made her bite her lip to keep the laughter at bay. "Thanks," she said. "I'll call you when I get home, Faye. The men will probably be on the ice."

"Sure will," Gus said.

"After church," Faye reminded him, with a meaningful glance at Sheila.

And while you're in church I'll be living in sin, Sheila thought to herself. She must truly be Myrna's child, she decided, because she felt absolutely no regret at that notion.

BY NOON on Saturday Douglas thought the nervous anticipation churning in his gut would rip him apart.

"Go split some firewood," Charlie advised when he found Douglas pacing the makeshift parking area. The lot was near the encampment site but screened from it by a copse of trees that helped the reenactors block out the twentieth-century view of automobiles. "Do you really want her to pull in and find you wandering around like an idiot waiting for her to arrive?"

Douglas grinned. "It's too late for nonchalance, buddy. She knows I'm her slave."

"Well, you don't have to look so damned pathetic, at any rate," Charlie said. "And we need your muscles on the other end of the sledgehammer."

"I guess it would give me something to do until she gets here."

Charlie glanced up at the sun as it peeked out from a gray cloud and disappeared again. No watches were allowed in the encampment, and everyone had learned to tell time by the sun. "If she left at noon, you have at least an hour before there's any chance she'll show."

"I was hoping she'd get an early start."

Charlie gazed at him and shook his head. "You *are* pathetic. In fact, I've never seen you act like this. I suggested you find a good woman to love, not a goddess to worship."

"Oh, she's no goddess. But there's something..." Douglas smiled softly as he recalled his last glimpse of Sheila on the veranda of the lodge Friday afternoon, her enthusiasm for life seeming to make her glow against the rustic backdrop.

"Oh, jeez, there you go again, off in space." Charlie grabbed his arm. "To the woodpile with you, my boy. And don't smash your kneecap, or any other essential part of your anatomy, while you're drifting in la-la land."

"It's just because you've forgotten what it's like," Douglas said as he walked beside Charlie through the encampment. "Marriage has dulled your romantic spirit."

"And the romantic spirit has dulled your wits," Charlie replied. "I told everyone you'd be a great addition to this planning session because you—a history teacher with some honest-to-goodness Sauk Indian blood in your veins—have all this background on the Black Hawk War. So how much did you contribute to the discussion around the campfire last night? Zip, that's how much. Just sat there staring into the flames with that dopey smile on your face, not a brain cell working.''

''She has this way of looking at a person,'' Douglas said, ''with this mischievous sort of smile, and you just wonder what she'll be up to next.''

Charlie lifted his eyes heavenward. ''Don't know why I bother flapping my gums. Nothing gets through.''

''What?'' Douglas turned toward him. ''Did I miss something?''

''Not a thing, Wagner.'' Charlie clapped him on the shoulder. ''Just let me identify the woodpile for you. It's about three feet high, about six feet in diameter and contains these round things we rational humans call logs. Your mission is to split them so they'll burn more easily. The wedge and sledge are right next to the woodpile. You swing the big thing and hit the little thing. Want to repeat that back to me so I know you've got it?''

''What's wrong with you is jealousy, pure and simple.''

Charlie stroked his beard and studied Douglas. ''Jealous? Nah. I'd rather be in love than fall in love any day. Now go make yourself useful while I find Cathy and give her a big, uncomplicated kiss. Watching you suffer has given me a whole new appreciation for seasoned relationships.''

Douglas thought about that as he loosened the laces on his buckskin shirt and placed the first log on the chopping block. In theory he agreed with Charlie—this turbulent excitement could wear people out if it lasted forever. Yet he was enjoying the ride despite being thrown around emotionally like an astronaut in zero gravity. He couldn't tell Charlie, but he'd never experienced such intensity, even with Joanne. He wondered if the life he and Joanne had lived together could have been considered a seasoned relationship. If so, it sure as hell had lacked some essential spice.

He tapped the wedge into a crevice in a log and swung the sledgehammer. The impact felt great as the wood split cleanly down the middle. Charlie had been right about this activity. It was a decent substitute for what he needed. He reached for another log.

Half an hour later, despite the cold day, he'd begun to sweat. Laying down the sledgehammer, he stripped off the buckskin shirt and draped it carefully over a nearby branch. The chill slapped his bare skin at first, but he picked up the hammer and started working again. Soon the comforting rhythm had warmed him right up.

SHEILA'S HEARTBEAT quickened when she spied the red barn Douglas had described as the landmark for the turnoff. Almost there. On the seat next to her rested the small gym bag she'd packed with underwear and toiletries, but she wasn't even sure she could use the twentieth-century items she'd brought. Douglas had told her to arrive with nothing, but she'd found that difficult to accept.

She slowed the car, put on her turn signal and swung onto a recently plowed side road arched over with the icy tentacles of leafless trees. The road headed gradually downward, and the trees packed in tighter around her. A few evergreens presented the only color relief in a world dominated by gray and white. Even the sky had turned the color of pussywillows, blotting out the sun. Sheila thought of buffalo robes and glowing embers, and a steady heat licked through her. Somewhere in all that grayness was a warrior chieftain named Black Hawk. And he was waiting for her.

She found the parking lot, a snowplowed meadow containing about twenty vehicles, included Douglas's pickup truck. At the sight of it her stomach clenched with excitement. She parked the car, got out and locked it before putting the keys in her jacket pocket. The gym bag and her purse could stay there until Douglas filled her in on protocol and gave her some clothes to replace the jeans, sweatshirt and turquoise-and-purple ski jacket she'd worn to the encampment.

As she continued down the plowed road on foot, the scent of wood smoke drifted toward her. She took a long, steadying breath to calm her jumpy nerves. Once she made contact with Douglas, she'd settle down, she told herself. Anticipation had keyed her up beyond all belief.

The road led straight down to the river, which appeared through the canopy of icy branches ahead of her. Most of it was iced over, but a small rivulet still ran free, where the current was strongest. The encampment, arranged essentially as it had been on the Timberlake grounds, was to her left in a meadow that she guessed was used for campers during the summer.

Yet now it looked like a window into another time as men in frontier soldier uniforms and women in long prairie dresses moved around a large campfire in the center of the settlement. A few men and women in Indian attire mingled with the soldiers and frontier ladies of the night, but Sheila didn't see Douglas.

As she started toward the encampment, she recognized Charlie coming toward her, a smile of welcome decorating his bearded face. Some of her nervousness faded.

"I ordered him over to the woodpile," he said as he approached and shook her hand. "He was driving us all crazy. If you hadn't arrived soon, we might have had to send him out to hunt wild game or something. The boy's a mess."

Sheila laughed, because she thought Charlie expected her to, but his words made her quiver inside. She liked knowing Douglas was strung as tight as she was over this weekend rendezvous. "Where's the woodpile?"

"Go around these wigwams here and follow the sound of metal hitting metal with an unholy force. I glanced over there a few minutes ago and noticed he's split enough logs to supply all the fireplaces in Milwaukee for a week. If we could harness that kind of enthusiasm, we could eliminate the energy crisis."

"So it's okay if I interrupt him?"

"I think it's imperative that you interrupt him." He looked over her jeans and ski jacket. "I think the dress Cathy found will fit perfectly. I hope you like it."

"I'm sure it'll be great. Thanks, Charlie."

"You're welcome. Now go find that log-splitting maniac before he starts in on the live trees, okay?"

"Okay." She headed off in the direction Charlie had indicated, her fur-lined boots crunching through the crusted snow, which lay about six inches deep. She shoved her hands into the zippered pockets of her ski jacket to keep them from trembling. On the other side of the wigwams she saw some motion through a wiry tangle of leafless bushes. The steady clink of metal and the clean sound of splitting wood carried through the crisp air.

She skirted the barrier…and came face-to-face with her fantasy.

CHAPTER FOURTEEN

DOUGLAS HAD RESTED the sledgehammer on the ground and was reaching for another log when he saw Sheila at the edge of the clearing, her cheeks pink from the cold and her cornsilk hair lifting in the slight breeze from the river. The log dropped from his nerveless fingers and he straightened. Until he saw her standing there, he hadn't truly believed she would come.

He started toward her at the same moment she moved in his direction. He covered the distance quickly and swung her up in his arms, lifting her off her feet and whirling her around in his joy. She was here! She was really here. She smiled down at him as he held her tightly, compressing the bulky ski jacket against his chest. Gradually he allowed her to slide down until he could kiss those smiling lips. Her soft hands curved over his bare shoulders before moving down to grasp his biceps. Desire surged through him like a freight train.

He groaned and plunged his tongue into her mouth. Now. He wanted her now. He fumbled for the zipper on her jacket and pulled it down to eliminate one more barrier between them. She cooperated by nestling closer and wrapping her arms around his bare back while her kiss invited him deeper. Yet despite her obvious willingness, she eventually eased away from him. He let her go with reluctance and took comfort in the fact that she was having trouble catching her breath.

"Charlie said…there was an outfit for me," she said, her chest heaving.

"Yes. In my tent." He knew if he went in there with her, they might not come out for the rest of the weekend.

Her smile told him she understood the same thing.

"I'll leave you alone to change," he said. "Then there's a planning session I'm expected to attend. You can sit in on it if you like or help the women get dinner ready."

She raised an eyebrow. "The men plan and the women cook? Isn't that a wee bit sexist?"

"Probably." He couldn't resist touching her cheek and watching the light come on in her eyes. "But it's also a historically accurate division of labor. You're in 1832 now."

"Is that why you're splitting wood? Because it's man's work?"

He stroked one finger along her jaw. "I'm splitting wood because while I was waiting for you I was useless for doing anything else."

She gave him that impish look that turned his knees to jelly. "So Charlie said."

"Charlie's a blabbermouth." He took a long, shaky breath. "I'm glad you're here."

"So am I." She met his gaze and allowed him to see passion lurking in the depths of her hazel eyes. "Better put on your shirt."

"Right." He forced himself away from that tempting gaze and walked over to retrieve his shirt. As he came back, he gave her a wry grin. "Think I'll also carry some wood into camp. I seem to have split a few logs while I was waiting for you."

"A few. Hold out your arms and I'll stack them up."

He enjoyed the easy way they worked together as she loaded the wood in the curve of his arms. When they were up to his chin, she settled a few logs in the crook of her own arm before they started back to camp. "Squaws are expected to carry firewood, right?"

"Yes, but you aren't a squaw this weekend," he said, thinking about what lay spread out in the tent on the buffalo robes.

"I'm not? But Charlie said that Cathy found me a dress."

"She did. I told her to locate a white woman's outfit." He paused to see if she'd pick up on the significance of that.

She stopped walking and gave him a long, assessing gaze.

"You're not only in 1832," he said quietly. "You're Black Hawk's captive."

BLACK HAWK'S CAPTIVE. She'd asked for that once, and he'd granted her wish. Moments later Sheila let the tent flap close behind her as she stared at the long white dress laid carefully across the soft fur of Douglas's bed. Long-sleeved and high-necked as well, it was demure, the dress of a proper lady, with a row of tiny buttons running from the neck to below the waist. Even the sleeves each had a row of six buttons on the wrist. It could have been someone's wedding dress, Sheila thought, her mind a swirl of sensuous impressions. A pile of underthings sat next to the dress— bloomers, petticoats, a delicate silk chemise to wear next to her skin and another one of wool to keep her warm. A heavy cape and lace-up shoes completed the outfit.

Douglas had instructed her to take off all her twentieth-century clothes, including her watch, and bundle them up. He would transfer them to her car later. He'd stationed himself outside the tent to make sure she wouldn't be disturbed while she changed clothes. She imagined him poised there, his arms crossed and his look haughty as he stood guard over his captive.

The embers in the small fire circle were cold, and she shivered in the chilled air as she exchanged her jeans, sweatshirt and underwear for the layers of fashion that women wore in the eighteen-hundreds. The lavender-scented garments were more cumbersome than her own clothes, but far more feminine. As she laced and buttoned, she thought of the infinite patience a man would need to undo it all again. And how the anticipation would build...

At last she swept the navy wool cape over her shoulders and stooped to walk through the flap opening. As she straightened on the other side, Douglas turned, and his green eyes darkened with excitement.

"Hold out your arm," he said.

"Is that an order?"

"Yes."

"Will you torture me if I don't obey?"

"Yes." His lazy smile and intense gaze promised a torture she'd find very pleasing indeed, but she held out her arm, anyway. He tied a circlet of braided leather around her wrist.

"What's that?"

"It shows that you're mine," he said, giving the knot a final tug.

Her heart fluttered. "A slave bracelet?"

"Precisely."

Delicious tension coiled within her. "Silly me. I was worried about the sexist nature of your work schedule around here, but as a captive, I have no rights at all, have I?"

"Only what I give you."

"And are you feeling generous?"

His glance slid over her, warm and proprietary, but he didn't answer.

Black Hawk didn't have to answer impertinent questions from his captive, she realized. "What now?"

"The women are preparing the evening meal in there."
He pointed toward one of the Army tents.

"While the big strong men plan?"

He lifted an eyebrow. "I can see you're going to be a
smart-mouthed captive."

"It's the only kind I know how to be." She deliberately
fingered the top button of her dress until she'd brought his
attention to the motion. Then she unfastened the first button. He swallowed. She refastened it. "Have fun planning," she whispered before she slipped away toward the
women's cooking tent.

Three hours later the entire encampment was gathered
around the bonfire, seated on upended tree stumps as they
shared the beef stew, biscuits and coffee that made up the
evening meal. Sheila sat next to Douglas, and under cover
of a general discussion about whether to have an encampment at Prairie du Chien over the Fourth of July weekend,
she turned to him.

"I thought you might make me wait on you during dinner, O Great Chief," she said, smiling slightly. "But instead you helped yourself to the meal. Why is that?"

He glanced at her. "Only a weak fool would waste your
services on food," he murmured.

A shiver passed through her. There was no doubt that
his manner had shifted from that of a high-school history
teacher to an Indian chief. The pale light of day was dis-
appearing rapidly. Soon it would be dark. She'd had fun
working on the stew and biscuits and getting to know Cathy
and the other women better, but that wasn't why she was
here. She and Douglas both knew that.

The discussion turned to historical accuracy for the next
battle, and someone suggested they might want to stage
something in Illinois, which made up a great part of the
disputed territory during the Black Hawk War. Sheila listened to the stories, many contributed by Douglas, of the

courage and tenacity of Black Hawk, warrior chief of the Sauk Indians.

"He was quite a noble figure, wasn't he?" she said to Charlie at one point.

Charlie laughed. "Why do you suppose Douglas agreed to portray him? I couldn't interest him in playing one of the soldiers, who basically helped take the ancestral lands away from the Sauk and Fox Indians. Our Douglas believes in fighting for the underdog."

"Aw, he just likes that costume," Cathy said, a teasing light in her eyes.

"That's it," Douglas agreed with a smile. "Without the costume I'd walk."

Sheila had to agree the costume was important. Douglas had pulled a buffalo robe around him as he sat near the fire, and she couldn't admire the fit of the buckskin quite as well now. She was feeling a little deprived. "I think a movie should be made centered around the story of Black Hawk," she said. "Has anyone every considered that?"

"Only educational filmstrips," said John, a history teacher from Milwaukee.

"From what you've said tonight, the story has the makings of a terrific screenplay," Sheila said.

Douglas turned to give her a long look. He started to say something and seemed to catch himself.

She interpreted the look and wanted to kick herself for starting such a discussion. In his mind, the topic of screenplays would lead logically to the topic of writing. Her writing.

The conversation shifted from history to children. Douglas joined in from the perspective of a teacher, but Sheila had nothing to contribute, so she remained silent. Douglas's thigh brushed hers as he moved on his makeshift seat. The simple contact started a chain reaction within her, and soon she wondered if she'd be able to hold her coffee mug steady.

She glanced at Cathy. "Is there a place where we can wash these dishes?"

"Sure thing. We might as well do that now." Cathy stood, and as if on cue the rest of the women around the circle began gathering dishes.

"I'll heat some water, Cathy," Charlie said.

"Maybe some of the other men can help you," Sheila said, tossing Douglas a challenging look before she walked toward the cooking tent with Cathy. "Honestly. We all clear dishes while they stare into the fire. They might as well have a television set and a remote."

Cathy laughed. "Take it easy, Sheila. The men don't help with the dishes because they're in charge of the wood and the bonfire. Charlie and the soldiers will prepare metal warming pans for our bedrolls, so the women don't have to climb into cold beds. The men staying in wigwams are stoking up the fires in those, so they'll be all warmed up by the time the dishes are washed."

"Oh." Sheila was glad darkness hid her flush Douglas was warming up the tent. Their tent.

"I've studied the subject of gender equality on the frontier," Cathy said as she led the way into the tent, which was lit by a kerosene lamp. "From what I've read, pioneer women were treated with equality because they performed meaningful, essential work. The times our freedoms become endangered are when we're pampered and patronized." She deposited her burden of dishes on a trestle table. "It's empowering to be expected to pull your own weight."

Sheila watched as the rest of the women came into the tent, laughing and talking. None of them seemed oppressed. "You're right. I was too quick to assume something."

"Better to be that way than clueless about women's

rights," Cathy said. "But then, if you were some simpering baby doll, Douglas wouldn't be interested."

Sheila accepted the compliment with a smile. "I know I've already thanked you for this dress…and all the rest of the outfit. Where did you find it?"

"In a resale shop. Don't worry. It's not an original from that time period, so it wasn't terribly expensive. I think it might have been used in a play or something." She glanced at Sheila. "I wasn't sure how you'd feel about white, though, with its…implications."

"It does look a little like a wedding dress," Sheila admitted softly.

"Yes, it does, more than a little. And…I'm not sure how important this relationship is to you."

The implied question about her depth of commitment made Sheila's chest tighten. Douglas was becoming more important than she'd been willing to confess, even to herself. His empathy toward his students and his sensitivity with her father had demonstrated that this was the sort of man with whom she would gladly spend a lifetime.

Cathy leaned close and put a hand on Sheila's arm. "You don't have to respond to that. Your face tells me everything I wanted to know. I'm glad I bought the white dress."

"What did Douglas say?"

"Not much. But his expression was exactly the same as yours." Cathy squeezed her arm. "I wish you both the best of luck."

Charlie appeared at that moment with a steaming kettle of water, and the women formed an assembly line that dispensed with the dishes in record time. Sheila was reminded of quilting bees and barn raisings. Sharing chores was another concept that had disappeared in the twentieth century as families operated primarily in isolation from one another, she thought. She could understand the appeal of these encampment weekends as a chance to break that lonely pattern.

When the dishes were done, she stepped outside the tent, expecting to find Douglas seated by the fire. He wasn't there. In fact, not many people were left.

"He's probably already in the wigwam, nursing the fire," Cathy said, coming up behind her. "I'd go look for him there."

Nursing what fire? Sheila almost asked, as her blood pumped hot in her veins. But she didn't know Cathy that well. "Thanks, I will." She was proud of herself for sounding almost normal when she said it.

She walked toward the wigwam. It glowed amber against the darkness, a honey-colored pleasure dome beckoning her forward. She pulled her cloak around her shoulders with trembling fingers. Nothing in her experience had prepared her for being the white captive of a Sauk chieftain.

She lifted the tent flap and ducked inside. Waves of heat rose from the fire circle, making Douglas's image shimmer on the far side of the wigwam. Clad only in his buckskin breeches, he lay on the buffalo robes, his head propped on his fist as he gazed at the doorway.

A braided leather band circled his temples, and another enclosed the muscles of his upper right arm. Both were of the same design as the one Sheila wore on her wrist. She touched it involuntarily as she gazed at him in speechless wonder.

"Your cloak, first," he said in a throaty whisper.

And she understood then that he would not require patience to undress her, because she would do it for him. At his command. She unfastened the loop holding the cape, and the garment crumpled in a circle at her feet. "I know it's a little late to discuss it, but I didn't bring birth control," she said.

"I did. Now your shoes."

She dropped to one knee and eased back the layers of petticoats until she'd exposed the lacings of the high-topped shoes. Her fingers shook so much she fumbled with the job. "I...might need help," she said, glancing through the shimmering heat to gauge his response.

He seemed carved of stone. "No."

"Then you'll just have to wait."

"I have all night."

Her throat went dry. *All night.* She'd imagined what it would be like to make love with him, but she hadn't considered all the hours they would have to accomplish that. At his words, the night stretched vividly ahead of her as a dark, seemingly endless river of promise. She managed to remove the first shoe and started to unroll the stocking on that foot.

"Not yet."

She stopped and bowed her head in obedience before shifting to the other knee and unlacing her second shoe. That gone, she rose to her stockinged feet and waited.

"The dress."

She watched him as she unfastened the buttons on the sleeves. A muscle twitched in his jaw. Perhaps he wasn't as controlled as he looked. She finished with the sleeves and began slipping loose the buttons at the high neck. Her gaze swept over his tight breeches. No, he wasn't as controlled as he looked.

As the buckskin stirred with his growing arousal, she began to ache in response. The dress, the petticoats and both chemises grew too warm and confining, but she was hampered in her desire to be rid of them by the delicate line of buttons that had to be carefully, painstakingly, unfastened. At last she finished and slid the shoulders of the dress from her arms. She started to step out of the dress and petticoats all at once, but he held up his hand.

"Now the chemises, one at a time."

Leaving her dress dangling from her hips, she lifted off the wool chemise. She could hear the sound of his breathing. No, he was not controlled at all. Then she swept off the silk one and tossed it aside. He drew in his breath.

Feminine instinct made her throw back her shoulders and lift her head. "Is Black Hawk pleased?" she asked.

He started to speak but had to clear his throat first. "Yes."

She smiled with delight. "Good."

"The rest, now," he said with a wave of his hand.

So perhaps he grew impatient, she thought with a thrill of satisfaction. Instead of removing the dress and petticoats, she lifted her skirts and leaned down to roll away a stocking. Then she carefully removed the other, allowing him a glimpse of her bare calf before the petticoats drifted back into place.

He groaned.

She took her time easing her dress over the petticoats and laying it on a mat nearby. The petticoats she untied and took off one at a time, and there were four. At last she stood in the silk bloomers and gazed across the fire at him. His eyes burned hotter than the coals in the fire circle. She pulled the end of the tie holding the bloomers in place, and they slipped partially down her hips, stopping at a very strategic point. Then she untied the ribbons holding them at her knees and slowly, very slowly, stepped out of them. Now she wore nothing but the leather braid around her wrist.

His voice rasped in the stillness. "Come to me."

Her bare feet sank into the fur matting as she walked around the fire circle, her heart pounding in an ancient rhythm. Kneeling beside him, she looked deep into his eyes. "What is your wish, my chief?"

He was trembling, and his skin shone as if covered with

a fine dew. He didn't touch her. "Unlace my breeches," he said in a strained voice.

Blood roared in her ears and she moistened her dry lips. She reached for the leather lacings that bound his swelling manhood. As she freed him from the buckskin, she learned for certain what she'd suspected before. He wore nothing beneath the breeches. When the buckskin parted, she found herself gazing at a thoroughly aroused man—a man she wanted more than she'd ever wanted anyone in her life. She reached to touch the velvet shaft.

"No."

She looked up into eyes darkened by a passion barely under control.

"Lie down," he whispered hoarsely.

Holding his gaze, she stretched out beside him. He reached for her wrist that was bound with the leather circlet and brought it to his lips, kissing the band and the quickened pulse beneath it. She drew in a long, shaky breath.

"Close your eyes."

"But—"

"Close your eyes," he murmured.

She obeyed. Obedience had been the unspoken bargain, after all. Movement beside her told her he'd peeled away the buckskin. Then he returned to her. The warm suppleness of his mouth found the pulse at her throat and marked it as the beginning of a journey that carried him to every sensitive spot of her firelit skin, as if he were creating her anew with his kisses. With her eyes closed she became pure sensation beneath his mouth and the molding touch of his gentle hands.

She began to quiver, vibrating each time he touched her, Gradually the sweep of his hands became bolder until at last he parted her thighs and the movement of air told her he was poised above her.

"Now open your eyes."

She felt as if she were rising from a deep pool as her eyelids lifted and she gazed up into his beloved face flushed with desire. She reached to frame his face between her hands as he began slowly, surely, to enter her. Her world seemed to stand still, waiting for the completion of that joining. He pressed deep and she gasped with pleasure. With a small movement of his hips, the vibrations he'd begun earlier gained momentum.

"Oh," she whispered, grasping his sweat-slicked back. His movements were almost imperceptible, but he'd built her response to a level that needed no more than a gentle push. And another. And she lost control.

He covered her mouth with his and drank in her cries of completion as her existence dissolved into a whirlpool of color and light. And feeling. Such feeling. The captive flew free.

CHAPTER FIFTEEN

DOUGLAS HELD BACK until the last shudders of Sheila's climax subsided. The restraint nearly cost him his sanity, but at last he lifted his lips from hers and gazed down into hazel eyes misty from the aftershock. He couldn't suppress the smile of triumph that curved his mouth. That was the sort of expression he'd wanted to see after he'd loved her, after he'd fulfilled what he hoped was her cherished fantasy.

Her hands, which had been firmly grasping the muscles of his back, slipped down to his hips, and she arched upward, snugging him in closer. He groaned softly as he recognized that she was about to return the favor. She wrapped her legs around his and drew his head down for her kiss.

It was the openmouthed kiss of a woman well loved, a woman whose inhibitions had been burned away in the fires of satisfied desire. She explored deeply with her tongue, nibbling and teasing. Then she drew back a fraction to whisper outrageous things that set his blood boiling. Her hips rotated against his in open seduction, and her laughter bubbled forth, low and throaty, incredibly sexy.

She urged him forward with insistent hands, and he gave up all pretense of control as a basic rhythm took hold, bringing him into her again and again. As the pressure built, taking away all reason, a cry of release formed deep in his chest and rose as surely as his seed within him. When the moment arrived, he pressed his mouth to her smooth shoulder to muffle the expression of a pleasure more intense than any he'd ever known.

Many long minutes later, when his heartbeat slowed, he lifted his head and saw in the glow of firelight that he'd marked her. A reddened spot on her shoulder had to be the result of his teeth against her soft skin. At least he hadn't drawn blood. Considering the cataclysm she'd helped bring about, he might easily have forgotten himself enough to do that, too. He kissed the spot. "I didn't mean to hurt you," he whispered.

Her voice was soft in his ear. "I didn't feel a thing."

He propped himself on his elbow and gazed down at her. "I hope that's not true."

Her smile was lazy, almost feline in nature. "I was referring to when you bit my shoulder. Is that some sort of ancient Sauk ritual?"

"No. Your shoulder substituted for the pillow I should have used to keep me from rousing the whole camp when I..."

"Yes, you certainly did," she murmured, tracing his lips with her fingertip. "And so did I. Tell me, do you treat all your captives this way?"

"I've never had a captive before. I'm playing it by ear."

"Your ear? I could have sworn that was a different part of your anatomy that saw the most action just now."

He tweaked her chin. "You are a saucy captive, aren't you? You don't seem the least bit cowed by your perilous position."

"Am I in peril?"

"Haven't you been listening to the discussions about Black Hawk? I'm a tough customer." Amazed at how he could heat up again so fast, he eased himself away from her and used the towel he'd laid nearby. Terrycloth wasn't exactly a nineteenth-century convenience, but neither were condoms. Some concessions had to be made. He turned back to her. "No telling what could happen to you in this tent, young woman."

She regarded him earnestly. "You know, for a while there, I almost believed you were an Indian warrior. Thank you for giving me my fantasy, Douglas. It was very exciting."

"Was?" He leaned across her and fingered the leather bracelet around her right wrist. "What makes you think it's over?" he said, lifting her wrist over her head and pulling the other one up to join it. "Seems to me you're still my captive."

Her breathing grew shallow and her eyes bright. "You don't scare me."

"No? I warned you about being impertinent. Now you'll have to pay the consequences." Anchoring her wrists with one hand, he moved to her side and held her ankles with one muscled leg braced across them. "Black Hawk has methods for dealing with women like you."

Her lips curved in a smile. "You'll never break me."

"That's fine. I just want to bend you a little." He cupped her breast, lifted so nicely by the way he'd positioned her beside him. "And perhaps hear you beg for mercy." Ah, she was soft to the touch. He caressed her breasts until her nipples tightened and she arched into the curve of his hand, wanting more. "See, you're already bending," he murmured.

Stroking past the valley between her ribs, he moved across her flat belly and lower, seeking out the moist channel that had given them both so much pleasure. She was ready for him again, and as he teased her gently and persistently, she whimpered and writhed next to him. Then he paused.

"Please," she whispered urgently. "Please."

"And begging," he said softly. Releasing her wrists, he slid down and boldly claimed her in the most intimate of embraces a man could give a woman. And she surrendered in the most ultimate of surrenders. His heart rejoiced at her complete acceptance of his caress. The barriers were all gone, swept away by the fantasy of an Indian warrior and his willing captive.

SHEILA CAME half-awake snuggled inside soft fur, with only her nose exposed to the cold air. She turned sleepily and the fur caressed her bare skin. Then her knee bumped a very solid thigh and memory returned. Black Hawk.

She opened her eyes and found his green gaze trained on her in the dim light of early morning. Coaxed by the intensity in his eyes, she replayed the memories of what they'd shared during the night, and her body warmed. She moved her arm and the leather bracelet shifted on her wrist.

She pulled her arm out from under the buffalo robe and held it up between them. "I guess I'm still your captive."

He placed his palm against hers and interlaced their fingers. "White woman," he murmured. "You've given Black Hawk such pleasure that you've earned your freedom."

A sudden pain sliced through her. "You're dismissing me?"

"No!" He released her hand and pulled her roughly against him. "God, no." He smoothed her tousled hair away from her face. "That was just my clumsy way of trying to find out…where you wanted to go from here."

She hesitated. "I wish we could stay in this tent forever."

"So do I. But we can't. We both have to go back."

"I guess we do."

He stroked a possessive hand down her hip. "But I won't be satisfied anymore with a few stolen kisses while we sit on your living-room sofa. Not after I've held you like this."

She grinned up at him. "You were never satisfied with a few stolen kisses in the first place."

"True." He took a deep breath and leaned his forehead against hers. "I'm worried, Sheila. I wonder what will happen between us when I'm back in my role as a history teacher and you're the manager at Timberlake."

"It will be different," she admitted.

He looked deep into her eyes. "I don't want to lose what we found last night."

"We could set up a tent in your backyard and play dress-up."

He smiled. "If I thought that would help, I'd do it. We've begun something wonderful, and we need time and privacy to nurture it. I don't think we'll get much of either one in Tyler."

"I'm afraid you're right." She rubbed the frown creasing his forehead. "But we're not there yet, are we?"

"You're right. We're not." He cupped her bottom and brought her against his arousal. "And I think it's time to show you the way the Sauk Indians welcome the dawn."

He loved her thoroughly, and then dressed and left the tent to get a kettle of warm water. When he returned, he made her promise not to tell Charlie that he'd brought soft towels and washcloths instead of the burlap towels purists like Charlie used.

"I wasn't about to use burlap on skin like this," he said as he washed her tenderly. Then she insisted on applying the warm water and washcloths to him, and they very nearly ended up back on the soft buffalo robes, bodies entwined. Only the sounds of activity outside the tent prevented them from making love again. Somehow they dressed, although the process took a long time, interrupted as it was by kisses and spontaneous caresses. Douglas had few garments to fasten and was ready first.

"Go ahead." Sheila glanced up at him as she buttoned

the dress over the silk chemise. Sunlight filtering through
the hides of the wigwam had convinced her she didn't need
the wool one this morning. "I'll be out in a minute. I'd
rather you broke the ice with everyone, anyway."

A corner of his mouth tilted up. "Just to put you at ease,
lots of lovemaking usually goes on at these encampments.
We're not the only ones who are turned on by the fantasy
of meeting in another time and place. Charlie told me the
reenactment weekends have rejuvenated many a stale marriage."

"That's a nice thought. And it does help me feel less
embarrassed about facing everyone after…"

He stepped toward her and gathered her close. "After a
night I'll never forget as long as I live."

"Neither will I."

"A good beginning," he said, and kissed her gently.

Her heart soared with hope that the magic wouldn't disappear in the midst of the modern world. If Douglas believed it, she would believe it. "A good beginning," she
whispered against his mouth.

Later, when she emerged from the wigwam, she saw evidence of what Douglas had said about renewed marriage
vows. Wives flirted openly with husbands, and she
glimpsed more than one pat on the bottom or stolen kiss
as breakfast was prepared and eaten. No one seemed particularly interested in how she and Douglas had spent the
night.

Only Charlie made a comment as he came around the
fire circle, filling everyone's cup with coffee. "I doubt if
you two need the caffeine," he said with a wink. "You're
both higher than a kite as it is."

"Careful, Charlie," Douglas warned.

"Just glad to see you happy, old buddy." Charlie poured
coffee into his tin cup and turned to do the same for Sheila.
"I keep thinking about what you said last night about mak-

ing a movie about Black Hawk. It would make a terrific story, wouldn't it?''

"Maybe," Sheila hedged. "I'm really no judge. It was just an idea."

"A dynamite idea," Charlie said, lifting the spout of the pot away from her cup. "If we could find a writer, the reenactors would make a fantastic research team. What a blast it would be if we could get someone in Hollywood to look at it. Stories like that are hot right now. It just might go."

"Sheila's a writer," Douglas said casually. Too casually.

She glanced at him and knew from his expression that he understood what he'd done.

"Really?" Charlie set the pot on the ground and crouched in front of her. "I didn't know that! Hey, this could be great. If you'd—"

"I'm not a professional writer," Sheila declared, interrupting him. "I'm not qualified to take on a project like this."

"Yes, she is," Douglas said in the same quiet tone.

Charlie looked from Douglas to Sheila. "A beautiful woman who's also modest. You've found quite a gem, Wagner."

Panic rose in Sheila. She felt exposed and frightened. "I'm not modest," she said more forcefully. "And I could no more take on writing a screenplay for this group than fly to the moon." Clutching her dishes in her trembling hands, she stood. "You can't listen to Douglas, Charlie. He's not the least bit objective about my abilities, or lack of them."

Douglas stood, too, and seemed to tower over her. "That's bull, Sheila. You're perfect for a project like this. Your intuitive grasp of fantasy would fit right into what's happening in films these days."

She couldn't believe he'd go this far. No one knew about

her writing except Douglas, and he'd revealed his knowledge without asking. Now he was subtly alluding to the night they'd just spent together. "You're wrong," she said, fighting to keep her voice steady. "I know nothing about fantasy. Now if you'll excuse me, I'd better start on these dishes." She glanced into his eyes, as filled with anger as hers. "If you'll get my clothes from the car, I'll change when I'm finished. It's late."

Had Douglas followed her into the cooking tent and tried to apologize, the fragile bond they'd formed might not have snapped completely. But he didn't follow her, and she felt the break as if the jagged edges had punctured her heart. Holding back her tears while she washed her breakfast dishes made her throat ache, but she repressed her emotions as other women came into the tent, happy women full of renewed love for the men in their lives.

Cathy put an arm around her shoulders and gave her a friendly squeeze. "I hope you're planning to come to the next reenactment weekend," she said. "It's been fun having you here."

"Thanks, Cathy." Sheila didn't dare look at her for fear she'd burst into tears. "I—I'll have to see. I've enjoyed...meeting all of you."

Cathy took her by the shoulders and gazed into her face. "Something's happened. A moment ago you were fine. You and Douglas were like a couple of turtle doves."

Sheila gazed at her helplessly. Cathy was a dear woman who had only the best intentions, and Sheila hated to brush her off. But a moment more and the dam would break. "I'm sorry," she whispered. "I have to go." She pulled away and hurried out of the tent.

Inside the wigwam, Douglas waited, his expression thunderous. He kept his voice low, but the intensity made it seem as if he were shouting. "Dammit, Sheila, it's criminal to waste talent! Your mother's journals are fun, but probably not worth publishing, considering they might cause embarrassment. But your work is a different matter. It deserves to be seen!''

''Did you get my clothes?''

He pointed to a bundle next to the door of the wigwam.

''Then if you'll leave, I'll put them on.''

''It's my tent and I'm not leaving.''

''All right.'' She took off the cloak and the shoes while he stood silently watching her. Finally she started on the buttons of the dress, her jerky movements a mockery of the sensuous moments she'd used undressing for him the night before.

He braced his feet apart and rested his hands on his hips. ''For the love of heaven, will you explain to me why you can't consider writing that screenplay?''

''Apparently you failed to understand that my writing is private. I have no intention of subjecting it to public scrutiny. And Hollywood! That place can chew writers up and spit them out. You might as well just throw me to the lions and be done with it.'' She pushed the dress and petticoats over her hips, glancing at him as she did so.

Anger smoldered in his eyes, but that wasn't the only emotion lurking there. Apparently even anger couldn't block out the attraction that sizzled between them. ''I didn't take you for a coward,'' he said.

Dressed in bloomers and silk chemise, she walked over to pick up her bundle of clothes. ''Well, I am.'' She located her bra and turned to face him. ''Yellow, through and through.'' She pulled the chemise off, blatantly taking advantage of the fact he still wanted her. He deserved to be tortured with what he'd lost by his stubborn insistence on pushing her in directions she didn't choose to go.

''I don't believe you.'' His voice and even his belligerent stance had softened. ''Use a pen name if you have to, like your mother did, but at least try!'' His gaze filled with yearning as he watched her fasten her bra in place.

Her movements stilled and new fury boiled within her. She'd trusted him with her secrets, and now he was using them against her. ''You have no shame, Douglas Wagner, if you'd stoop to bringing up my mother's true-confession stories to get me to come around.''

''Dammit, you're wasting your potential!''

She'd had enough. ''That's my business. And you have no right to tell me otherwise.''

''Of course I have a right.''

''Have you? Then so have I. What about the scuba club, Douglas?''

He looked as if she'd slapped him hard across the face. She had little time to feel her regret before he eliminated the distance between them and gripped her in his strong arms. The muscles bunched in his jaw. ''That isn't the same thing.''

She met his gaze head-on. ''I say it is. I say you're depriving those kids of an experience many of them desperately need because you're afraid. So watch who you're calling a coward.''

''My God.''

As she absorbed his stricken expression, she resisted the urge to take the accusation back. But she believed every word, and in the end she stood her ground.

''You are merciless,'' he whispered, nearly lifting her off her feet as he brought her closer. ''I must be crazy to still want you.''

''Is it me you want, or some creature you can shape the way you want?''

He uttered a soft oath and his mouth descended in a punishing kiss that aroused her more than she'd ever admit to him. But she couldn't control her response, and she pressed against him, crushing her breasts against the muscled wall of his chest. His fingers bit into the soft flesh of her upper arms, and he groaned deep in his throat.

When he lifted his head, his eyes blazed with a ferocious passion, as if he'd reverted to his role as Black Hawk, and she was the luckless woman upon whom he would exact his revenge. She half expected him to rip her clothes away and take her. Instead he released her and left the tent without another word.

CHAPTER SIXTEEN

THE MINUTE SHEILA got home on Sunday she called Abby at the lodge and suggested the two of them take in a movie that night in Sugar Creek. That way she wouldn't be home when Douglas came over for the chess match with Emil. Douglas probably would appreciate her absence, anyway. Then she managed to keep busy with chores and avoid Emil's questions until it was time to go pick up Abby.

Abby, empathetic friend that she'd become, didn't probe when Sheila refused to discuss Douglas or her weekend. She sat through a double feature without remembering what she saw and arrived home late.

Douglas's pickup was still in the drive.

She considered driving back into town for a cup of coffee at Marge's, but she was tired and wanted nothing more than to crawl into her bed and sleep for hours. If she allowed Douglas to keep her from doing that, she was giving him far too much power. She parked the car and went into the house.

The kitchen light was on, and she assumed her father and Douglas were still sitting in there playing. Not even glancing their way, she started for the stairs.

She had her hand on the newel post when Douglas called her name. There was no anger in his voice, only a soft plea. Heart pounding in trepidation, she turned and looked into the kitchen. Dressed in a moss green turtleneck and jeans, he sat alone at the table, a mug of coffee in front of him, the chess set put away for the night. He'd waited for her.

The arrogance of Black Hawk had been replaced by a vulnerability that shook her. His eyes were shadowed, his expression subdued.

Sheila walked into the kitchen. "Has my father gone to bed?"

"About an hour ago. Would you like some coffee?"

"No, thank you."

"Then I'd appreciate it if you'd sit down for a minute. I have a few things to say."

She eased into the chair opposite him.

He stared into his coffee mug and ran his finger along the handle. Now that his anger appeared to be gone, she couldn't dredge up any of her own. Instead she wanted to reach for his hand and offer comfort. Yet his distress had to do with her.

"You were right," he said, glancing up at her. "I have no business telling you what to do with your talents if I can't face my own handicaps. I probably don't even belong in the classroom."

A cry of protest rose to her lips.

He shook his head. "I'm half the teacher I used to be, Sheila. I've kidded myself in the past four years that giving my all in the classroom is enough. Maybe for some people it is. But I've known the satisfaction of doing more than that." He pushed his coffee aside. "There's a kid in one of my classes who's crying out for some personal attention. He may come to me for help and he may not. If I had him in the scuba club I could guarantee he would. I've failed that boy."

Sheila's heart wrenched. "I never meant to imply that you were a failure at teaching. No one would ever say that."

"Except me." His gaze was bleak. "And until I can beat this thing, I have no business influencing other people's lives...including yours."

She reeled from the pain of that statement. They'd quarreled, but the heat of quarreling had generated a certain amount of energy, and she hadn't really believed their relationship would end on that note. But this cold logic could build a permanent wall between them. "What are you going to do?"

"I'm not sure."

She fought the urge to reach across the table and touch him. Something in his demeanor warned her that he wouldn't welcome softness and comfort right now. "Is there anything I can do?"

"Unfortunately, no. I allowed myself to escape into a wonderful fantasy with you, and it felt great to be so alive again. But as you so rightly reminded me, I have unfinished business to take care of."

Regret formed a lump in her throat. "I should never have said anything. I was angry, and I grabbed the first thing at hand to hurt you with. I think you're being way too hard on yourself. You'll probably get over this problem if you give yourself time, if we can—"

"I've had time. Four years is plenty. I've made no progress." He pushed back his chair and stood. "Don't worry about your father and the chess. I'll still come over for that. But I wanted you to understand why I won't...why I can't..." Anguish shone from his eyes.

"Don't shut me out," she whispered.

His jaw clenched and he started out of the kitchen.

"Douglas." She followed him, but she wasn't quick enough. He'd grabbed his jacket and was out the door before she could catch him. He closed it with a decisive click. He obviously didn't want her around.

She leaned her back against the door and gradually slid down to a sitting position on the floor, where she stared into space. Idly she fingered the leather bracelet she still wore, the bracelet she'd been unable to take off, despite their harsh words to each other earlier in the day. How self-righteous she'd felt then, how sure that she had an excellent argument he couldn't refute. And he couldn't. She had the miserable satisfaction of being right. The damage of that might never be repaired.

"Is he gone?"

Sheila looked up. Her father stood at the top of the stairs in his red-and-white-striped nightshirt, his brow creased in a frown. "Yes," she said with a sigh. "He's gone."

"Why aren't you going after him?"

"Because he doesn't want me to."

Emil came down the stairs. "That's what you think."

"Pa, I saw his face. He wants to be alone."

"Hogwash." He walked over and folded his gangly body until he sat beside her, his skinny legs stretched out in front of him. "He's plumb in love with you, Sheilie. A man in love don't want to be alone."

She took a long, shaky breath. "You didn't see him, Pa. Or hear what he had to say."

"Don't hafta. When your ma and I had fights, and we had some beauties, I was usually the one who'd stomp out to the barn. I always acted like I wanted to be alone. But I didn't."

"I don't know that Douglas is like you, Pa."

"He is."

The first glimmer of hope lit a small place in her heart. "Why are you so sure?"

"Been playin' chess with him, haven't I? You can tell a lot about a man from that. Or a woman."

"But you never talk!"

"We might not talk, but we know what the other one's thinkin' mostly. I read his face. He reads mine. I'm bettin' he's a lot like me, and you should handle him just like your ma handled me. She didn't let me get away with that stompin' out business." He chuckled. "Nope, sir. Didn't never get away with nothin' with your ma. She played chess like that, too. Aggressive as all get-out, always doing the unexpected to keep me on my toes.''

''So you think I should get in the car and follow him?''

''That's exactly what your ma woulda done.''

Sheila turned her head and looked at him. ''I tell you something else she would have done. She would have told you to stop going out on that ice, as of this minute.''

He faced forward and didn't look at her. ''Maybe.''

''So don't go out there anymore, Pa. It's crazy.''

''I almost got Jumbo today. And I'm losing the day tomorrow for those dad-blamed new teeth.''

''Pa, give it up. Win the flag back in the summer season.''

Finally he turned his head. ''Give me until Friday, Sheilie. If I don't get Jumbo by Friday, I'll let Gus-Gus win.''

''Friday? You promise?''

''On the memory of your ma.''

''Okay. Friday.'' It was a small victory, but a victory nevertheless, and she needed one right now.

''Gonna go after Douglas?''

She hesitated, achingly unsure of herself. ''I guess I will.''

''Just barrel in there, like your ma woulda done, and you'll be fine.''

ALL THE WAY into town Sheila worked on her entrance speech. She'd probably have to rouse Douglas out of bed to answer the door, but that was okay. If all went well he'd be back in it soon enough—with her. After all, love was all about facing problems together.

And love was what she felt for Douglas. What else would bring her out in the middle of the night to bang on this stubborn man's door? What else would twist her heart in knots when she realized the same stubborn man was hurting so bad he growled and tried to push her away like a wounded animal? She hadn't used the word *love* during their time together and neither had he, but her father had said Douglas was in love with her, and Emil was a perceptive man. She'd cling to that belief. And the memory of her feisty, spirited mother.

A light was on in Douglas's small, nineteen-thirties-style bungalow when she pulled into the driveway. At least he was still awake. His truck wasn't visible, but he'd probably put it in the garage. Her chest heavy with tension, she got out of her car and climbed the small stoop to ring the doorbell.

When he didn't answer, she rang again. And again. She didn't picture Douglas with a nonworking doorbell, but just in case, she banged on the storm door. No doubt the neighbors would hear her. No doubt there would be gossip in the morning. She no longer cared. She banged harder and called out his name. If he was in there refusing to answer the door, she had a few choice words for him!

Finally it dawned upon her that he might not be home. She trudged around the side of the house to the detached, one-car garage and pressed her nose against one of the panes of glass in the garage door. No truck.

She sagged as all the buoying energy of an impending confrontation seeped out of her. He wasn't even here. She'd nearly made up her mind to go home again when she thought about her mother. Her mother wouldn't have given up now.

At this hour on a Sunday night he had only a few choices in Tyler. Sheila couldn't imagine him barging in on a friend when he hadn't wanted any consolation from her. So he could be at Marge's Diner, or he could be driving aimlessly around the countryside, or he could be at the high school. The school was only a block away, the diner a little farther on. She headed for the school.

She found his truck parked, not in the faculty lot, but in the large area in front of the indoor pool adjacent to the school. Lights were on in the building. Owned jointly by the school district and the county, it provided a place for the Tyler High swim team to practice in the winter and the community to cool off in the summer. Once Sheila saw Douglas's truck, she knew why he was there.

She raced for the closest double doors and found them unlocked. The strong smell of chlorine assaulted her as she stepped into the bright interior, and ripples of light waved across the ceiling from the recently disturbed water. Douglas sat on a bench down by the deep end of the pool, his muscular body enclosed in his black scuba suit. He was heaving as he gasped for air. His fins were tossed to one side and his air tanks rested against the bench next to him. He'd had his head in his hands, but he jerked upright when she came through the door.

She circled the perimeter of the pool while keeping her gaze on him. He was very pale. The scene was self-explanatory—he'd obviously tried to use his scuba gear in the relatively harmless confines of the community pool. And he'd failed, succumbing to some sort of panic attack.

She walked toward him, wanting nothing more than to gather him into her arms, wet suit and all. Instead she sat down next to him.

"You'll get wet." His voice revealed the strain he was under.

"I don't care." She stuffed her hands into the pockets of her ski jacket to keep from grabbing him and shaking him until his teeth rattled. As she stared at the choppy water, it began to smooth into gently shifting swells. "You can't get rid of me that easily, Douglas." She held out her wrist and pulled back the sleeve of her jacket. "I'm still your captive."

"I released you," he said softly.

"You don't understand." She turned slightly and studied his set profile. "I have nowhere else to go."

Slowly his gaze came around to meet hers. "Sure you do. You're beautiful and talented. You don't have to settle for a man who's less than he could be."

She longed to tell him she would gladly take him if he never made another dive in his life, but she knew he wouldn't come to her on those terms. "What happened just now?"

"Sheila, go home. This is my private hell. You don't have to immerse yourself in it."

"Dammit, Douglas." Without giving it much thought, she did exactly that, jumping up from the bench and hurling herself into the pool. The weight of her snow boots and her ski jacket sucked her under.

She didn't intend to drown. If he didn't respond, she could kick off her boots and wiggle out of her jacket, but she was gratified when a surge of water beside her indicated Douglas had come in after her. He hauled her to the side of the pool and pushed her unceremoniously over the cement coping. Then he pulled himself out after her.

"You're crazy," he said, gasping for air.

She struggled to a sitting position, her clothes squishing beneath her. "I had to get your attention somehow."

As his breathing steadied, he regarded her with a level stare. "Don't kid yourself that this was some sort of breakthrough. I don't like getting in the water at all these days, but I can do it if I have to. I don't start to panic until I put on the breathing apparatus and go under. That's what I'd tried just before you got here, and I nearly blacked out from an anxiety attack."

"Do you want to try again while I'm here?"

He looked at her, and a ghost of a smile tugged at his mouth. "Are you going to be my lifeguard?"

"That's me."

He leaned a little closer to her. "You look like a toy I had when I was a kid. I put it in the washing machine to see what would happen."

"And what happened?" Her clothes squished again as she edged nearer to him.

"It came out looking like you."

"I'm a mess, huh?"

"Yes." He cradled her head and brushed her wet hair from her cheeks. "The most beautiful mess I've ever seen," he murmured, lowering his head.

His kiss started out as a tender gesture, but she wanted more than tenderness from him. She taunted him, making a sensuous foray into his mouth with her tongue. He moaned and took the kiss deeper. But as he wrapped his arms around her and tried to bring her in closer, she seemed to adhere to the concrete coping around the rim of the pool.

He drew back and took her chin in his hand. "I feel as if I'm hugging a sponge."

"And I feel as if I'm hugging a giant condom."

He started to grin, and soon the grin became a chuckle, and the chuckle turned into laughter that brought tears to his eyes. "Come home with me," he said at last, caressing her cheek.

"I thought you'd never ask."

"Does Emil know where you are?"

"Approximately. He told me to come after you."

He raised an eyebrow. "I have your father's permission to take you home with me?"

"Yes."

"That's a pretty heavy responsibility."

"You can handle it."

He gave her a wry smile. "I'll give it a try. Can you walk?"

"If I take off these boots and wring out the jacket, then maybe I can."

"I'll help you. Then if you'll go into the men's changing room and put on my clothes, maybe you won't get pneumonia on the way over. I'll drive home in my wet suit."

"I do hope Brick Bauer isn't patrolling this street right now," Sheila said.

"He's already been by. Stopped to make sure I was okay. That was before I'd put on the air tanks, and I could tell him in all honesty that I was fine."

She gazed into his eyes. "You will be."

"I wish I could believe that."

For an answer she gave him another kiss.

THE MANY GUISES of Sheila Lawson, Douglas thought as she came out of the boys' locker room in his jeans and turtleneck. Of all the strange and seductive things she'd worn recently, he'd be hard-pressed to name his favorite. This one made her look like an urchin in need of tender loving care. She had to hold his jeans up at the waist, and she'd rolled the cuffs several times. It looked as if two people her size could fit inside his shirt.

He'd found a plastic bag for her wet clothes, and he held it out while she dropped them in. He had already transferred his air tanks and fins to the truck and found a blanket to wrap her in so he could wear his coat. It was still damned cold out there. That was good, he supposed, considering that Emil was still going out on the ice every day.

"I'll carry you out to the truck," he said.

"What about my car?"

"I'll bring you back early in the morning, before the kids get here." His blood warmed at the thought that he would have her all to himself for another night. He had no business taking her home, making love to her, winding her tighter around his heart. But when he swung her up in his arms and she snuggled against his chest, he had no will to resist.

CHAPTER SEVENTEEN

DOUGLAS LEFT SHEILA in the truck while he unlocked the house. Then he returned and carried her inside. She couldn't avoid the feeling of being a bride transported over the threshold, and the idea gave her such a case of delicious shivers that she trembled in his arms.

"You're cold." He deposited her gently on a sofa in front of a brick fireplace. "Let me get out of this wet suit and throw your clothes in the dryer. Then I'll make us a fire."

She glanced at the firewood in a metal holder on the hearth. Old newspapers and a container of fireplace matches sat beside it. "I can do it."

"All right," he agreed easily. "I'll be right back."

She liked the fact that he'd turned her loose with the fireplace and hadn't issued any instructions. He was a man who would expect a woman to pull her weight as an equal partner. No pampering and patronizing.

She and Emil hadn't built a fire in their fireplace all winter, she realized, as if it would be a sacrilege to have a cozy fire when Myrna, who'd loved a cheerful blaze, couldn't enjoy it. That type of thinking would have to change, she decided.

She crumpled newspaper and arranged the wood on the grate. She wasn't really that chilled, but a fire might reestablish some of the atmosphere she and Douglas had created in the wigwam, and she was feeling nervous about making love in this house—which seemed to belong less to Black Hawk and more to Mr. Wagner. Once the wood on the grate began to crackle, she sat back on her heels and glanced casually around, wondering if she'd come face-to-face with a picture of Douglas's late wife.

But there were no photographs in the living room. There were, however, books. Floor-to-ceiling bookcases flanking the fireplace overflowed with hardbacks, paperbacks and two entire shelves of *National Geographic*. Piles of books sat on end tables on either side of the deep-cushioned sofa, and several issues of *Time* and *Newsweek* covered the top of the coffee table. Newspapers from several cities were stuffed into a magazine rack next to a leather easy chair. Sheila hadn't been so surrounded by the printed word since her last visit to the new Tyler Public Library. Evidence of Douglas's scholarly mind intimidated her a little.

He returned dressed in gray sweats, his chest unselfconsciously bare. As he walked into the living room he pulled on a blue-and-gold Titans sweatshirt, tousling his dark hair in the process. The momentarily bare chest and the tousled hair helped, but she still had the unsettling feeling she was paying a visit to her teacher.

He paused and studied her for a moment. "You look as if someone just caught you smoking in the girls' bathroom."

"That's sort of how I feel."

He crossed to her, his bare feet making no noise on the carpet, and crouched in front of her. Taking her hands, he brought them to his lips and brushed feathery kisses across her knuckles. "I can take you back, Sheila. Just say the word."

She decided boldness was in order. "Which word is that?" she murmured. One word could save them. One word could wipe away the clandestine feeling of this tryst. And now, in this room filled with words, it was the only one she wanted to hear, needed to hear.

His gaze searched hers. Then, with a muttered oath, he released her hands and stood, turning away from her and massaging the back of his neck. He apparently couldn't, or wouldn't, say it.

Her heart felt like a hunk of Wisconsin limestone. "That wasn't the word."

"I know."

She got to her feet. Her throat hurt. "The word is *love*, Douglas."

He whirled, his expression tormented. "I know that, too, dammit! And twelve hours ago it was on the tip of my tongue. But now...now I feel that saying it would be unfair to you."

"Why?" Her anguish echoed through the simple question.

"Because my love can make you do things you don't want to do! You've said it yourself—I have this confounded urge to teach, never stopping to think that someone could get hurt...or even...die."

Her heartbeat thundered in her ears. "Like Joanne?"

"Yes, like Joanne."

"You're still insisting it was your fault?"

"Absolutely." His green eyes grew murky and cold. "I talked her into learning how to dive, and of course, I, the great instructor of the universe, taught her how. I pushed and pushed, and she went along, because she loved me. All the trips were my idea, but especially that last one to the Truk Islands. Ever heard of them?"

She nodded, bracing herself to withstand this story, one she didn't want to hear, but one he had to tell, perhaps for the first time.

"For a diver who loves history, the lagoon is Shangri-la," he said. "Our Air Force sank an entire fleet of Japanese ships there in 1944. Tanks, supplies, even a complete Zero plane, are all down there to explore. Joanne didn't care about any of it, but I did. So she went on the dive with me, to be a good wife.''

''That was her choice,'' Sheila said.

''A choice she thought she had to make.''

''Why?''

''Because our marriage wasn't working. We both suspected we weren't compatible, but by God, she tried to be. And when your heart's not into something, you tend to get careless.'' He finished the story in a monotone that cut more deeply than a scream. ''If I'd taught her better how to react when she ran out of air, or if I hadn't insisted she learn to dive in the first place, she'd still be alive.''

Sheila took a few moments to digest the whole horrible impact of his confession. Finally she swallowed and looked directly at him. ''So how long have you had this God complex?''

His gaze narrowed. ''What do you mean?''

''You seem to think you have all this power to influence people. Have you always felt that way or—''

''Don't you see? She went on that dive to please me! Out of love.''

''Which was also her choice! She was an adult, Douglas.''

''I've told myself that, too. And sometimes it even helps a little. But high-school kids aren't adults. When they join a scuba club they want to have fun and learn to dive, but they also want to please the teacher. I had girls in that club who joined for no other reason than that they liked me. It took Joanne's death to show me how dangerous that can be, and how helpless you are when disaster strikes. When I put on the scuba gear and slipped under the water at the pool tonight…I was terrified.''

''I know.''

''And the problem is, I'm beginning to understand why I'm terrified. When Joanne died, I decided to put my gear away forever. I thought if I never put it on again, if I never taught anyone else to dive, I could go on with the rest of my life as it was. But that's not true.''

"But you've been doing a good job.''

"No, I haven't. Once I believed I had the right to teach, that I would make lives better if I did. Joanne's death destroyed my confidence in that, but I haven't been willing to admit it. Then you came along and reminded me of the time I failed you. Have you noticed how I tried to fix that? By pushing you the same way I pushed Joanne.'' He paused. "I have no business teaching anyone.''

She stared at him as despair elbowed hope from her heart. "Why did you bring me here tonight?''

"I was fool enough to think making love to you tonight would keep away my demons. I was wrong. They're here and howling for blood.''

"Douglas, no,'' she whispered, taking a step closer. "We can work this out. Together we can—''

He backed up an equal distance and gave her a sad smile. "Your clothes should be dry by now. I'll get them for you.''

She felt as if he'd hurled her against a cement wall. Dazed, she tried to comprehend that he was giving up, ending their relationship.

"I'm sorry, Sheila.''

At last fury anesthetized her against the pain. "Not half as sorry as you will be,'' she said fervently.

When he went back to the laundry room, she fumbled with the knot on the leather bracelet. Tears and anger didn't help the process.

Holding up the waist of Douglas's jeans, she stomped into his kitchen and met him coming from the laundry room carrying her clothes. "Got a knife?'' she asked.

His eyes widened.

"Don't worry. I'm not going to slit my wrists or stab

you, although that second thought has some appeal." She thrust out her arm. "I want this off and I can't untie the knot."

He deposited her clothes on the kitchen table and walked toward a drawer. After taking out a paring knife, he came over and handed it to her, handle first.

She refused to take the knife and held out her wrist instead. "I can't cut the leather and keep up these jeans at the same time. You do it."

A muscle twitched in his jaw. He took her wrist and carefully slid the knife under the leather bracelet. He hesitated.

"Get it over with, Douglas."

In one clean motion he sliced upward, and the bracelet fell to the tiled floor.

Sheila didn't even glance at it. Scooping up her clothes, she turned to him. "Where's the bathroom?"

"Down the hall to the left." His gaze was devoid of all feeling.

On her way out of the kitchen Sheila held her head high, never indicating for a second that when he'd sliced through the bracelet he might as well have sliced her heart in two.

DOUGLAS FAKED his teaching duties on Monday and Tuesday. A few of the more perceptive kids, like Matt Hansen, gave him puzzled looks when he responded to a joke a few seconds late or failed to complete a sentence, staring into space. But so far none of his students had asked any questions. He figured the whole student body had somehow found out about his lost weekend with Sheila and were cutting the lovesick teacher some slack.

By the end of classes on Tuesday he faced another unpleasant fact—he'd promised Emil Lawson a chess game that night and it looked as if no one from the Lawson household was going to call and cancel. He'd thought maybe Sheila would talk her father out of the game, but either she had failed or hadn't tried. In either case she would probably leave as she had on Sunday night. Still, he didn't look forward to a night with Emil, who seemed to see right through him when it came to his feelings for Sheila.

He surveyed the paperwork on his desk. All of it appeared trivial, but the administration wouldn't appreciate his throwing away test papers instead of grading them. He picked up a stack of the multiple-choice quiz papers from his third-period class and slipped them into his briefcase, in preparation for taking them home, just as Clint Stanford walked into the room.

Douglas gave Clint a controlled smile. They still hadn't regained their easy camaraderie, and Douglas now doubted they ever would. He planned to return his teaching contract unsigned this spring. "What can I do for you, Clint?" he asked.

"I have an emergency situation and I need your help tonight," Clint said without preamble. "Are you free?"

"Not really." Douglas wished he didn't have a conscience. Clint was handing him an excuse not to play chess with Emil, and he wasn't even going to take it. "What's up?"

"The Tyler police pulled Matt Hansen and Jack Patterson over for a minor traffic violation when they were leaving school." Clint rubbed his jaw. "It seems in the process of issuing the ticket they found a joint on the floor of the car."

"Aw, hell." Douglas reevaluated his options for tonight.

"Neither one of the boys will admit to it being his. They swear it was planted by somebody else. The parents are going crazy, especially Patterson's folks, because it was his car. He's supposed to be the valedictorian this year. Unless this is cleared up, he won't be."

"I believe those kids, Clint. They aren't the type to mess around with pot. They're athletes, and good students, and too damned smart for crap like this."

"I guess that's why both boys asked that you be at the conference we're having with them and their parents tonight. I set it for seven-thirty, hoping you didn't have anything going. Is there any way you can reschedule your... commitment?"

Douglas grieved for the days when Clint would have followed his first impulse and said "hot date" instead of "commitment." But Clint was all business now. "I think maybe I can," Douglas said. "Where's the meeting?"

"In my office. I don't know how long it will take, either. But I'd really like you there. As an administrator I'm probably viewed as an adversary in a situation like this. You can serve as an advocate for the kids."

Douglas made his decision. "I'll be there."

"Thanks." Clint started out the door. Then he paused and turned back. "You might be interested to know that when I asked the boys if there was a teacher they'd like to have sit in on the conference, you weren't just the first choice. You were the only choice."

ON TUESDAY AFTERNOON Sheila sat in her office rewriting a memo. It was a simple memo to the head groundskeeper asking him to order two lilac bushes for a bare spot near the lodge entrance. But she couldn't seem to get the words in the right order, or even the letters. She'd had similar difficulties all day.

At least she was back at work, away from her father's persistent questions about Douglas. Monday she'd driven Emil to Sugar Creek to be fitted with his new teeth. In between his complaints about the expense of the dentures, he'd used her forced captivity in the car to press her for details of what he called "another spat with your friend Douglas."

She knew he meant well, and that he was probably worried he might lose his chess partner. Finally, in exasperation, she'd promised him that her problems with Douglas had nothing to do with the chess games, and that she was confident Douglas would show up as he always had. Although Emil had protested that that wasn't his reason for being interested, he hadn't brought up the subject again.

When Sheila's extension buzzed, she picked up the receiver gratefully. Maybe she'd be able to talk better than she could write memos. Or maybe she should just give up and string paper clips all afternoon. At least she'd lined up another movie date. Abby was busy, so Sheila had called Sandy Murphy, who'd been delighted to get together again. Drew was out of town on a sales trip, she'd related—a detail Sheila had already heard via the grapevine.

"This is Sheila Lawson. How may I help you?" she answered with brisk efficiency.

The pause on the other end should have alerted her, but she was still sucker-punched when Douglas's voice came across the line. "Hello, Sheila."

"What's the problem, Mr. Wagner?" she said, striking out instinctively. In the two days since she'd talked with him, she'd clung to her anger like a life raft. "Did I leave too much lint in your dryer?" Silence. She'd made a direct hit. Good.

He drew in a breath. "Something's come up at school and I won't be able to make the chess game tonight. We'll have to reschedule. I know your father's probably out on the ice, so I wonder if you'd tell him for me."

"Not a chance, buster."

"Excuse me?"

"Tell him yourself. He's been worrying himself sick that you won't come because of our problems, but I assured him you wouldn't let that get in your way. I want you to look into his face while you give him your miserable, cowardly excuse for not fulfilling your obligations to someone who's counting on you. And I don't believe that nonsense about rescheduling, either. Don't you dare string that poor old man along, Douglas Wagner, or I'll come after you and nail your worthless hide to the nearest tree."

"I'll take that as a no."

"Good call."

"All right," he said quietly. "I'll drive out there."

"Fine." She started to slam the phone down, but caught herself and replaced it gently in the cradle. She hadn't thought she could be any angrier, but the more she thought about Douglas disappointing her father, the more her fury grew. She wanted another go at him when he came back from her father's fishing shack. After giving him some driving time, she pulled on her coat. On her way outside she stopped by the desk and told Julie, the registration clerk, that she was taking a brief walk by the lake.

Her timing was excellent. Douglas had just started down the path to the lake as she left the lobby and stepped out on the veranda. She gripped the railing and fought back her longing. He'd really gotten under her skin. His loose-hipped stride, the broad set of his shoulders beneath his black ski jacket and the way the cool breeze played with his hair made her knees weak. Remembering his gentle humor and quiet compassion filled her heart with regret. She'd have to work on those inconvenient reactions if she intended to tell him off in a few minutes.

He paused at the edge of the frozen expanse and seemed to be studying the best route to Emil's canvas shack. Sheila had a moment of disquiet as she remembered Gus's carefully drawn diagram. There were some rotten spots on the ice. Maybe she'd been hasty to send Douglas out there without some instruction. Then again, he'd been around frozen lakes all his life. Surely he'd be able to figure out a safe route.

She relaxed a little when she saw him picking his way across the ice with caution. But she'd be glad when he was safely back on shore. She started down the veranda steps so she could be waiting for him. Then she'd give him a piece of her mind for his despicable behavior toward her father. Not only was he lying to that poor old man, he was being untrue to his own finer nature. He was a better person than that.

Something at school had come up, he'd said. Oh, sure. How dumb did he think she was? The fact that he'd made up some excuse instead of coming right out and saying he wouldn't play chess with her father anymore was the most infuriating thing of all, she decided as she walked more quickly along the path. Mr. Douglas Wagner was about to get a tongue-lashing he wouldn't forget.

She estimated that he'd covered about half the distance to the shanty when her father flung open the flap of the canvas structure and let out a shout of triumph.

"I got'm!" he hollered, stepping out with his fishing pole in one hand and a very large walleye flapping in the other. "Hey, Gus-Gus! I got Jumbo! Get ready to streak nekked…" He stopped and stared across the ice at Douglas. "Hey! Whatcha doin' out here, Douglas?"

"Coming to congratulate you!" Douglas called back.

Gus emerged from his shanty. "What the hell's happenin'?"

"I got Jumbo!" Emil said.

"I see that, you old fool!" Gus pointed at Douglas. "What's he doin' out here?"

"He's my chess partner!" Emil said. "Hey, Douglas, don't walk over there!" Emil started moving toward Douglas at a trot. "That's a rotten spot. Don't—"

His feet went out from under him all at once, and his

forward momentum caused him to slide nearly ten feet. It was about three feet too far. Sheila began to run as a loud crack echoed over the lake. With a startled yell Emil plunged straight through the jagged hole that opened up like the gaping jaws of a shark. He bobbed up for a moment, and it looked as if he might stay afloat. Then, with no warning, he disappeared under the dark surface.

CHAPTER EIGHTEEN

WHEN EMIL WENT UNDER, Douglas's first impulse was to race forward and dive in after him, but he checked that instinct. Instead he kept his gaze on the sloshing water as he moved quickly yet cautiously to the most solid-looking side of the jagged hole. Easing to his stomach, he peered into the dark water. A red stocking cap floated on the surface, but he couldn't see Emil.

"Get a rope!" he shouted over his shoulder, figuring Emil's fishing buddy had to be within earshot. Precious seconds passed as he strained to see something, anything beneath the surface. Failing that, he eased away, still keeping an eye on the hole as he pulled off his boots and shucked off his jacket. "Where's the goddamned rope?" he yelled.

Then he heard the slip of hard-soled shoes on the ice and he glanced up. Sheila. "Go back!" he called.

"No," she gasped. She reached the far side of the hole and crouched down, her face as white as the ice that was slowly numbing his chest and groin.

Fear for her clawed at his throat. "I said *go back*," he said, forcing the command past constricted vocal cords. "The ice is rotten."

Her voice was choked with unshed tears. "Not here." She copied his former position and lay flat on the ice. "Pa!" she cried, a note of hysteria in her voice. "Over here, Pa!"

Images of Sheila crashing through the ice made his head

spin. He couldn't save them both, and he knew which one he'd choose. Emil would die. "Get help, Sheila. We need help." He issued the order as if she were a recalcitrant student, hoping she would obey out of habit.

Gus crawled up beside him with a coil of nylon rope looped over his shoulder.

As Douglas took the rope and tied it around his chest, under his armpits, he looked across the black water toward Sheila. She had backed away from the hole and was getting to her feet.

"Go!" he shouted. "I'll get Emil. You call an ambulance. And for God's sake be careful crossing that ice."

Her eyes wide with horror, she gave him one last glance. He didn't try to mask his love and concern as he gazed back. Then she turned and started toward shore.

"Let the rope play out as I go in," Douglas said to Gus. "I just need it to find my way home."

"I'll pull you out if I hafta," Gus said grimly.

"Let's hope you don't." Douglas filled his lungs, let out the breath, filled his lungs again and jumped in. The water seemed to freeze his blood. What he wouldn't give for a wet suit. And a large dose of luck.

GET TO SHORE, Sheila told herself. Somehow she had to block the terrified child within her who threatened to become hysterical at the prospect of losing another parent so soon. *Get to shore. Get help.*

She couldn't think of anything else. Not of Emil under the water all this time, or of Douglas going in after him, or of the panic that might overcome Douglas and render him unfit to perform this rescue—a panic that could take Douglas's life as well as her father's. She shut down all thought except the image of a telephone, an emergency number and the welcome sound of a siren. Douglas would do his part; she would do hers. Emil would make it.

When she reached solid ground she started to run. She slipped twice on the icy path but didn't fall. Tearing up the steps to the veranda of the lodge, she burst into the lobby.

"Call an ambulance," she told Julie. "My father's fallen through the ice." She waited only long enough to register Julie's nod and her hand reaching for the telephone. Then she whirled and headed back toward the lake.

At a spot on the path where she could see through a break in the trees to the shanties, she paused, breathing heavily. Her heart jolted in her chest. Her father lay faceup on the ice, with Douglas and Gus leaning over him. He was lying very still.

This time as she ran she did fall, but she scrambled up again, not even feeling the pain from her bloody knee and scraped palm. Douglas was alive. But her father...

Tears blurred her vision and she brushed them impatiently from her eyes. She had to see to stay on the path across the frozen lake. Douglas wouldn't want her out there again, but she was going. She had to make damn sure she didn't fall through the ice and cause more problems.

As she drew closer, she could tell that Douglas was giving Emil CPR, alternately blowing into his mouth and pushing on his chest. Her father wasn't breathing. Her own breathing seemed to stop as she gazed across at the huddled men.

Douglas leaned down, pinched Emil's nose and blew into his mouth. Then he leaned back and pressed down firmly on the older man's chest. "Come on, Emil," he said, his voice raw, urgent. "I need a chess partner, dammit."

"Open them ornery eyes!" Gus said, his face contorted with grief.

Breathe, Pa. Sheila concentrated on her father's chest and willed it to move on its own. It didn't.

Then she remembered that Douglas had to be frozen and exhausted. He hadn't even put his coat back on, and the wind had to be cutting right through his soaked clothing. She knew CPR. She'd relieve him. The sense of purpose released her from her paralysis, and she moved carefully around the hole in the ice until she reached them.

Gus glanced up as she approached, and the self-blame in his eyes made her look away. There would be time later for recriminations, and the worst culprit in this disaster would be her. Right now they had to save Emil. His face was the color of a winter sky, and he was so still. So very still.

"Come on, buddy." Douglas pushed with the heels of both hands. "Sheila needs you, guy."

"Hell, *I* need you, you piece of crow bait," Gus said.

Sheila picked up Douglas's coat and wrapped it around his shoulders. She didn't realize she was sobbing until she tried to tell Douglas she'd take over. She was furious with herself and struggled to get her emotions under control. A sobbing person couldn't administer CPR. She crawled next to Douglas and choked back another sob. "Let—let—"

"Yes!" Douglas shouted. "That's it, Emil!"

Sheila's attention flew to her father, and she saw it, too—a slight movement of his rib cage. "Pa! Breathe, Pa!" she cried as fresh tears streamed down her face. A siren wailed in the distance.

Emil sputtered and coughed. Gus shouted something indistinguishable and began to cry in great, heaving gasps.

Sheila couldn't prevent the sobs of relief that shook her. Gus squeezed her shoulder with a trembling hand as Douglas got an arm under Emil's shoulders and elevated his head. The siren drew closer and stopped. Emil coughed some more and his eyes flickered open.

"Welcome back, partner," Douglas said with a tired grin.

Emil looked around the circle of faces. "Lost my danged

teef again!'' he muttered, and closed his eyes once more. But he kept breathing.

Douglas started to laugh, and soon Sheila and Gus joined in.

When the paramedics arrived, they looked worried as they surveyed the helpless mirth that had taken control of everyone except Emil. They moved cautiously around the hole, and after some consultation decided all four people needed to be transported to Tyler General—one for getting lungs full of water and possible hypothermia, and the other three for uncontrolled hysteria.

THE AMBULANCE RIDE was short and filled with bustling activity as the paramedics clapped an oxygen mask on both Emil and Douglas. Once the ambulance pulled in to the emergency entrance of Tyler General, everyone was separated and assigned to curtained cubicles. Sheila tried to convince the nurse who insisted on treating her scraped knee and hand that she didn't need medical attention, but the woman didn't pay any attention and bandaged her anyway.

After Sheila had been released, she inquired about her father and discovered he'd been admitted for observation. Gus had been released, and a doctor was checking Douglas over for any ill effects of being immersed in the icy water and then exposed to the cold air for many long minutes. Sheila went in search of her father's room and met Gus in the hall going in the same direction.

His round face had lost all trace of merriment. He looked at her bandaged hand and knee. ''You got hurt, too?''

''Not really.'' She smiled. ''People around here are trained to slap a compress on anything that bleeds. All I have is a skinned knee and hand. I've done worse falling off my bike when I was a kid.''

Gus didn't smile back at her. ''I feel awful, Sheilie,'' he said. ''You was countin' on me, and I let you down.''

She wrapped an arm around Gus's substantial waist as they walked. "No, you didn't. If Pa hadn't caught that fish right at the moment Douglas showed up, he wouldn't have become so distracted and careless. And I'm the one who sent Douglas out there, so if anyone's to blame, it's me."

"You sent him out there? How come?"

Sheila sighed. "It's a long story, Gus-Gus." And despite the dramatic rescue scene, nothing had really changed between her and Douglas, she thought. There was always the chance that saving her father had renewed Douglas's confidence in himself, but it probably hadn't. He hadn't had to put on a wet suit to do it, for one thing. But whether Douglas wanted anything more to do with her or not, she owed him a tremendous debt. She would find a way to tell him of her gratitude, even if she could never tell him of her love.

"This here's the room number," Gus said. "Want to go in by yourself?"

"Now why would I want to do that?" Sheila asked.

Gus looked uncomfortable. He lowered his voice and leaned close. "Sometimes you get mad because me and Emil say things to each other. No tellin' how he'll insult me this time, mad as he is about his teeth and losin' that fish. Knowin' me, I'll probably say something back to that dang fool for lettin' hisself fall in the water, so maybe I should wait out here for a while so you can talk to him in peace."

"You know something, Gus?"

"What's that?"

"I'd like nothing better than to listen to you two pick at each other for another thirty years, starting right this minute."

Gus's eyes began to twinkle, and the smile on his round face returned to its full wattage. "I'd vote for that, myself. I'd be plumb lost without that old geezer."

"And he'd be plumb lost without you, Gus-Gus. Now let's both go in and give him hell."

AFTER SPENDING a half hour with her father, Sheila wondered if the hospital staff would reconsider their decision to detain him overnight. Emil Lawson was not a cooperative patient. He questioned every procedure and demanded to know the cost of everything from X rays to cotton swabs.

A tall man with chestnut hair that needed trimming strolled into the room in the middle of one of Emil's tirades. Sheila recognized him as Liza's brother, Jeff, chief of staff at Tyler General, but the only thing that marked him as a doctor was the stethoscope hanging around his neck. Despite his position of authority he dressed as Jeff Baron had always dressed—in running shoes, jeans and a cotton shirt.

"I heard we had a little problem down in this wing," he said with a wink at Sheila. "So I came to see what the fuss was all about."

"Highway robbery," Emil pronounced. "Shouldn't keep me here."

Jeff braced both hands on the rail at the end of Emil's bed. "If it were up to me, we wouldn't, Mr. Lawson, but I've had several female nurses who specifically requested that you stay, and I like to keep the staff happy."

"Nurshes?"

"Yes, sir." Jeff's lips twitched, but he managed to keep a straight face. "They said you were the cutest thing they'd seen all week and they begged to have you admitted. So I gave in."

Emil chuckled, revealing his bare gums. "I know you. You're Alyssha Baron's boy."

"Guilty. Except she's Alyssa Wocheck now."

"Right. Married to Sheila's bossh." Emil eyed the tall man at the foot of his bed. "You in charge here?"

"So they tell me. Personally, I think the nurses are just humoring me, and they're the ones who really run the place. At least that's what my wife, Cece, says."

"Anybody around here play chessh?"

"Come to think of it, we do have someone on the night shift who plays a mean game of chess. As far as I know, nobody on the staff has been able to beat him."

"Ha!" Emil said with a disdainful sweep of one hand.

"Want me to set something up?"

Emil nodded, then glanced at Sheila. "Guessh I'll hafta shtay, then."

"Looks like it," she replied, grateful for Jeff Baron's kindness. "Speaking of Cece," she said, turning to him, "how are the twins?"

Jeff rolled his eyes. "They just turned three. Need I say more?"

Sheila laughed. "All I know is that those girls have Mr. Wocheck wrapped around their pudgy little fingers. He's always pulling out a new set of pictures. In fact, it was seeing those identical faces so often that gave me the idea of setting up the convention of twins at the lodge."

"Oh, yeah. The twins convention." Jeff nodded. "Would you believe that Cece wondered if we should sign the girls up for that? I suggested they might be a tad young to attend workshops and sit in the bar trading stories all night, so she decided to wait a few years."

"Good move," Sheila said.

"But she's counting on you still having the convention when the girls are old enough to go."

"I'll make a note of it," Sheila said with a smile. But the comment had an unsettling effect. When Jeff's twins were old enough to attend a convention at the lodge, she hoped she wasn't still a resort manager booking fascinating groups into Timberlake Lodge. She wanted more....

Jeff pushed himself away from the bed rail. "Guess I'd

better walk the halls and look important for a while," he said. "I'll set up your chess game, Mr. Lawson."

"Thanksh."

"No problem." Jeff gave them a wave as he walked out of the door. "Makes me feel useful."

When he was gone, Sheila glanced over at Gus, who'd appropriated a chair in the corner. "Liza told me Jeff works the longest hours of anybody around here," she said. "Yet the way he talks you'd think he barely lifts a finger."

"He's a nice kid," Gus said.

"Highway robbery," Emil said again, but the edge was gone from his complaint. "Hey, Sheilie, were thosh teef inshured?"

"Oh, for pity's sake." She gave him a look of pure exasperation.

"Well, were they?"

"I don't know. I'll have to check with our insurance agent."

"Shoulda kept your mouth shut when you fell in," Gus observed from his chair over in a corner of the room. "But then, you never could get the hang of that."

"Don't you shay nothin'!" Emil said. "And I won the flag, Gush-Gush."

"You won?" Gus surveyed the room. "I don't see no fish, Emil."

"I had him!"

"Doesn't count."

"Does sho." Emil pushed the button that raised the head of his bed and kept talking as he motored upright. "Had him out of the water, Gush. Caught him with my lucky pole. I…" He paused and his head sank back against the pillow. "Pole's gone," he said with a sorrowful look at Sheila.

"I don't care, Pa. All I care about is that you're alive."

He reached out and gripped her wrist, giving it an impatient tug. "But that pole's a Lawshon tradition, Sheilie." His eyes were bright, and if she didn't know him better, she'd swear he was about to weep. "I need that pole. I need it for...the grandbabies."

"Oh, Pa." She swallowed a lump in her throat. "It's okay." *And there may never be any grandbabies.* Logically she knew there were other men in the world besides Douglas Wagner, but she doubted any of them would interest her in the slightest. Douglas was the one she wanted, and he didn't want her.

DOUGLAS COULD HEAR Gus and Emil arguing about the fish as he walked down the hospital corridor. He smiled with relief; Emil was okay. When Douglas heard that his chess partner had been admitted, he'd been a little worried, but maybe the doctor just wanted to keep the old guy under observation for a few more hours. Douglas could understand the staff's caution with Emil. A man his age shouldn't be immersing himself in ice water.

Douglas wanted to see Emil and make sure he was recovering. He'd prepared himself to treat Sheila with polite concern, nothing more. She might have the crazy idea that he'd overcome his phobia in order to rescue her father, but he knew he hadn't. With no time to think he'd been forced into action, but plunging into the lake had been a reflex. Once the emergency was over and he'd been put in a private cubicle, he'd begun shaking like a leaf. He'd refused the tranquilizer the doctor had offered him, but he'd been strongly tempted to take the pills. He was back under control now, but he knew his reactions still couldn't be trusted.

He reached the open door of Emil's room about the time the old man mentioned losing his lucky fishing pole. He sounded truly distraught about it. Douglas glanced in and saw Sheila leaning over the bed, trying to console him, and his heart swelled. No matter how much he tried to shut down his feelings, he was in love with that woman. He loved her laughter, her intelligence, her giving nature. He'd been kidding himself that he could walk into the room and remain emotionally aloof. One look into her sweet eyes and he'd be on his knees.

Gus glanced toward the door and noticed Douglas standing there, but Douglas put a finger to his lips and turned away. He had what he'd come for—the knowledge that Emil was recovering nicely. As he started back down the hall, he heard Emil explain that he needed the fishing pole for his grandbabies.

Grandbabies. Sheila's children. Something gave way inside him and he leaned against the wall for support. Closing his eyes, he struggled with a longing that threatened to suck him under. How he wanted to father those children! He could see them so clearly. His arms ached with the need to hold them, to hold Sheila. Now and forever.

Anger and frustration burned in his gut as he pushed away from the wall and strode down the hospital corridor. He'd found the woman of his dreams, the woman he could imagine loving for the rest of his life. And he didn't have the courage to claim her.

He clenched his hands into fists. If he planned to keep facing himself in the mirror for another fifty years, if he hoped to salvage any respect for himself as a man, he had to find that courage. And he knew exactly where to look.

CHAPTER NINETEEN

SHEILA HAD THOUGHT about calling her aunt Gracie and
had decided against it. Later, when Emil was home and
everything had returned to normal, she would call and fill
her aunt in on the incident. She'd forgotten how fast news
traveled, even to the communities surrounding Tyler, until
her aunt walked into the hospital room.

Gracie had Emil's fair coloring. She wore her blond hair
short and feathered around her face, but other than her hair,
the sibling relationship wasn't obvious. Her eyes were a
warm brown and her petite, curvaceous figure was the exact
opposite of Emil's tall, gaunt frame. Gracie had developed
the habit of comparing people to dog breeds, and she'd
dubbed Emil a greyhound.

She laughingly referred to herself as a *papillon,* a toy
spaniel whose name translated to "butterfly." The spaniel
looked small and delicate but was in fact a strong-willed
individualist that was a lot tougher than its size suggested.

Gracie burst into the room, pulling off her driving gloves
and unzipping her leather bomber jacket. "What in
heaven's name is going on?" she demanded, striding over
to Emil's bedside. "You may have the body of a greyhound, but you seem to have the brain of an Afghan hound,
Emil Lawson."

"Hello, Grashie." Emil's toothless grin flashed.

"Where are your teeth?" She turned to Sheila. "He
needs his teeth. Without them he looks at least a hundred

and twenty years old. Oh, hello, Gus-Gus. Didn't see you sitting there.''

"Hello, Gracie." Gus gave her a little wave from his chair.

"Pa lost his teeth in the lake," Sheila said. "But don't get him started on that subject."

"Dang new teef!" Emil said. "Tried to get'm."

"So *that's* why you disappeared under the water so fast." Gus leaned forward in his chair. "I wondered why you didn't float awhile. You dang fool, you! You *dived,* didn't you?"

"Thosh teef cosht a lot!" Emil said, his eyes snapping.

"Emil, you're ridiculous," Gracie said. She slapped him lightly with her driving gloves. "Giving us all the scare of our lives because you were trying to save a pair of dentures. Honestly. I wouldn't even compare your brain to an Afghan hound's. It would be an insult to the hound." With a shake of her head she turned back to Sheila and held out her arms. "Thank goodness you have this girl to look after you, Emil." She gave her niece a warm hug.

Sheila hugged her back with a quiet sort of desperation. It had been a rough few days, and the strain was beginning to get to her.

Gracie seemed to feel the tension and leaned back to gaze into Sheila's face. "Are you okay?" she asked softly.

Sheila didn't trust herself to speak without bursting into tears, so she just nodded.

"I don't think so," Gracie said. She glanced past Sheila to Gus. "How about if you take this girl down to the cafeteria for a cup of coffee and maybe a bite to eat? I'll stand watch over this crazy cheapskate and make sure he doesn't shimmy down the drainpipe to save himself the cost of a night in the hospital."

Sheila gave a watery laugh. "If he didn't have a hot

chess game set up with a member of the staff, he just might.''

Gracie released her and pointed her toward the door. ''Take a break, sweetie.''

Gus pushed himself out of his chair. ''Yeah. Come on, Sheilie.''

They were waiting for the elevator when it slid open and Faye Lemke stepped out, her coat buttoned up wrong and her purse clutched against her chest like a shield that would protect her from the unexpected disasters of life.

''There you are!'' she said, puffing. ''No sooner did I get in the house from shopping in Sugar Creek, but Annabelle Scanlon called with the news!'' She glanced at Sheila. ''Is Emil all right?''

''Yes, he is, Faye,'' Sheila said, reaching to pat her arm with her bandaged hand.

''Good heavens! You're hurt, too!''

''Just a few scratches. I fell on the path when I was running back to the lake.''

Faye heaved a huge sigh and looked at Gus in silent rebuke.

''It was just one of them things that happens, Mother,'' Gus said. ''Didn't lose nothin' but Emil's new teeth and his fishing pole.''

''That's beside the point,'' Faye said. ''This stupid rivalry has gone too far, Gus.''

''I think maybe they both learned a lesson today,'' Sheila said.

Faye glanced at her. ''I wouldn't count on it. Well, Gus, are you ready to come home with me?''

Gus shifted his feet. ''I was going to get Sheilie something to eat in the cafeteria.''

''Oh.''

''That's okay,'' Sheila said. ''You two go ahead. I'll grab something and go on back to the room.''

"No, that's silly," Faye said. "We'll all go to the cafeteria. My macaroni-and-cheese casserole will keep."

Sheila protested some more, but Faye had decided on a course of action and wouldn't be dissuaded. Finally Sheila gave in. "Why don't I meet you down there?" she said. "I haven't talked to Douglas since we were brought in, and I want to thank him for all he did."

"I should go with you and thank him, too," Gus said. "Don't know what we'da done without him."

Faye gave Sheila an assessing glance. "No, you let Sheila go by herself this time," she said. "You can thank Mr. Wagner later."

Sheila didn't know if Faye truly understood or if she'd rather not be party to a conversation that included the man Sheila had spent a sinful weekend with. Either way, she was relieved to proceed on this mission alone. "I'll be there shortly, then," she said, and walked over to the nurses' station to see if she could locate Douglas.

A nurse called down to the emergency room for Sheila and relayed back the message that Douglas had been released more than an hour earlier. Sheila accepted the news in silence. An hour ago. Douglas hadn't even bothered to come upstairs and check on her father. Or perhaps his aversion to seeing her had prevailed, and he'd found out Emil's condition from one of the doctors, maybe even Jeff Baron. In any case, he was gone.

Gone.

SHEILA ATE VERY LITTLE in the cafeteria. Then she returned to her father's room with Faye and Gus. She tried to remain upbeat, but Gracie seemed to see right through her. Eventually Emil told them to all go home before the hospital started charging extra for the number of people occupying the room.

"Come on, kiddo," Gracie said, taking Sheila's arm as

they left Emil's room. "I'll drive you back to your car. I assume it's still parked at the lodge."

"It is." She could hardly believe that only five hours had passed since Douglas had called to say he couldn't play chess with her father. Sheila felt as if she'd lived a lifetime since then. Her emotional balance was destroyed. In the past few days she'd experienced peaks of ecstasy and depths of despair that had left her disoriented and exhausted. On the drive from the hospital to the lodge she slumped in the bucket seat of Gracie's sports car, too numb to make conversation.

"This Douglas character who pulled Emil from the lake," Gracie began. "Isn't he your old history teacher, the one who plays chess with Emil?"

"Yes."

The headlights of an approaching car illuminated Gracie's face as she glanced at her niece. "Pretty athletic behavior for an old history teacher, isn't it?"

"He's only thirty-five," Sheila said.

"Hmm. A few rumors reached my neck of the woods, believe it or not. Rumors that my niece was dating her high-school history teacher. I was afraid you'd become involved with some old goat, but apparently he's a young goat."

Sheila smiled faintly.

Gracie gunned the motor and passed a slower vehicle on the two-lane road leading to the lodge. When she returned to the right-hand lane she resumed her questions. "Seeing as how he wasn't hanging around Emil's room, I take it the romance isn't going well?"

"There is no romance," Sheila said.

Gracie was silent for several moments. "Oh, I think there is," she said. "You should have seen your face every time someone mentioned this Douglas guy tonight. And he's obviously upset, too, considering that he didn't pay a visit to the man he risked his life to save."

Sheila stared out the window at darkened fields dotted with the occasional lights of a farmhouse.

"I wish I could help," her aunt said.

Sheila sighed. "I wish you could, too, Aunt Gracie."

"Want me to stay overnight with you since Emil's not here?" Gracie turned down the tree-lined lane leading to Timberlake Lodge. "I could call somebody and have them check on the dogs."

Sheila weighed the comfort of Gracie's sympathetic presence against the urge to nurse her grievances in private. The need to be alone won out. "Thank you for offering, Aunt Gracie, but…"

Gracie pulled up next to Sheila's car and switched off the ignition. She turned to her niece. "I understand, sweetheart. Some kinds of pain need solitude to heal." She smiled. "Besides, maybe he'll come to his senses and reach out to you. I wouldn't want to be in the way."

"I'm afraid there's no chance of Douglas reaching out." Sheila opened the car door. "I've finally given up on that fantasy."

Gracie gave her arm a quick squeeze. "Come and visit me soon, okay? I'm expecting a litter of puppies in a few weeks. Well, *I'm* not. Hortense is. They're going to be very cute. I think you might have to have one."

Sheila leaned over the console and gave Grace a quick hug. "That sounds fun. And thank you, Aunt Gracie. For the ride, and for coming to see Pa. I could see it meant a lot to him, even if he doesn't always show it."

"Couldn't help myself," Gracie said, a tremor in her voice. "You and Emil are my only family. I need you guys."

"And we need you." Touched by Gracie's brief show of vulnerability, Sheila gave her another hug before scooting out of the car and closing the door. Gracie waited until she'd unlocked her car, gotten behind the wheel and started the motor. Then, with a flick of the sports car's pop-up headlights, Gracie zoomed out of the parking lot.

Sheila took her time driving home. Once there she needed something to do, so she hauled in wood from the wood box outside, opened the chimney flue and built a fire. The activity reminded her of Douglas and the night at his house, but everything in her existence reminded her of Douglas. She resigned herself to running into memories at every turn and touched a match to the crumpled newspaper.

Once the kindling caught, she sat on the braided rug in front of the fireplace and stared into the flames. The shock of Douglas's leaving the hospital so abruptly was wearing off, and pain was setting in. He'd really dismissed her from his life. If only she could do the same with him. She'd have been better off if Douglas Wagner had never walked into Timberlake Lodge that fateful afternoon.

No, that wasn't true, she admitted. Despite the way the relationship had ended, she wouldn't give up the night they'd shared at the encampment for anything in the world. Her ultimate fantasy had come alive that night. Not many women could say that.

He'd also forced her to reexamine her beliefs about her writing. She thought about Glenna's success with her videos, and the uneasy feeling she'd had when Jeff mentioned repeating the twins convention for another twenty years.

On an impulse she climbed the stairs to her room and retrieved her cardboard box of manuscripts, including those she'd given Douglas. Sitting in front of the fire once more, she picked up the envelope and took out her work. To her surprise it was covered with comments in Douglas's handwriting. She'd never thought to look at it.

Reading through his remarks was a bittersweet experience. He'd loved everything, especially her play about two old codgers with a fishing rivalry that lasted for sixty years.

He'd seemed to understand the humor and compassion she'd tried for and had congratulated her for achieving it. Knowing that his perceptions matched hers was a heady feeling. She wanted to thrust the entire box of her writing into his arms and ask him to read all of it.

But of course that was impossible now.

She hugged the manuscript pages against her chest, as if she could somehow absorb Douglas's presence through the words he'd written. Tears filled her eyes, but she blinked them back as a decision solidified in her mind. She would submit her work to a publisher. Douglas might never know that he was the catalyst for that decision, but she would dedicate her first published manuscript to him, anyway. How ironic that a man who had lost confidence in himself had given so much to her.

When a knock sounded at the door, she glanced at the clock. It was late for visitors. Her heartbeat quickened. *Maybe he'll come to his senses.* But she'd raised her hopes before, only to have them dashed. Best to prepare herself for the sight of Gus, or Abby, or Sandy. Maybe even Mr. Wocheck had come to make sure she was all right. She opened the door.

Douglas stood in the pool of light by the front door, her father's fishing pole in his hand.

Sheila gasped and looked into his eyes. His gaze was triumphant, telling her more than words ever could. There was only one way he could have retrieved that pole. With his scuba gear. The blood roared in her ears as she stepped back and he walked through the door. She closed it behind him and leaned against its solid support. She felt as if she'd been running.

He turned and held out the pole. "I understand your father needs this."

"Yes," she whispered, taking it from him.

"For his grandbabies."

"Yes." Her eyes searched his and found there everything she'd ever wanted in the world.

"I love you, Sheila."

The fishing pole clattered to the floor as she launched herself into his arms.

He caught her easily and gazed down into her face as if he couldn't get enough of looking at her.

Belated fear for him made her shiver. "You should never have tried that. Not in the dark, with nobody around, when you could have panicked..." Her throat closed in terror at the realization that he could have died getting the stupid fishing pole.

"If I hadn't done it, my life was worthless, anyway," he said gently, smoothing her hair back from her temples. "You're my salvation. I had to conquer my problem because I had to have you."

She hugged him with fierce urgency. "You have me."

"That's good." He sighed as he looked deep into her eyes. "That's very good."

"And I'm going to be a writer, Douglas."

"Correction. You are a writer."

"I mean a published writer."

His smile was filled with love. "I never had a doubt. Now will you kiss me before I become so passion-starved I can't see straight?"

She gave all her attention to the assignment and was gratified by the rapid warming of his body pressed against hers.

Finally he drew away enough to begin unfastening the buttons on her blouse. "I know two is the recommended number these days," he murmured, "but once we get started, we may find that's not enough."

"Two?"

"Grandbabies," he said softly, scooping her into his arms.

Sheila wrapped her arms around him as he carried her effortlessly up the stairs. Two fantasies fulfilled, she thought. Two fantasies...and counting.

HOMETOWN REUNION

continues with

Those Baby Blues

by Helen Conrad

Here's a preview!

THOSE BABY BLUES

"I THOUGHT YOU were a burglar. I almost called the police."

"I wish you had called them. Maybe they would let me sleep in a cell." He tried again to force the key into the lock.

"How did you get here?" she asked, still confused.

"Ernie drove me over. He's offered to be my personal cabby any time I'm in need. He's a great guy." He turned and stared at her. "Hey, I'll bet you have a key, don't you?"

She nodded, thinking fast. So many conflicting feelings were rattling around inside her. Rosemary hated Paul for the past, but felt responsible for him and his broken foot. She wanted to fight him because of the house, wanted him out of her life, wanted to keep him close so that perhaps she could talk him out of his plans. In less time than it took to tell about it, she resolved everything in favor of control.

"Come on into my place," she ordered, leaning down to pick up the crutch and handing it to him with a stern look. "I'll fix you a place to sleep."

He was still frowning, but he let her lead him into her apartment, then sat on the straight-back chair she indicated at her kitchen table while she went around turning on lights and putting on the gas under the teakettle.

"I need to ask you a question," she said, her soft voice belying the anger simmering below the surface. "Just where do you get off throwing tenants who've lived in this house for years out in the street?''

He turned to look at her, startled. ''I told the rental agency to offer each of you a bonus. Didn't they tell you?''

''A bonus!'' She tossed her head and glared at him. ''You think money will make up for destroying a home?''

His dark brows drew together quizzically. ''But this is just an apartment. There are apartments all over the place.''

''Not like this one. Can't you see that I've made this place my own?''

He looked about at the gleaming counters, the plants in every corner, the collection of porcelain teacups on a shelf.

''You've done a very nice job,'' he said politely, though it was clear these individual touches didn't mean a thing to him. ''I'm sure you can recreate it all in some other nice apartment.''

She resisted the urge to yell, biting her lip to keep the lid on. ''Haven't you ever had a home that you loved?'' she said at last, her voice slightly shaky. ''A place that was the center of your life?''

He thought for a second and yawned. ''No, not really.''

''Never mind,'' she told him quickly. She would have to think this over, find an angle of attack that had a better chance of working. She could see this wasn't going to get her anywhere.

''Never mind,'' she said again, moving briskly. ''And you can sleep on the couch. I'll get you some bedding.''

''Here?'' He turned to look into her living room, remembering that he hadn't wanted to do this. ''What a great idea,'' he murmured, following her lead.

The couch was more comfortable than it looked, and he sank into the pillow with relief. It had been a long day. He needed sleep, and he got it. In less than a minute he was fast asleep.

Rosemary hesitated, reluctant to put herself in the position of caretaker. But that was basically what she was, whether she liked it or not. She finally relented, leaning down to spread a blanket over him and pretty much tuck him in. Then she stood looking down at him for a few minutes.

There was no denying Paul Chambers was an attractive man, even with those beautiful blue eyes closed. The hard angles in his face softened as he slept, and his long dark lashes rested on his cheeks, making him look even younger than he did when awake. She could see why women fell for him in droves.

It was a good thing she herself was immune to the disease. With a shrug, she turned away from him and switched off the light.